MURDER IN THE QUEEN'S ARMES

A GIDEON OLIVER MYSTERY

AARON ELKINS

THE MYSTERIOUS PRESS

New York • London

Tokyo • Sweden • Milan

All of the characters in this book are fictitious. The Queen's Armes is a real hotel in the village of Charmouth, and it is as described. The landlord, Peter Miles, who is nothing like Andy Hinshore, has graciously allowed my use of his establishment for deeds sinister and foul.

MYSTERIOUS PRESS EDITION

Copyright © 1985 by Aaron J. Elkins
All rights reserved.

This Mysterious Press Edition is published by arrangement with the author.

Cover design by Stanislaw Fernandez

Mysterious Press is a registered trademark of Warner Books, Inc.
666 Fifth Avenue
New York, N.Y. 10103
A Warner Communications Company

Printed in the United States of America

First Mysterious Press Printing: September, 1990

10 9 8 7 6 5 4 3 2 1

CRITICAL ACCLAIM FOR

Aaron Elkins and Gideon Oliver

1

EDWARD HALL-WADDINGTON, O.B.E., M.A., Ph.D., F.S.A., ran his hand nervously over a pink and liver-spotted pate, absently brushing back a lock of hair that had been gone for almost forty years.

"Oh, dear," he said in tremulous distress. His white eyebrows knitted atop a beaky, jutting nose that was at odds with an otherwise frail and retiring face. "My word, Professor Oliver! Only an hour? But there's so very much to see..." His words trailed sorrowfully off, and the hand moved from his brow to take up the burden of his message, gesturing vaguely at the dusty glass cases and musty corridors that lay beyond the door of his tiny, cluttered office.

"I wish I had time to see everything in the museum, sir," Gideon Oliver said courteously. He sat, more than a little cramped, in a small side chair at the elderly archaeologist's desk, his shoulders too wide for the narrow space between desk and wall, his long legs twisted out of the way off to the side. "Actually, Dorchester wasn't on our itinerary at all, but I couldn't imagine being in England without paying my respects."

"To be sure, to be sure," Professor Hall-Waddington said, pink cheeks showing his pleasure. "And to Pummy as well, no doubt?'' The eyebrows went up, and cheerful blue eyes twinkled out from under them.

"Pummy, too,'' Gideon said, smiling.

The prize possession of the Greater Dorchester Museum of History and Archaeology was a six-by-eight-inch piece of curving, darkened bone, most of the back of a thirty-thousand-year-old human skull that had been unearthed by a World War II bombing at nearby Poundbury and fortunately recognized for what it was by the amateur but competent Greater Dorchester Historical and Archaeological Society. Poundbury Man was of considerable anthropological significance because Britain, so rich in archaeological sites, was notably lacking in actual skeletal remnants of ancient man. From the first, the fragment had affectionately and quite naturally been dubbed "Pummy.'' (With typical English disdain for the middle parts of names, Poundbury is pronounced "Pum'ry.'')

It was extraordinary to have such an object housed in a provincial museum run by an amateur antiquarian society, but Professor Hall-Waddington had lent his considerable weight to the society's claims when the find had been made. In 1944 he had been one of England's foremost archaeologists, a colleague of Grahame Clark, V. Gordon Childe, and Leonard Woolley, and Dorchester had gotten to keep its find. When the professor had retired from the British Museum more than thirty years later, after the death of his wife, the society had timidly invited him to become curator of the museum. He had accepted with gratitude, and the collection had become the love of his life.

"Well, let's go and see him, shall we?'' he said, rising with unexpected sprightliness. "We'll follow the well-worn path to his case. Old fellow gets quite a lot of attention, you know. You're the second American to pay him a visit this week, as a matter of fact.''

"Oh? Another anthropologist? Someone I might know?''

"No, no, I doubt it. I didn't get his name. Student, from the look of him. Spent most of the morning slouching about.''

When they walked from the little office into the nearly

deserted exhibit rooms, Gideon saw that the museum wasn't dusty at all, and certainly not musty. It only looked as if it should be: a hodgepodge of waist-high glass cases with row upon dull-looking gray row of projectile points and stone flakes, each one painstakingly identified and cataloged on its own typewritten card. Improbable and seemingly inapposite objects stood in dark corners, leaned against the walls, and even lay unprotected on worn tables of dark wood. It was, Gideon admitted to himself, a look that he liked, for he was not a champion of the museum-as-entertainment-center, with buttons to push, levers to pull, and slick, nonexplanatory placards. They taught little, and they attracted hordes of marginally interested kids who jumped from contrivance to contrivance, comprehending nothing worth knowing. No, *this* was the way a museum ought to look, as old-fashioned as it was. He even liked the smell: a chalky, flinty mixture of old, worked stone and floor polish.

Their progress toward the Poundbury exhibit was slow and halting. Professor Hall-Waddington paused at almost every object they passed to murmur a few words about it and, if it was not encased, to run a hand lovingly over it.

"Fragments of a bell mold. Cast in 1717. Don't see many of these."

"Ah," said Gideon.

"Romano-British sarcophagus here. Found in 1925. Body'd been completely packed in chalk, except for the head. What do you make of that? Quite curious."

"Huh," Gideon said. "Interesting."

"And these are the old borough stocks. Used to stand against the side of the town hall. They'd put their feet in the holes, of course. Do you have any idea when that all began?"

"Uh, no, I'm afraid I don't," Gideon said.

"Ha! Thought you wouldn't. Have a guess."

"Sixteenth century?"

"*Six*teenth century!" cried Professor Hall-Waddington, delighted. "My word, no! It's from Anglo-Saxon times. And in 1376, Parliament decreed every town had to have a set of them. Decree's never been abolished, you know. This is ours.''

"Is that so?" Gideon breathed politely, looking with secret longing toward the case in which he knew the famous skullcap lay.

The old man shuffled a few steps on, but stopped rather firmly ten feet short of the goal. "Now here," he said, placing his hand tenderly on a monstrous, grimy pair of bellows standing on end against the wall, as if some fifty-foot giant of a blacksmith had leaned it there for a few seconds while he had a sip from a bucket of water. "Now here are the actual bellows from the Downtown Forge."

"Mm," Gideon said. "Ah."

"Most bellows authorities claim these were manufactured in 1792, you know, but I hold firmly with 1796 or even later. What would you say, Professor?"

The fact that there was such a thing as a bellows authority came as news to Gideon. "Well," he said, "uh . . . I'd say 1796 or 1797."

'Ah, and quite right you'd be. Quite right. No question about it in my mind. I'd be curious about your own rationale, however." He turned his frank, clear, blue eyes expectantly on Gideon.

"Well," said Gideon. He coughed gently and looked surprised. "Is that the Poundbury skull over there?"

"What?" Professor Hall-Waddington looked over his shoulder at the case with the golden fragment of bone in it. "Why, yes, of course it is. I keep forgetting you're a physical anthropologist and not another fuddy-duddy old antiquary like me." He chuckled pleasantly. "Here you are, come all this way to pay homage to old Pummy, and I've been prattling on about bellows."

"Not at all," Gideon said quickly. "It's been fascinating."

"Kind of you to say so, but now let's have a look at him, shall we?"

There was, however, one obstacle still to be negotiated— an exhibit consisting of what seemed to be two vicious-looking pitchforks chained together scissors-fashion, and

Professor Hall-Waddington was unable to ignore it in passing.

"Know what this is?" At the absence of Gideon's usual courteous murmur, he spoke a little louder. "It's an old hay-devil. Used for bringing hay from wagon to rick, you see . . ."

Gideon hardly heard him. He was staring at the Poundbury skull fragment only a few feet away. Something was wrong with it, so wildly wrong that it had him momentarily doubting his senses. "Poundbury Man," he whispered, unaware that he was speaking aloud. "Isn't it supposed to be an elderly man, long-headed . . . ?"

"Supposed to be?" Professor Hall-Waddington echoed, bewildered. "Of course it is. Le Gros Clark himself aged it, and sexed it, and estimated the cranial index. Sir Arthur Keith verified it, and so did your own Hooton."

Gideon was well aware of all this. He had himself studied photographs and casts of Poundbury Man and had never doubted the original analysis. "Professor," he said, "would it be possible to take it from the case—to handle it?"

The curator used a key at his waist to unlock the small, ordinary padlock, and raised the glass lid of the case. He turned aside four simple spring-clips that held down the black-velvet-covered block to which the time-stained bone was attached by two loops of wire. Looking oddly at Gideon, he stepped back and gestured politely at it. "Please," he said.

Gideon picked up the block and turned it so that he could look at the back of the fragment more closely. He needed only a second to confirm his impression.

"It isn't Poundbury Man, sir."

"Not Poundbury Man?" The old archaeologist laughed tentatively. "Not Poundbury Man?"

"I'm afraid I don't see how it can be." Poundbury Woman, maybe, or Poundbury Girl, but not Poundbury Man. There was no doubt in Gideon's mind that what lay in his hand was the left rear half of a woman's skull—not elderly at all, but in her twenties. And clearly broad-headed, not long-headed.

"Look at the nuchal crest," he said, "or rather, the absence of it—and the supra-auricular ridge. They're not nearly pronounced enough to be male—"

"But Le Gros Clark himself stood right here, right where you are . . . Or was it in my office . . .? Yes, in my office—"

"And look, sir," Gideon persisted gently, "you can see for yourself that none of the sutures show even incipient closure, so she's probably no more than twenty-four or twenty-five—"

"But of course it's Poundbury Man. It *must* be Poundbury Man. Why, what else would it be?" His thin, brown-flecked hand made an uncertain movement toward his lips.

"Hard to say," Gideon's fingers brushed the fragment's edges with seeming carelessness. "It's old, all right. Not thirty thousand years, but a good two or three thousand anyway. On a guess I'd say she might be from one of the brachycephalic Beaker populations, one of the later groups, maybe 1400 or 1500 B.C."

"No, no." Professor Hall-Waddington shook his head querulously. "It's quite impossible, I tell you. How could . . . how . . .?"

His voice sputtered to a stop as he took his first good look at the skull. "Why," he said, pointing an accusatory finger at it, "that's *not* Pummy."

He snatched it from Gideon. "Do you know what this is? It's from Sutton Bell—you know Sutton Bell? A later Beaker site near Avebury—1500 B.C. or thereabouts. Look here." He hunted briefly along the skull's jagged perimeter and found some faded, tiny numbers written in pen: SB J6-2. "You see? But how very odd! How did it get into Pummy's case? And where's Pummy?"

"This fragment—is it from the museum's collection?"

"Yes, of course, but it ought to be in storage in the basement." The tense skin around his eyes relaxed slightly. "Someone must have accidentally exchanged the two, don't you think? Why, Pummy must be right downstairs in the basement."

The run to the basement was made with a speed and directness of which Gideon had thought Professor Hall-Waddington incapable. Once there, the doors of a metal storage cabinet were thrown ajar, the contents hastily rummaged through, and finally the lid of a dusty cardboard box labeled SB J6-2 was flung heedlessly across the room. Professor Hall-Waddington thrust his face into the box.

"Empty! Pummy...Pummy appears to have been..." He held the box in trembling hands and looked up at Gideon with wondering eyes. "But why would anyone steal a thirty-thousand-year-old parieto-occipital calvareal fragment?"

❑ 2 ❑

"WHY *WOULD* ANYONE steal a thirty-thousand-year-old whatzit?" Julie asked, her black eyes no less wondering.

"Beats the hell out of me," Gideon said.

She stopped walking and tilted her face upward. "Ooh, that smells wonderful. Whatever it is, let's get some."

He agreed readily, delighted to see her healthy appetite returning. She had felt the lingering effects of jet lag through three wet and gloomy days in London, and their stay had left her a little dispirited, not a typical condition with her. He, too, had been depressed by the huge city—perceptibly grungier than the last time he'd seen it six years before—and was happy to get out of it.

Once they'd rented the little Ford Escort and driven west past the dormitory towns and through Hampshire, and then into the green and rolling hills of Dorset, they'd begun to cheer up, and now, guidebook in hand, they had just embarked on the agreeably small-scale adventure of exploring Dorchester.

The aroma that had caught their attention turned out to be coming from a bakery a few doors away on the High Street, and they went in and sat themselves down at a tiny wooden table, for two big wedges of warm Dorset apple cake and a pot of tea. They were both coffee drinkers, but this was England, after all, and what was the point of foreign travel if you carried your old tastes and prejudices around with you? Besides, they'd tried English coffee.

As they ate, Gideon took the opportunity to watch Julie and to congratulate himself on his good luck, both of which he'd been doing a lot of lately. And why not? Life was full and sweet, sweeter than he had any right to expect. When Nora had been killed four years before, he couldn't imagine ever loving again; he could barely think about living. And now, astoundingly, he was married. There was Julie at his side, munching away; bouncy, pretty, bright, robust Julie, whom he hadn't known a year ago, and who was now the center of his existence. She had left her Park Service job; he was on leave for the fall quarter; and they were spending a rambling, come-what-may honeymoon in England. And it was as if his life were starting over again.

"You know," she said suddenly, putting down her fork and brushing back a tendril of dark, glossy hair, "you sure don't look like a world-renowned anthropologist." She'd been studying him too; the thought was absurdly pleasing.

"I'm not a world-renowned anthropologist."

"Yes, you are. You told me; twice, at least. And you're certainly the world's best-known skeleton detective." This referred to an unfortunate label that had appeared in a magazine article about his identification of some human remains that had been buried for thirty years. The sobriquet had clung, and Gideon spent considerable effort among his colleagues at Northern California State University trying to live it down.

"Bite your tongue," he said. Then, after a moment: "What's a world-renowned anthropologist supposed to look like?"

"Not like you. He's not supposed to be big and broad-shouldered, with a prizefighter's nose and a beautiful, warm, hairy chest, and—"

"Hey, finish your tea," he said, ridiculously happy. "I think we'd better do some sightseeing."

They went back out into the venerable and bustling High Street with its pleasing jumble of old cottages, staid Georgian bow windows, ancient, lichen-stained church walls, and

twentieth-century facades. Inside of an hour they'd visited
the Thomas Hardy statue at Top o'Town, admired the
remains of the Roman wall, crossed a stone bridge on which
a notice informed them that it was off-limits to "locomotive
traction engines and other ponderous carriages," and looked
at various sites purported to be models for the settings in
Hardy's *Mayor of Casterbridge*.

Docilely following the terse instructions in their guidebook, they turned left at the County Laboratory, walked
down the narrow, high-walled passage to its end, and mounted
the flight of steps. When they had done so, they found
themselves in a parking lot.

This, their book informed them, *is the site of No. 7 Shire
Hall Place, where Hardy lived from June 1883 until June
1885—now,* it added unnecessarily, *a car park.*

From there they were directed to a gray stone mansion
called Colliton House, *the prototype for Lucetta's house,
High Place Hall*.

Gideon read aloud from the guidebook. " 'The arms over
the front entry are extremely interesting: Sable, A Lion
Rampant Argent, Debruised with a Bendlet Gules—' Julie,
are you really enjoying this?"

"Are you?"

It didn't take them long to agree that they weren't, and a
quick skimming of the rest of the book gave them the happy
information that *nearby the river Frome, with its many
Hardy associations, wends its peaceful way between shaded
banks, followed closely by a rustic river path.*

They decided to let the Hardy associations go for the
moment and to stroll the bucolic, deserted path for its own
pleasures. At their feet the tiny river babbled and purled,
while a few yards beyond it rose the mossy base of the
flat-topped mound on which Dorchester—or Durnovaria, as
it was called in Roman times—had first been built. On the
other side of the path were tidy little vegetable gardens, one
after another, and beyond them, in the distance, lay lonely
Durnover Moor, hazy in the pale afternoon light.

"I keep wondering why anybody would take that darn

skull," Julie announced abruptly, once they'd walked quietly for a while.

"Me too."

"It's famous, isn't it?"

"To physical anthropologists, yes."

"Well, isn't it worth money then? Couldn't it have been stolen to be sold?"

"To another museum, you mean? Well, a museum would pay for something like that, sure—a lot of money. But Pummy wouldn't be sellable. Any decent physical anthropologist who took a good hard look at it would know it's Poundbury Man, and he'd know that Poundbury Man belongs in the Dorchester Museum. So even if some shady museum was willing to buy stolen materials, there'd be no point."

"Do you mean there's only *one* Poundbury Man? Aren't there others from the same . . . the same population, that look more or less like him?"

"No," Gideon said, pausing to watch some skinny children feed bread chunks to some fat ducks, "he's one of a kind. He's Homo sapiens, of course, but no one else from *that* time and *that* place has been found. And he *is* remarkably dolichocephalic—long-headed. Whether he was just an oddball that way, or whether all his people looked like that, no one knows, because he's the only one we've got. There are even some anthropologists who want to dub him a separate subspecies—Homo sapiens poundburiensis, or some such."

"Really? They want to postulate an entire subspecific population on the basis of a single fragmentary—" She burst into sudden laughter, startling the ducks. "Good gosh, I'm starting to talk like you!"

"That's what happens to married people."

"After five days?"

Gideon shrugged. "You must be a quick study."

"I guess I am." She reached out for his hand as they moved on over a low stone bridge. "Well, anyway, if not a museum, what about a private collector? Aren't some fabulously rich eccentrics supposed to have their own collections of stolen Rembrandts or Vermeers, even though they can't show them to anyone? Wouldn't this thing be worth money to someone like that?''

"Rembrandts I can see, but a broken old piece of skull? He'd have to be pretty eccentric, all right.''

"Mmm,'' Julie said, thinking. "Okay, could it be some kind of joke? Maybe Pummy's just been hidden, not stolen, and the other skull was put in the case as a hoax.''

"The same thing's occurred to me. But what for?''

"To make Professor Hall-Waddington look silly? Maybe you weren't supposed to find it and tell him in your nice way. Maybe there was supposed to be a big scandal.''

"Possibly. . . This is all pretty conjectural, isn't it?''

"Yes, but it's fascinating.''

They crossed a final footbridge and found themselves with surprising suddenness out of the dappled shade and back on the High Street, a few blocks from where they'd started.

Gideon looked at his watch. "Feel like walking some more?''

"'Uh-uh.''

"Want to drop into a pub?''

"They don't open for another hour.''

"That's right. Well, let's see, what can we do?''

She cocked her head at him. "Here you are on your honeymoon, with your beautiful young bride at your side, and your hotel less than two blocks away. . . and you can't think of anything to do?''

"Nope,'' he said blandly, "not a thing. But why don't we go up to our room, take off our clothes, and lie down? Maybe something will occur to me.''

It was two hours before they arrived for dinner at the Judge Jeffreys on the High Street, an ancient inn with a grim past, having been the lodging of Baron George Jeffreys, the presiding judge at the Bloody Assize of 1685, when seventy-four of Cromwell's royalist opponents had been executed. Nevertheless, the dining room was cozy and country-pubbish, a centuries-old room with rough-beamed ceiling and stone-mullioned, multipaned windows of wavy, leaded glass.

"What would you think," Gideon said as they settled into a black, gleaming wooden booth, "of spending the next day or two in Charmouth? Since we're in the area anyway, I'd like to drop in on a dig near there—Stonebarrow Fell. I thought maybe I'd better stop in and see how Nate Marcus is doing."

"Here we are then," said their hurried waitress, and laid the pints of bitter they'd ordered on the table. Julie and Gideon clinked the heavy glass mugs in a wordless toast.

"Why '*better* stop in'?" Julie asked. "And who's Nate Marcus? An old friend of yours?"

Gideon nodded. "I haven't seen him a few years, but we were both graduate students at Wisconsin, under Abe Goldstein. He's head of the anthro department at some place called Gelden College in Missouri. When Abe heard you and I were thinking of coming this way, he suggested I stop by and see if I couldn't keep him out of trouble."

"What kind of trouble?"

Gideon sipped the cool, soothing bitter. "The same as always," he said. "Nate rubs a lot of people the wrong way. He can be pretty. . . well, abrasive."

"Abrasive? You mean rude?"

"Yes, rude. And flip and sarcastic, and aggressive and thin-skinned. Know-it-all . . . arrogant . . ."

"This is one of your old friends? I'd love to hear you describe an enemy."

Gideon laughed. "To tell the truth, I do like him—most of the time anyway—even if I'm not exactly sure why. He and I sat up a lot of nights, over a lot of pitchers of beer, at the old Student Union in Madison, arguing anthropological trivia until four in the morning. Those are good memories."

"Well, he still sounds awful. What's he doing in charge of a dig?"

"For one thing, his excavating technique is impeccable. For another, the Stonebarrow Fell site is his personal discovery. As I understand it, he took one sharp-eyed look at the place—undug, mind you; just a grassy hilltop—and announced there was a Bronze Age burial mound there, even though the mound itself had weathered away. And on top of

that, he said it was Wessex culture, to be exact; circa 1700
B.C.''

"And was he right?"

"He was this time—which, as you can imagine, irritated
a lot of people. You can guess how the Wessex Antiquarian
Society, which is a very sober, professional group of archaeologists, feels about some brash, belligerent American—
which Nate is, I'm afraid—stomping in and finding the
mound in their backyard."

Julie frowned as she sipped from her glass. "But if he
was right, he was right. It doesn't seem very professional
to keep a grudge over it."

Gideon laughed. "I hate to disillusion you, but anthropologists are people like anyone else. The thing is, you see,
that the site's now been radiocarbon-dated at 1700 to 1600
B.C., exactly as he predicted, which makes it the earliest
accurately dated Bronze Age barrow in England; it's a heck
of a find, and it could answer a lot of questions."

"Well, that's good for all concerned, isn't it? I still don't
see why this Wessex Antiquarian Society should hold a
grudge."

"They don't. In fact they're very honorably cosponsoring
the dig, although the Horizon Foundation is putting up most
of the money. But it still has to rankle, and Nate, as usual,
is blowing his own horn, so the squabbling goes on and on."

The waitress brought menus, and they ordered smoked
mackerel followed by steak-and-kidney pie, with another
round of bitters. The little room was filling up, and Gideon,
for once, was enjoying the closeness of others. The soft
British laughter and the polite, civil English speech created
an agreeable, unintrusive ambience.

The mackerel was brought out immediately, a whole
dusky fish on each plate, and they set silently to work,
peeling back the golden skin and separating the tender flesh
from rib and backbone. They were hungrier than they'd
realized and didn't speak again, except for murmurs of
appreciation, until they'd turned the fish over and scraped
the last shreds of meat free with their forks.

Julie wiped her lips and pushed away a fish skeleton so

perfect it might have been dissected, then took a sip from the new glass. "Ah," she said contentedly, "my mind is clear again. But I still don't understand why they're quarreling. If your friend was right about this Bronze Age thing, he was right. Right? What is there to fight about?"

"As usual, Nate's found something." Gideon absently fingered the smooth, round dimples in his beer mug. "From what I understand, he claims to have come up with incontrovertible evidence that Wessex culture is the direct result of Mycenaean diffusion, and—this is what's got everyone excited—he's not talking about plain old cultural diffusion, but actual, physical transmigration from the Peloponnese directly to England."

"Incontrovertible evidence of Mycenaean diffusion!" Julie exclaimed, her eyes wide. "In direct transmigration! My goodness, no wonder everybody's excited."

"Yes—" He looked at her over the rim of his glass, one eyebrow raised. "Young woman, are you having sport with me?"

Julie laughed. "I wouldn't dare. But what in the world are you talking about?"

"I'm talking about the fact that Nate is one of the few Bronze Age archaeologists who categorically reject parallelism as a mechanism for the transmission of cultural—"

"Gideon, dear, have mercy, please."

Gideon groaned. "My gosh, weren't you an anthro minor? What do they teach you in Washington? All right, let me try to make it simple; no theoretical stuff."

"That would be nice."

"In England, the main Bronze Age culture is called 'Wessex,' okay?"

"As in Thomas Hardy's Wessex."

"Right. Well, this Wessex culture appeared fairly suddenly and overran the earlier Beaker culture—the Beakers being the last of the Neolithic people, the ones who built Stonehenge. You've heard of Stonehenge?" Julie rightfully ignored this, and Gideon continued. "Now, the question is: Just how did this advanced Wessex culture, with its metal technology, get here? Where did it come from? Who brought it? Was it an actual migration of people, or was it simply the adoption by the Beakers of some of the technology and social customs of the Europeans they traded with? Nowadays, it's the latter that's generally accepted."

Any teacher of even minimal perception knows the signs of lack of interest in an audience that does not wish to offend. There is an intense fixity of gaze; brows are knit with expectancy and concentration; chins are supported on hands, the better to permit leaning attentively forward. But the gazes are glassy and unwavering, the rapt expressions vaguely unfocused, the postures rigid rather than alert. So sat Julie across the table.

"As we all know," Gideon went on, "the Wessex people were the inventors of the video game. They wore polyester pantsuits and lived in four-story houses made from abandoned escargot shells."

For a moment there was no slackening in her enthralled and unrelenting attention. Then she spluttered into laughter. "You rat! All right, you caught me. I'm afraid I go a little blank at words like 'metal technology.' But really, tell me about Nate Marcus. I'm interested, truly." She blinked her eyes severely to demonstrate.

Gideon smiled. "Okay, in a nutshell: Nathan Marcus is probably the only anthropologist who believes that some seafaring bunch of Mycenaeans set out from Greece and settled in England, where they singlehandedly started the British Bronze Age in about 1700 B.C. Now, there isn't too much doubt that the British Bronze Age had its roots in the Aegean, but the evidence points to its spreading to England slowly, over centuries, via Europe, possibly without any migration of people at all."

"Without any migration? How could that be?"

"Well, just through cultural diffusion. The same way you find English rock music all over Russia today, or French wines in Kansas and New Mexico."

The waitress brought their steak-and-kidney pies. It was the first time Julie had tried one. She broke the crust with a fork and gingerly sniffed the pungent steam.

"It smells all right," she said doubtfully, and enlarged the hole to peer inside. "Which pieces are kidney?"

"The kidney sort of disappears in the cooking. All those chunks are beef." A white lie, but she would thank him for it.

She speared a tiny piece of meat, put it in her mouth, and chewed tentatively. "It's not bad."

"Of course not." He scooped up a forkful of his own thick pie. The English, he felt, were somewhat maligned in the matter of their food. There were, of course, grotesqueries like baked beans on toast and those unfortunate, unavoidable breakfast sausages, but he found the cuisine generally mild and inoffensive: plaice, hake, gammon, beef, and pile upon bland pile of peas and chips.

"So is that what the argument's about?" Julie asked. "The dispute over the Bronze Age?"

"That's it. Nate thinks that Wessex culture—and therefore the British Bronze Age—was personally introduced by the Mycenaeans, and everybody else says it came through slow diffusion."

"It hardly seems like anything to get fighting mad about."

"Anthropologists are funny people, as I'm sure you're coming to realize, but where Nate is concerned, there's more to it. Since the respectable journals won't touch his theory, he's been out pushing it anywhere he can—magazines, newspapers, talk shows—and that doesn't help his credibility among anthropologists."

"What about his theory? Do you think he could be right?"

"I doubt it, but I don't know enough about it to have a legitimate opinion. To tell the truth, I can't say I find the Bronze Age all that fascinating myself. Too recent."

"Seventeen hundred B.C. is recent?"

"Sure, to an anthropologist. Didn't you ever hear what Agatha Christie said about being married to one?"

"I didn't know she was."

"Yes, a famous one: Max Mallowan. She said it was wonderful—the older she got, the more interesting he found her."

"I hope it's true," Julie said, laughing. She pushed aside her not-quite-finished pie. "That was good," she said a little uncertainly, "but I think you have to acquire a taste for it." She sipped her bitters and looked soberly at him. "Gideon, you're not going to let yourself get involved in a theoretical argument, are you? It's our honeymoon."

He cupped his hand over hers on her glass. "Do you really think I'd rather get into an academic fracas than spend my time with you? I love you, Julie Tendler—"

"Oliver."

"Oliver... I forget what I was going to say."

"How much you love me."

"Oh, yeah. Well, let's see. On a scale of one to ten I'd say a, well, um, maybe a, well . . ."

"I'm going to hit him," she muttered into her glass.

He took her hand from the glass and brushed the backs of her fingers over his lips. Her eyes glowed suddenly in the semidarkness of the restaurant, and he felt his own moisten. How extraordinary it was to be married to this marvelous woman. For a moment he held her hand against his cheek, then replaced it on the glass, recurving her fingers around the handle.

"Never mind how much I love you," he said, "I'm not about to encourage complacency. Anyway, all I intend to do when we get to Charmouth is to pay an hour's visit to the site and say hello to Nate. That's it."

"And after that we're on our own? No more bones? Just cream teas and country walks and pub lunches?"

"No bones, no stones, and, thank God, no corpses. The skeleton detective is traveling incognito and nobody knows where to find him." He put down his nearly empty mug with a thump. "And now, if you think steak-and-kidney pie is good, wait till you try treacle!"

□ 3 □

THE WALK FROM Charmouth to Stonebarrow Fell was so magnificent that Gideon almost went back to the Queen's Armes Hotel to bring Julie along, but she had been adamant. He was making a professional visit, she had pointed out, and she wasn't going to tag along to hang around like an ignoramus while everyone else was chattering on about Mycenaean transmigration and cultural diffusion.

"Besides," she'd said, "we've been married six days and I have yet to perform a single wifely function."

He grinned at her, but she laughed before he had a chance to say anything. "Fun things don't count; I mean chores. Do you know, I have yet to do the laundry? We've been washing our stuff in sinks, and things are getting grubby. I want to go to an honest-to-goodness Laundromat."

She seemed to mean it, and Gideon had let it go at that. After lunch he had left her to her wifely chores and walked out Lower Sea Lane, past the bright, clean bed-and-breakfast houses and private cottages of the village, to the sandy beach. There, in its grander days, the River Char had worn a soft, lush U-shaped valley down to the sea between the towering coastal cliffs. High up on those cliffs, reachable by a gentle but relentlessly ascending path, was the prettily if redundantly named Stonebarrow Fell—Stonehill Hill, in modern English.

He crossed the wooden footbridge over the now-tiny River Char and headed up the green, sweeping slope at a good, swinging pace, enjoying the crisp ocean air and the welcome sensation of muscles working. It was a cool, cloudy day, with an immense fog bank a few miles offshore, but the air was clear, and the sea was green and silvered, lit by narrow columns of sunlight that slid over its surface like spotlights. To the east, behind him, was Charmouth in its picture-book valley, and a mile beyond it, down the curving coast, there was Lyme Regis, compact and pretty, with its famous stone breakwater—the Cobb—snaking out into the ocean. Ahead of him the green, round-shouldered hill rose to the top of the fell, and a few miles farther on, the aptly named Golden Cap loomed, solid and squarish, over the Dorset coast.

Near the top of the hill, the path swung out to the very edge of dizzyingly sheer cliffs and Gideon instinctively moved back. He was a good four hundred feet above the beach, and the land under him was obviously unstable. The rim of the path had crumbled away in places, and even while he looked, a few pebbles dropped free to start a small, slithering landslide. Still, he paused to take in the scene. These were famous cliffs to anyone who knew something about fossils. It had been here at the base of this wall of blue lias clay, about half a mile beyond Charmouth, that ten-year-old Mary Anning had chanced upon a twenty-five-foot icthyosaurus skeleton and set the scientific world of 1811 on its ear. Which was just what Nate Marcus hoped to do with his "incontrovertible evidence" of a Mycenaean landing. Well, good luck to him, but Gideon would be very surprised if he had that evidence, or if it existed.

A hundred feet from the crest of the hill, where the path cut through a dense thicket of gorse, was the last of four stiles. Here a ten-foot wire fence had been put up, and on it was a stenciled sign: *Archaeological excavation in progress. Visitors admitted only with prior authorization. Wessex Antiquarian Society.* A heavy padlock on a thick chain made good the warning.

There was no information on how to get authorized, and he was thinking about climbing the fence and taking his chances with the wrath of the Wessex Antiquarian Society when a puff of wind carried a few syllables of barely audible conversation down from above, from the far side of the summit.

"Hi!" Gideon shouted. "Anybody home?"

Within a few seconds a husky, pink-faced young man came trotting down the path and up to the other side of the fence.

"Hiya," he said. "Want in?" He was an American in his midtwenties, thick-necked and slope-shouldered, with downy cheeks and a healthy farm boy's smile. A scant blond mustache, painstakingly groomed, but obviously never going to amount to much, glistened on his upper lip.

"Yes," Gideon said. "I'm an anthropologist; an old friend of Dr. Marcus's."

"Sure. no problem." From the pocket of his jeans he produced a key. Once Gideon was through the gate, the young man closed and locked it again, shaking the lock to test it.

"I'm Barry Fusco," he volunteered.

"Glad to know you, Barry. You're a student at Gelden?"

"Uh-huh, all of us are. The workers, I mean: me, and Sandra, and Leon, and Randy. Dr. Marcus and Dr. Frawley are profs, of course." He flashed his engaging smile. "Not that they don't work. I just meant that the ones who do the real work—you know, the peon work—are the students. Not that I'm complaining . . . " He carried on in this affable if muzzy manner while they climbed to the crest.

Once there, Gideon saw that the summit of Stonebarrow Fell was a grassy, rounded meadow that seemed to be at the very top of a world of rolling green downs and endless sea, with cliff and hillside falling away in every direction. The dig itself was about a hundred feet from the edge of the cliff, and consisted of two wedge-shaped pits about twelve feet across at their widest points, situated like two great pieces of a pie that had been quartered.

There were three people in the shallower wedge, which

had been dug down about a foot and a half: a young man and woman about Barry's age who were on their knees scraping at the pit floor (peon work?), and an older man—not Nate Marcus—who leaned over them, watching closely.

"You just want to watch?" Barry asked.

"For a few minutes."

While Barry climbed down into the trench and got to work, Gideon walked up to the single strand of rope that protected the excavation from a listless group of nine or ten schoolchildren and a glum-faced woman. The rope restraint was hardly necessary: the onlookers could not have been less enthusiastic.

And no wonder. Archaeological digs did not very often turn up bronze masks, or cups of gold, or ancient skulls with jewels in their eyesockets. Mostly, a dig consisted of hour after slow hour of scraping gingerly away at the earth. When something was uncovered, the chances were ninety-nine out of a hundred that it was fragmentary, nondescript, and muddy-brown—a piece of a sooty cooking pot, a two-inch segment of a bone awl, a discarded flake of waste flint or granite; all unrecognizable and of no conceivable interest to the lay observer. And even then, one did not just "dig up" a piece of a pot or a bone tool. One cleared the area around it millimeter by millimeter, photographing it, drawing it, measuring and recording it as one went. The basic tools were the trowel, the hoe, and the brush, not the pick and shovel. As spectator sport, it was far from riveting.

"Mrs. Kimberly, may we please go now?" a fat boy pleaded fretfully. "I'm *awfully* hungry."

There was a round of stifled giggles, and the unhappy-looking Mrs. Kimberly lined the children up. "You'd think there'd be something to *see* after coming all this way," she grumbled querulously and marched them off. Barry ran after them to let them through the gate.

It was another minute before the older man looked up for the first time, lifting a pouchy face with eyes as mournful, moist, and droopy as a basset's.

"Yes?" he said morosely to Gideon.

"I'm looking for Dr. Marcus. Can you tell me where to find him?"

"And you are . . . ?"

"Gideon Oliver. An old friend."

The man sighed lugubriously and stood up. "I'll see if he's available." He climbed gravely from the far side of the pit, a small, soft man with little feet who seemed out of place on a field expedition, and made his way fussily around the backfill piles toward a prefabricated building of corrugated metal.

Barry had returned and was looking at Gideon with frank but somewhat puzzled awe on his open countenance. "Gee," he said, "are you *the* Gideon Oliver?"

Gideon was asked this from time to time, sometimes by a person familiar with his publications on Pleistocene hominid taxonomy, but a great deal more often by someone who'd read a lurid account of his consulting work with the police or FBI. He had never hit on a satisfactory response.

"Well," he said, smiling modestly, "I'm *a* Gideon Oliver."

Understandably, this seemed to confuse Barry, so Gideon added, "I teach anthro at Northern Cal."

The serious, friendly face cleared somewhat. "Gee, sir, I've sure heard of you."

From a slight vacancy in the smile, it was clear that the young man knew Gideon was *someone*, but didn't quite know who.

The rewards of fame, Gideon thought. "Thanks, Barry," he said. "How about introducing me to your friends?"

The other two were absorbed, or pretending to be absorbed, in their scraping, but Barry called to them enthusiastically. "Hey, guys, this is Professor Oliver from Northern Cal." Then, indicating the woman, he said, "This is Sandra Mazur."

From her knees she looked up, and Gideon saw a thin, pale face, long-nosed and elegant in an edgy, horsey way, with sharp, delicate cheekbones over which the skin was tightly stretched.

"Hi, there, Prof," she said brightly. With one hand she took a cigarette from the corner of her mouth. With the other she gave him a sober mock salute, tipping her trowel to her forehead. It seemed to Gideon there was something false in the casual, easy greeting, something that didn't go with the shadows under her eyes or the tense, almost haggard set of her thin lips. The trowel at her forehead tossed back a few pale, wispy strands that had straggled from under a woolen headband.

"Good morning," he said. "Looks like you have something there." He indicated a small black object before her, lumpy and shapeless, and still only partly coaxed from the earth.

"Yes, I think it's a leather belt buckle. What do you think?"

"Could be, or maybe a wristguard—you know, for an archer."

"Yes!" she cried. Again Gideon had the feeling she was overdoing it. "These holes could be where the thongs went, couldn't they?" She bent over it again, crouching to blow away the crumbs of dirt as she loosened them. Her teeth were sunk in her lower lip—to show her concentration? —and when the wisp of fine hair fell over her eyes again, she ignored it.

"And this," Barry said, "is Leon Hillyer."

The third person in the trench was already rising and wiping his hands on his jeans. There was something slightly familiar about the good-looking, self-assured face with its well-trimmed golden beard, the compact body, and the concise, almost prissy movements, but Gideon couldn't remember where he'd seen him before.

"The skeleton detective," Leon said—a little dryly, Gideon thought, but the intelligent face wore a cordial enough smile and the cleaned hand was extended.

"Right," said Barry, and then, with pleasure as it clicked, *"Right,* the skeleton detective! Damn!"

Gideon shook Leon's hand. "We've met, haven't we?"

"Not exactly," Leon said. "I delivered a Gabow Award

paper at last year's Triple-A meeting in Detroit. You probably saw me."

Gideon remembered. The Gabow Awards were three
one-thousand-dollar prizes given by the American Anthropological Association for the best student papers of the year,
and Leon's had dealt with the inferring of broad cultural
values from ceramic analysis. Gideon had found it rather
long on broad cultural values and short on ceramic analysis,
but it had been competently done. He remembered being put
off by a certain insolence in Leon's manner, a smug expectation of esteem due him from an audience composed of
distinguished men and women, many of whom were two or
three times his age.

"I did," Gideon said. "I thought it was a fine paper."

"Thanks. I sat in on your panel on Neanderthal population genetics the next day. I thought you made some damn
good points."

This was delivered man to man, one colleague to another,
and Gideon was freshly and unreasonably nettled by Leon's
offhand self-satisfaction.

While they had been talking, Barry had begun to pick up
crumpled gum and candy wrappers that had been left behind
by the school group. "You know the way Dr. Marcus is
about housekeeping," he said to Gideon.

"No, I don't. Is he a stickler?"

It was Leon who replied. "White-glove inspection every
day. One tool out of place, one shovelful of dirt where it's
not supposed to be, and we have to stay after class for a
twenty-minute lecture."

The three students snickered among themselves and settled back to work.

When the older man still had not emerged from the shed
after another minute or two—what was taking so long?
—Gideon said, "Looks like you have an interesting dig
doing. Mind if I come down and have a look?"

"Sure!" Barry said. "You can tell us about the ribs."

"Ribs?" Gideon ducked under the rope and dropped
easily into the pit.

Sandra pushed at her sandy hair with the back of her

wrist. "We uncovered a couple of broken ribs over there in the northeast quadrant," she said, squinting through cigarette smoke, "and we've been arguing about them for days. Everybody but Leon says they're human. And he won't give up, because he can't believe he could be wrong." She turned a bright, toothy smile on Leon.

Leon did not return it. He jerked his head petulantly. "It's just that I happen to be right."

"Well, let's have a look," Gideon said.

In the wall of the trench, two sections of rib had been carefully excavated, the dirt around them shaved away so that they lay like an offering to the gods on an eight-inch pedestal of earth. Gideon knelt to look briefly at them, then straightened up.

"What makes you so sure they couldn't be human, Leon?"

His lips pursed, Leon studied the bones with professional nonchalance. Absently, he took a roll of mints from the pocket of his windbreaker and pushed one into his mouth with his thumb. "It's the shape. It's hard to put into words, but they just don't look human."

"But they're the right size," Barry put in. "Too small for a cow, too big for a dog."

"No, Leon's right," Gideon said. "They're not human; not enough curvature. If you made a cross section of a human body and looked down on the ribs from above, the rib cage would be kind of heart-shaped, sort of like a big, fat apple, with the stem at the back, where the spine is. But a quadruped's rib cage—a deer, say, which I think this is—would be shaped more like a . . . oh, like an elongated egg—like a bucket, really."

"Gee," Barry said, "they sure look human to me."

"No, human ribs are more curved, like arcs of a circle. You can see these are much more flattened."

"Yes, it's obviously caused by evolution," Leon said easily. "In a four-footed animal, gravity would make the weight of the internal organs bear on the front of the rib cage, so it would naturally be shaped like a bucket to hold them in. But a human stands on his hind feet, so to speak, so his organs aren't supported by his ribs, and they spread out into a nice, roomy circle.''

He *is* quick, Gideon thought; no doubt about that. By comparison, Barry's glazed eyes showed that he'd been left far behind.

"That's right," Gideon said, "except that it isn't *caused* by evolution. Evolution isn't the cause of anything, strictly speaking; it's a set of responses, of adaptations—"

"Well, yes," Leon said, "that's one way of looking at it—" He stopped, seeing that the older man had returned.

"Golly, Dr. Oliver," the man said in mournful apology, "I must have been out to lunch when you said who you were. Nate's talked about you lots of times." His liquid eyes shone with abashed sincerity. The man really does look like a basset, Gideon thought. Even his ears were baggy.

He shook hands with Gideon, a sincere, confidential two-handed shake, the left hand gripping Gideon's elbow. "I'm Jack Frawley, Nate's assistant. I'm an associate prof at Gelden." He smiled weakly. "It's a genuine pleasure to meet you."

Although he'd never met him, Gideon knew who Frawley was. At one time he'd been a promising scholar, and he'd achieved his associate professorship by the time he was twenty-five. Two decades ago, however, he had published a paper in *American Antiquity* in which he'd made a string of elementary statistical errors. Published responses had been scathing and brutal, after the time-honored fashion of learned societies, and Frawley had never dared to publish again, as far as Gideon knew.

In the world of academia, that had meant a dead stop to his career, and for more than twenty years he had remained an associate professor at Gelden. When old Blassie had retired two years ago as head of the department, Frawley, the senior member of the faculty, hadn't even been considered as a replacement, and the younger Nate Marcus had been brought in from Case Western Reserve.

"Well, well, come on back," Frawley said with oily

hospitality that failed to convince. "I'm sure you want to see Nate."

Gideon turned to Leon. "Sorry, I hope we can finish this another time."

"Anytime, Gideon," Leon said. "Always glad to hear your views."

Gideon? . . . Hear your views? What the hell kind of way was that for a graduate student to talk to a professor he'd just met? But then, why shouldn't he be sure of himself? And why should he, Gideon, be ruffled by informality from someone not much more than ten years younger? Was he already looking jealously over his shoulder at the next generation of bright young anthropologists? Now *there* was a tendency to be watched.

As they walked toward the corrugated-metal shed, Frawley clasped Gideon's forearm and moved closer. There was stale pipe tobacco on his breath. "Now, Gideon," he said confidentially, "—may I call you Gideon?—I'd like to share some thoughts with you in all candor."

Gideon's vague unease defined itself more sharply. People eager to "share" things with him put him off—particularly after a one-minute acquaintance. So did people who squeezed his arm—men, anyway—conspiratorially or otherwise, and leveled shiny-eyed, straight-shooting gazes on him. And he'd never been much of a fan of the double handshake.

"Damn!" Frawley unexpectedly exclaimed. Not looking where he was going, he had stumbled over the corner of a narrow trench not far from the shed.

"What is it?" Gideon asked. "A test pit?" With a little luck, Frawley might forget about his candid thoughts.

"A test pit, yes. Nate thought there might be a barrow here, or some buildings, with their surface features obliterated."

Gideon could see no reason to think so, but then no one had believed there was anything at the site of the main dig either, except for Nate. "You didn't find anything?"

"Nothing. A foot and a half below the surface we hit glacial till. I mean the Riss glaciation—Middle Pleistocene. We certainly weren't going to find anything interesting under that; it'd be two hundred thousand years old, at least.''

Gideon smiled to himself. Two hundred thousand years. That was about where things began to get interesting, as far as he was concerned.

But not as far as Frawley was concerned. The older man urged him on—with a hand at his elbow—and then, as they approached the door to the shed, he squeezed Gideon's forearm once more. Whatever it was he wanted to tell Gideon in all candor, it looked like Gideon was going to have to hear it.

"Yes?" he said.

Frawley heard the coolness in his voice. The hand fell from Gideon's arm, and the sober face, which had been staring directly up into Gideon's, retreated with its sour tobacco smell.

"Well, it's only that you should know that, in all candor, Nate isn't quite himself. He's been very..." He pursed his lips, chewed his words. "What I mean to say is that he's, well, terribly determined to prove he's right about the Mycenaeans bringing the Wessex culture with them to England.''

"You don't agree with his theory?" Gideon asked.

Frawley looked aggrieved. "Do *you?*"

It was a fair if surprisingly direct question. "No," Gideon said. "It made a little sense in the thirties and forties, when no one realized the extent of Bronze Age commerce. But now it seems pretty simplistic to invent a three-thousand-mile sea voyage when long-term trade contracts explain things a lot better.''

"Well, there you are," Frawley said, vaguely mollified. "But that isn't my point. What I'm getting at is the idea—I think I might well say the fact—that this . . . obsession of his is getting in the way of his objectivity. All this defending himself, and this fighting with the Antiquarian Society. . . . Well, I think maybe it's affected his judgment, made him a little . . . well, paranoid.''

The hand darted out briefly to touch Gideon's arm again. "Now, I don't mean to imply he's not doing a top-notch job. No, sir, no way, not for a minute. What I'm trying to say is''—here the sincere and shining eyes were turned full on Gideon again—''that he needs help, your support. He's made some wonderful contributions. He's a wonderful person, a great man.''

What, Gideon wondered, was this all about? A little judicious, not-so-subtle backstabbing by the loyal, passed-over senior faculty member? But why to Gideon? What did he have to do with it?

Frawley drew himself up, manfully putting the lid on his emotions. ''Shall we go in now, Gideon?''

◻ 4 ◻

FROM JACK FRAWLEY'S tone, Gideon half expected to walk into the parlor of a funeral home, and was relieved immediately at the friendly, familiar clutter and jumble of an archaeological workroom. Most of the small interior was taken up by two pushed-together old tables on which were several newly put-together pottery sections, the beads of glue still fresh on them; a few blackened, unidentifiable scraps of metal; and five or six small paper bags labeled with thick, black numbers. There was also a corroded but impressive bronze dagger, next to which lay the golden nails that had studded its hilt and the few rotten slivers of wood that were presumably all that remained of the hilt itself. Obviously, it had been a productive dig so far.

Squeezed around the table were five or six folding metal chairs, and on one of them, near an electric heater, sat Nate Marcus. Frawley's warning notwithstanding, he looked very much like himself: small and wiry, intense and sarcastic. He was a man of extraordinary hirsuteness. Black and vigorous, his hair always seemed to be in the process of taking him over, gleaming blue-black and gritty on his spare cheeks, dipping low on his forehead in a thick, simian wedge, meeting above his eyes in a woolly, Cyclopean eyebrow that sent fuzzy feelers halfway down his nose. In the V of his open collar a glossy tuft sprouted like a nest of tangled wires.

I know just what he's going to say, Gideon thought, and exactly how he's going to say it. *Well, look who's here,* he'll say in that mocking, flip New York accent he'd never lost, *the famous skeleton detective.*

"Look who's here," Nate said flatly. "What a terrific surprise."

"Hi, Nate. It's nice to see you."

"Sure." Nate folded his arms. "Have a seat. Have some coffee."

"Thanks," Gideon said, unsure of himself, feeling as if he were accepting not a cup of coffee but a challenge.

Frawley scuttled to a corner. "I'll take care of the coffee," he said, heavily jocose. "That's an assistant director's primary responsibility." He busied himself with the coffee things that are as omnipresent as calipers or acetone in archaeology workrooms all over the world.

Nate stared at Gideon, his eyes inexpressive. "Okay, Gid, what do you want?"

Even for Nate this was pretty brusque, and there was an increasing prickle of irritation at the back of Gideon's neck. Or was he being unduly sensitive? He had been irritated by Leon; he hadn't liked Sandra; he found Frawley odious; and now Nate seemed even ruder than usual. Maybe Gideon was just having one of his misanthropic days and it was all in his mind. On the other hand, he reassured himself charitably, he hadn't disliked Barry, had he? No, it wasn't his perception; there was something uneasy, something off-key in the atmosphere of Stonebarrow Fell.

"I don't want anything," he said evenly. "I was traveling in the area with my wife, so I thought I'd say hello. And Abe Goldstein wanted me to give you his best."

There was a ponderous silence while Frawley brought back three mugs of coffee clutched insecurely in his white hands. He set them carefully on the table. "There we go. See, even assistant directors are good for something." He sat on Nate's other side, around the corner of the table.

Nate continued to glower at Gideon. "You thought you'd drop in," he finally said.

"Yes."

When Nate just kept staring at him with a crooked, unfunny smirk on his face, Gideon stood up, puzzled and angry. He had paid his duty call and had no wish to be glared at by a contentious and hostile colleague who might once have been a friend, but who clearly had no use for him at the moment.

"You don't have anything to do with the inquiry?" Nate said sharply as Gideon pushed his chair back. "Is that what you're telling me?"

"The what?"

"The Stonebarrow Fell inquiry," Frawley said.

Gideon shook his head. "I don't know what you're talking about."

"No?" Nate looked at him quizzically. "Okay, have a read." He reached to the shelf behind him, got a newspaper, and tossed it onto the table in front of Gideon, who dropped back into his chair. It was the previous day's *West Dorset Times*, and the headline ran across the two leftmost columns.

CRISES MOUNT AT STONEBARROW FELL

Professor Nathan G. Marcus, the outspoken and controversial director of the archaeological excavation at Stonebarrow Fell (Charmouth) is set for his most critical test thus far.

The *Times* has learned that the Wessex Antiquarian Society (WAS) and the New York–based Horizon Foundation for Anthropological Research, which cosponsor the expedition, will shortly conduct a joint inquiry, to be held in Charmouth, into charges against Professor Marcus of maladministration and unprofessional behavior. The charges stem from a confidential letter of complaint sent by the WAS to the Horizon Foundation.

The secret letter, of which the *Times* has managed to obtain a copy, protests Professor Marcus's "animadversions upon the Society in particular and English archaeology in general." It also alleges that "his unsubstantiated and incredible claims regarding a Mycenaean settlement of southern England discredit all concerned and tarnish the reputation of archaeology itself." Further, the unprecedented letter expresses "gave reservations about Professor Marcus's competence and objectivity."

Professor Marcus, in a statement to the *Times*, said that his claims are consistent with the facts, and that "the Wessex Antiquarian Society has been out to get me from Day One . . . They won't admit the obvious truth even when the d--n thing stares them in the face, just because an American came up with it. Look, I'm glad they've got a lot of practice eating their own words, because I'm going to dump a big plateful right in front of them."

These charges and countercharges fly amidst growing rumours of an astonishing and sensational new discovery at Stonebarrow Fell; one that will lend credence to Professor Marcus's unorthodox theories. When queried about these rumors, the American scholar would only smile.

The expected arrival on the scene of Professor Gideon P. Oliver, an internationally known authority on skeletal analysis and reconstruction, is believed by informed sources to suggest that the alleged new discovery consists of one or more human skeletons. Professor Oliver, it is believed, will play a significant role in the inquiry into his countryman's behaviour.

Gideon stared at he last paragraph a second time, then dropped the paper and looked up.

"How in the hell did *I* get involved? How could the . . . the . . ." He glanced at the masthead. ". . . the *West Dorset Times* even know I was coming? *Nobody* knew we were going to Charmouth."

This was virtually true. Gideon had talked about it with his old friend and teacher Abe Goldstein, but Abe was living in quiet retirement in Sequim, Washington, six thousand miles away. No one else could possibly know. They had not even made reservations at a Charmouth hotel, trusting instead to plentiful vacancies in the off-season.

"I'll be damned," he said. "Nate, I give you my word I don't have anything to do with any inquiry. I didn't even know there was one."

Again there was a burdensome silence. Against the one small window an unseasonable bluebottle fly buzzed and thumped sluggishly. Nate, who had been studying Gideon closely all the time he'd been reading, appeared to come to an abrupt decision.

"Okay, okay, I believe you. I'm sorry, pal, maybe I'm getting paranoid." He toyed with the old dagger blade, picking at the rough, green patina with thin, hairy fingers. "That damn WAS. They'll do anything to make me look bad. I'll bet anything they're behind it."

Paranoid, Frawley had said, and now Nate had said it too. Gideon began to wonder if there wasn't something to it. He glanced at Frawley and was met with the sort of knowing look that is generally said to be "fraught with meaning."

"Nate," Gideon said, "you know the WAS is a serious group of archaeologists. I don't think—"

"Don't give me that bullshit. Dammit, Gideon, I've got them so shook up with what I'm finding here they'd do anything to get me canned—so they can have all the credit for good old England. Bastards!" His hand closed around the blade, and for a second Gideon thought he was going to ram the fragile implement into the table, but he only gripped it a moment and tossed it down. "Hell, what am I getting so excited about? It's the same old story." He grinned suddenly, his teeth very white against his dark face, and tapped the newspaper. "I gave 'em as good as I got, though, huh?"

"Yes, it's great to see you out there winning friends for America."

Nate laughed, throwing back his head and barking at the ceiling. It was too loud and it went on too long, and in his throat the arteries stood out like fat worms. Again

Gideon found Frawley's doleful eyes fixed meaningfully on him.

Nate leaned over and slapped Gideon's arm. "Let me tell you, pal, I'm really glad you're not with them. I'd hate to think you were on their side."

Gideon returned his smile but was obscurely troubled. Were there sides? Whose side *was* he on? Nate's theory was cockeyed and deserved refutation, no question about that, but the man had once been close to him, and Gideon couldn't help being concerned. Abe Goldstein had been right, as usual; Nate Marcus was in need of being kept out of trouble.

"Nate," Gideon said softly, wishing that the mournfully attentive Frawley would go away, "this whole Mycenaean business. . . . Are you sure you're not getting yourself out on a limb? An inquiry by Horizon—that's serious stuff; it could affect your whole career."

"Everything I said is true," Nate said fervently. "Listen, I can *prove* the Mycenaeans brought the Bronze Age to England." He stared at Gideon, then turned suddenly to Frawley. "Right?"

Frawley was caught raising his mug to his lips. He spluttered and set it down, then drew from one breast pocket a metal-stemmed, stubby pipe, from the other a foil tobacco pouch. "Well, yes," he said, "I would certainly say that what we've found provides considerable confirmation of your theory, yes." His pouchy eyes lit glancingly on Gideon and then dropped to his pipe, at which he poked assiduously with a paper clip.

No wonder Nate was getting himself into deep waters. If the rest of his staff was like Frawley, he wasn't getting any honest feedback or argument.

"Look, Nate," Gideon said, "I know you're excited about this, but think about what you're saying. How can you *prove* something like that? At best—"

"All right," Nate snapped, "you don't need to lecture me." For a moment his hot, black eyes blazed, but the fire went out as quickly as it had come. "Sorry," he said. "I guess I'm a little edgy. You're right, you're right. We're supposed to be scientists; we deal in probabilities, not certainties. But it just seems as if it's so goddam obvious. . . ." He grasped the edge of the table and leaned forward. "Look, if there was no Mycenaean invasion, how do you account for the sudden introduction of a complex, multitiered society with 'Aegean' stamped all over it? Tell me that! Where did those incised geometric pottery motifs come from? The faience beads?" He snatched up the bronze dagger again. "This?"

Gideon spoke as gently as he could. "You know I'm no Bronze Age specialist, Nate. But even I know that the arguments you're making were laid to rest decades ago. As far as I know, you're the only modern scholar who still accepts them."

"And that makes me wrong?"

"Of course not. Look, you're the expert, not me. All I'm trying to suggest is that the way you're going about things has gotten the Horizon Foundation and the Wessex Antiquarian Society on your back, and you might want to be just a little less bellicose. If that inquiry goes against you and they relieve you here, you'll never get another legitimate dig."

Nate sighed impatiently, flicking a pottery fragment with the back of his finger. "Listen, you think I don't know you're trying to help me? I appreciate it, believe me. But I have to do this my own way. Do you want me to say I don't believe what I know is true? I *know* I'm right; Jack knows it; all of us here know it."

Frawley had continued to probe his pipe noncommittally. Angrily, Gideon rounded on him. "Jack, isn't there anything you'd like to say about this?"

Frawley shifted and shook his head, not meeting Gideon's eyes. "I may have certain, ah, minor points of difference, but what Nate says, ah, makes real sense." The pipe seemed to be ready, and he concentrated on searching for his matches, pocket by pocket.

It was amazing that Nate, never very kindly disposed toward yes-men, would tolerate Frawley's sycophancy, let alone encourage it. Or maybe not so strange. Nate *had* changed. He had, of course, always been intense, frequently ardent, and yet underneath his passion there had always been that healthy, self-mocking sense of humor that kept him on a reasonably even keel. But if it was still there, it hadn't surfaced so far. Was he so caught up in his strange theory that he didn't know a yes-man when he saw one—even one as pusillanimous as Frawley?

"Gid," Nate said, "you know what the *Times* said—rumors of a sensational new discovery? Well, it's true. I've got proof that nobody can argue with. You're not going to *believe* it!" He spoke with mounting excitement, as if he were about to hug himself or rub his hands together. Instead he jumped from his chair to pace restlessly up and down the narrow space behind the table. He'd gotten thinner, Gideon realized. His clothes flapped on him as if they were two sizes too large. This battle he was fighting was eating him up.

"Just wait," he said. "Wait till that damn inquisition convenes. What a kick in the ass they're going to get—what a surprise!"

"Would that be the human skeletal remains the paper mentioned?" Gideon asked.

"Right." He grinned wolfishly. "Jealous?"

"Interested. Do you have any physical anthropologists working with you?"

"No, and if what you mean is that, being an ignorant archaeologist, I might be misinterpreting the skeletal evidence, then come back in two weeks and see for yourself."

"I've got a better idea. Why don't I look at what you have right now?"

"Uh-uh, I want it to be a surprise for Horizon."

"I'll keep it a surprise; it's your baby, whatever it is. I promise not to tell anybody what I've seen. Look, for one thing, I really am damn curious to see what you have. For another, maybe I could point out some things you missed—it's my business, you know." *And for still another,* Gideon thought, *maybe I can show you you're heading for a hell of a debacle, and maybe you'll listen.* For whatever Nate had unearthed—and if he said it was sensational, it probably was—it could hardly confirm a theory that was untenable to begin with.

Nate had been shaking his head all the time Gideon was speaking. "Nope," he said firmly. "I think we'll just go ahead and have the official unveiling at the Grand Inquisition."

It was said with finality, and at that point Gideon gave up. He'd tried to help and been rebuffed. And when it came down to it, it wasn't his affair. Nate was a grown man, chairman of a department and director of an excavation, and he had more than once shown himself capable of getting out of his own difficulties as well as into them. Besides, Gideon told himself (only a little after the fact), he'd promised Julie to stay out of academic fracases on his honeymoon, and that was a promise he meant to keep—no matter how curious he was about Nate's mysterious find. He had no idea what sort of game Frawley was playing, but that, too, was Nate's problem.

He took his first sip of the tasteless, now-cold coffee and put the mug down. "Okay, Nate, do it the way you want. I wish you well; you know that."

"Hey, don't go 'way mad." Nate, more relaxed now, picked up a piece of pottery, rubbing it thoughtfully with his thumb. "Where are you going to be in two weeks? Still in Charmouth?"

"No, I'm leaving tomorrow. We thought we'd drive west, spend some time in Wales, see some of Ireland, and then head back to London in a couple of weeks."

"Well, couldn't you work it out to stop in Charmouth again on the way back? The inquiry's November twenty-ninth."

"I don't think—"

"Wait, don't say no. I'm in trouble, Gid. That inquiry board is dead set against me. They've already made up their minds. They'll find some way to twist—"

"I don't buy that, Nate. Horizon and the WAS are objective, knowledgeable—"

His protest was waved away. "They're archaeologists, like I am. What do they know about skeletons? Look, man,

we could use a good physical anthropologist there; somebody without an ax to grind, someone we all trust—because
we sure as hell don't trust each other.''

Gideon shook his head. ''Forget it. The last thing I need
is to be on a board of inquiry—into *your* conduct, no less.
No, thanks.''

''Listen, all I'm asking you to do is be there, maybe for
an hour, when I show them what I have. You know, just be
an expert resource; do your thing, give us your opinion.
Call it the way you see it.''

''Nate, I'm on my honeymoon.''

''Okay, let me put it this way.'' He looked soberly at
Gideon. ''I know you think I'm kidding myself, and maybe
I am. But I'm not crazy, you know. And what if I'm right?
What if the most important Bronze Age find of the century,
maybe of any century, is about to pop? I'm asking you to be
the first physical anthropologist to look at it. You'd be right
there at the grand opening; you'd be the one to do the initial
analysis. . . .''

Gideon sighed, then laughed. What anthropologist could
say no to that? Besides, it might give him a final chance to
help Nate, to keep him from doing anything more foolish
than he'd already done. ''Well,'' he said, ''when you put it
that way . . .''

Nate laughed and reached forward to shake hands. As he
did so, a cool draft from behind Gideon rustled the papers
on the table.

''Oh, sorry. I didn't know you were in conference.''

Nate looked up over Gideon's shoulder. ''No problem,
Randy, come on in. Gid, this is Randy Alexander, number-
one contender for the world's perennial-student title.''

Laughing offhandedly, a big, coarsely good-looking man
carrying a paper sack came in. He was about thirty-five,
only a few years younger than Nate and Gideon, with
longish, curling brown hair, a casual, loose-jointed gait,
and an air about him of indolent, somewhat studied
dissipation.

''Hiya, Prof. I think I heard of you.''

It was certainly his day for public acclaim, Gideon

thought, but even this dubious tribute, the second in an hour, was quickly retracted.

"Or," Randy said, "maybe I just heard Dr. Marcus talk about you being an old friend."

"My oldest," Nate said. "Gideon and I were chuga-lugging watered-down beer in the UW Rathaus fifteen years ago."

"No kidding." Randy went to a metal cabinet near the coffee paraphernalia and, whistling softly, began taking things from the sack and putting them on shelves.

"Did you get everything?" Frawley asked him.

"Yup. Coffee, notepads, mallet, chisels, string, the whole schmear."

"Well," Gideon said, rising. "I guess I'll walk on down now."

Randy turned with surprising speed. "I'll let you through the gate."

"Hey, Gid . . . ?" Nate said.

Gideon waited.

"I'm glad to hear you got married again." He smiled—the old smile Gideon remembered, shy and quick, and unexpectedly elfin in that intense, lean face. "You're the kind of guy who needs to be married, you know that? Congratulations and best of luck. What's her name?"

"Thanks very much, Nate. Her name is Julie." Gideon was moved; a glimmer of the old Nate had peeked through. "Nate, are you sure you wouldn't like me to take a sort of confidential look—"

"No way, pal. Trust me. See you on the twenty-ninth."

Outside, the thick fog had moved in. The ocean, the coastline and the surrounding hills were all invisible, and on the fell everything was indistinct and gloomy.

Randy conversed with mumbling indifference as they walked past the other three students, in the pit, but as soon as he and Gideon were shielded by a small, grassy rise he stopped. "Could I talk to you, Dr. Oliver?"

"Sure."

"It's about this Mycenaean thing. Look, if I tell you

something pretty wild, will you promise to keep my name out of it?''

"No, I won't, Randy. If you want to tell me something, go ahead. But no strings."

Randy's sleepy eyelids lifted. It wasn't the answer he'd expected. "It's really serious. I mean, I think you should know."

"I think you're talking to the wrong man. You probably know a lot more about the Bronze Age than I do."

"But this whole Mycenaean thing, it's all screwed up—"

"Randy, have you talked to Nate? His bark's a lot worse—"

Randy laughed. "Oh, sure, talk to Marcus about it. You don't know how funny that is."

"Frawley, then?"

He shook his head impatiently. "He wouldn't do anything about it. It's crazy. . . . Dr. Oliver, I know you can do something about it before anyone gets into real trouble. . . . I don't know, I just feel like I can trust you, you know?"

Gideon felt the same sort of ambivalence he'd had in the flower-child days when someone you'd never seen before would walk up to you with a smile, thrust a daisy into your hand, and energetically tell you to have a good day. Was Randy being as honest as he was trying to appear, or was this a put-on for his own amusement? Still, the gray eyes, on a level with Gideon's own, were imploring, waiting for a signal to continue. It seemed to Gideon he had been dancing and sidestepping all morning to stay out of the morass of Stonebarrow Fell, but now, reluctantly, he nodded.

"Okay, but no strings. If I can keep your name out of it, I will, but I can't promise."

"Uh-uh," Randy said, "no deal. If—" He stopped abruptly, his eyes focused beyond Gideon.

"Private discussion?" Nate asked dryly. He had just come over the rise.

"Nope," said Randy with smooth nonchalance, "just talking shop."

"Well, I was looking for you. When you're finished, come on over to the dig. Now that everyone's here, I want to go over our problems with level three. I think we need to talk about pseudostratigraphic indicators."

"Will do, chief; my favorite subject."

He was uncommunicative while he walked with Gideon down to the gate, and when they got there, he glanced behind them. There was Nate at the top of the crest, looking after them, almost hidden in the mist.

Randy unlocked the gate. "Okay, you win," he said hurriedly. "Can I talk to you later? Where are you staying?"

Gideon let out a long breath. He'd thought he'd managed to wriggle his way off the hook with honor reasonably intact. "The Queen's Armes, but we're taking off tomorrow."

"How about tonight? Five o'clock?"

"Okay," Gideon said resignedly, "I'll be there."

At 5:45 P.M. Gideon snapped shut the Ngaio Marsh novel he'd borrowed from the hotel library and tossed it irritably onto the low table.

"Let's go get some dinner."

Julie looked up from her own book. "I thought you said he really seemed to have something on his mind."

"He did, but he was pretty coy about it. I think he just changed his mind."

"What do you suppose it was about?"

"I don't know, but to tell you the truth, I'm just as glad not to hear it. There are some very funny dynamics going on up there."

"Maybe something held him up at the dig. Why not give him a few more minutes?"

"It's been dark for over an hour. They shut down long ago. Besides, I thought you wanted me to stay out of academic squabbles."

"I do, but you made it sound important. Do you know where he's staying?"

"No, and anyway, why the hell should I go chasing after him? He's the one who wants to talk to me, isn't he?"

Julie got up and came over to him. She leaned over the back of the big leather armchair and kissed his cheek. "Poor baby. He gets grumpy when he's hungry, doesn't he?"

Laughing, he stood up and hugged her. "I do, don't I? Come on, let's go get some honest English roast beef and ale. If something's held him up, he can call and leave a message.

"Oh, by the way," he said, as they shrugged into their coats, "speaking of academic squabbles that I'm so skillful at staying out of, there's this inquiry on November twenty-ninth . . ."

❑ 5 ❑

THEY ARRIVED BACK in Charmouth on November 27, after a full morning's drive over country roads. Gideon, cramped after all that time in the car, went for a long walk on the beach while Julie, hungry for some modern American fiction, left in search of a bookstore.

It was a good, muscle-loosening walk, made even more enjoyable when he found a small, perfectly coiled fossil ammonite among the pebbles. The wind began to sharpen after an hour, however, and the afternoon was fading rapidly to a dirty, sleet-spattered gray, so that by the time he got back to the Queen's Armes he was cold through and glad to close the wooden door of the old inn behind him. He was happy, too, to see the ruddy flicker on the wall of the long entryway opposite the Tudor Room. That meant that a fire had been laid in the snug, ancient chamber that served as a resident's lounge.

The little Queen's Armes Hotel was reputed to be over five hundred years old, and although the outside had been stuccoed and modernized many times through the years, the Tudor stonework and age-blackened woods inside gave credence to the reputation. Its owner, Andy Hinshore—a wiry, nervous, darting man, though affable and gregarious— had welcomed Julie and Gideon back as if they were his best and oldest clients.

At the moment, they were his only clients, and the absence of other guests had pleased them. Having the time-weathered old Tudor lounge to themselves, with glasses of sherry at their sides and a fire crackling in the great stone fireplace, had promised the most delightful way imaginable of spending a few wintry evenings in the quiet heart of the English countryside.

It was therefore with a sense of being disagreeably intruded upon that Gideon now heard voices coming from the lounge. Glancing in as he passed by, he saw two men in business suits sitting in armchairs—the very ones he'd had in mind for himself and Julie—near the fireplace. One was a spare man of forty in a flawlessly tailored gray suit, an elegant, long-limbed man with stylishly molded, graying hair and a lean-fleshed, aristocratic face. The other, hunch-shouldered and lumpy in an old tweed jacket, had his back to Gideon. They looked unpleasantly settled in, as if they meant to stay awhile.

Grumpily, Gideon climbed the stairs and opened the door to his room. On the bed was a note from Julie.

Dear Husband (What fun!):

Do mufflers fall off cars? Something fell off ours and it looks suspiciously like one. Mr. Hinshore recommended a garage in Taunton, so I've driven over there to see if they can stick it back on again.

Curses, we're not alone after all. A couple of archaeologists have moved in and one of them (I forget his name*) says he knows you. They told me to tell you they'd be in the Tudor Room this afternoon and would like you to come by. One of them is a sexy, interesting Englishman who looks like Sherlock Holmes (Razzle Bathbone, I mean), but the other one (the one who knows you) is kind of a dud, I'm afraid.

I should be back by 5:30, I hope.

I love you! I love you! I love you!

With sincere regards,

(Mrs.) Julene T. Oliver

*Barkle? Arkle? Carbuncle?

P.S. I was thinking about making love to you on the Tudor Room hearth tonight. Do you suppose your friends would mind?

P.P.S. See page 2 of newspaper for more on Stonebarrow Fell.

Holding the note in his hand, Gideon frowned apprehensively. She hadn't driven alone in England before. Would she remember that you drove on the wrong side? She'd be coming back on slippery roads after dark; he didn't like that. And where the hell was Taunton? He found himself gnawing his lower lip with concern, smiled, and put the letter down. She was a perfectly competent women of thirty, a former senior park ranger who had once coolly rescued *him* in the depths of Olympic National Park. She had gotten along just fine without him all her life, and to worry now because she was driving alone was nothing but a reprehensible, condescending, and atavistic sexual chauvinism, to be discouraged before it got started. Never mind that it felt so good.

A copy of the *West Dorset Times* was on a corner of the bed. Gideon turned to page two and found the brief article at the top of the page.

STONEBARROW FELL AGAIN

The controversy-plagued archaeological excavation at Stonebarrow Fell continues to be the focus of interest in another matter: the mysterious disappearance of Mr. Randall Alexander, a staff member. Mr. Alexander has not been seen or heard from since November 13. Fears of foul play are mounting, and Chief Constable Kevin Blackmore yesterday requested the assistance of New Scotland Yard in the matter. It is understood that Detective Inspector Herbert T.M. Bagshawe is already on the scene.

He sat down on the bed with a queer, uneasy sense of misgiving. Randy had never shown up that night and had failed to leave a message, so that he and Julie had left the next day—November 14, was it?—without hearing from

him. Gideon had been a little concerned at the time, but
he'd forgotten about it before the day was out. But now he
suddenly felt ... responsible? Guilty? As if by being more
receptive to Randy he might have prevented ... what? The
thought, ill-formed and obscure, skittered away from him.

He got up and went to the dark window, staring out but
seeing only his own reflection, with the comfortable room
behind him. Absently tossing and catching the small, heavy
fossil he'd found on the beach, he tried to sort out his
thoughts.

"Do I think he's been murdered, is that it? Is that what's
bothering me? That someone killed him—Frawley? Nate,
even?—flung him from the cliffs to keep him from telling
me whatever secret he was going to reveal at five o'clock?"
He said it aloud to see what it sounded like, and it sounded
silly. There were a lot of explanations to sift through before
getting to that one. Not that it was his responsibility to do
any sifting. Still ...

He looked in the tiny telephone book and, standing at the
window, dialed the number for the county police. Inspector
Bagshawe of Scotland Yard, he was told, was handling that
particular case, but the inspector was gone for the day.
Would he mind speaking with Sergeant Fryer?

Gideon told Sergeant Fryer as much as he remembered of
his conversation with Randy, feeling more ridiculous by the
second. The sergeant was courteous but not overly animated,
and appeared to lose all interest when Gideon explained that
it had to do with an alleged Mycenaean settlement in 1700
B.C.

"Ah," he said in his northern accent, "you're an anthropologist yourself, are you, sir?"

"Yes."

"Oh, aye," Sergeant Fryer said, as if that explained it.

When he asked Gideon how long he would be in Charmouth
and where he could be reached afterward, Gideon could tell
that he did so more out of politeness than relevance.

If he had any duty in the matter, he had now performed it,
yet he still felt unsettled and on edge. He picked up the
telephone book again, turned to "Hotels and Guest Houses,"

and began dialing. He got Nate on the third try, at the Cormorant.

"Nate, I was just calling to see if there was any news."

"News? What kind of news?"

"About Randy Alexander."

"Randy?" Nate said in a sort of disgusted disbelief. "Who knows where the schmuck is? I've had it with him."

"You're not worried? The paper seemed to think he might be dead."

"Oh, come on . . . the *Times?* They jump on everything they can to make the dig look screwed up. I told you, they've got some kind of vendetta against me."

"Well, what do you think happened to him?"

"I think he just got bored and took off again. Probably rented a motorcycle somewhere and went tooling around the country."

"*Again*, did you say?" He felt as if someone had lifted a weight from his shoulders.

"That's what I said. He once did it for two *months*, never mind two weeks, in Missouri—had to make up a whole semester, not that he gave a damn. And then he did it for two or three days during our first week here. But this does it. He's through. He can go find someody else to bug. Hey, how'd you like a nice new graduate student?"

"No thanks. Nate, that same day he disappeared—"

"Took off," Nate said peevishly.

"He made an appointment with me for five o'clock that day. He said he wanted to tell me something he didn't seem to feel comfortable talking to you about. Do you know what that was about?"

"No, what was it about?"

"That's what I'm asking you."

"How should I know?"

"Okay, never mind. I guess I was worried about nothing."

"You sure were, buddy. Listen, Gid, this guy isn't one of your typical graduate students. He's a drifter, a bum. He's just playing around in school. You know what he really wanted to be? A pitcher. The guy spent six years in the minors. He was a southpaw, supposed to have a great fast ball, until he wore his arm out. Then he was a drummer in a rock band. Then he claims he was a mercenary in Africa—''

"And now he wants to be an archaeologist?''

"Don't ask me, man. You know what he does back home? He rides with one of these so-called outlaw gangs— all middle-aged nerds, like him. You should see his chopper— it's about twenty feet long; you practically have to lay on your back to ride it.''

"Is he making it at Gelden?''

"Well, he's not really that dumb,'' Nate allowed grudgingly. "He can read and write, more or less, and he's loaded; his old man's Alexander Toilet Tissue—not that the old guy isn't always yelling about cutting him off. Anyway, that's enough to get into Gelden—in fact, never mind the read-and-write bit. I voted against admitting the guy in the first place, but I got overruled. But this time I'm kicking his ass out of the department. The dean can stick him in classical lit if he want to. Look, why are we talking about him? What's the big deal?''

"Well, he just seemed so anxious to talk to me.''

"I'm telling you the guy likes to put people on. He really made an idiot out of Jack Frawley once; he even tried to do it to me. Forget him, will you? Hey, you're gonna be there Thursday, aren't you? Ten o'clock?''

"That's why I'm here. Nate, are you still feeling good about this? Are you sure you don't want me to have a private look before the board meets? I could come up tomorrow.''

"You kidding, you want to ruin the suspense? No, you be there at ten, and bring your calipers and stuff. I'm gonna make you famous.''

Gideon hung up, not as relieved as he might have been. For one thing, his concern over Nate's coming disaster had been freshened, even though the man was so damn *confident. Could* there have been a Mycenaean migration? *Could* Nate refute the accumulated wisdom of the specialists? Gideon shook his head, wishing he knew more about Bronze Age anthropology. All he'd be able to do Thursday would be a conventional skeletal examination and analysis;

someone else would have to do the interpretation. Deep down, he wasn't sorry. He didn't want to be the one to tell Nate he'd made a fool of himself.

Something else was bothering him. Despite everything Nate had said, Gideon still had an unsettling sense of foreboding about the fate of Randy Alexander. And it wasn't simply the unkept appointment; it was the very atmosphere of Stonebarrow Fell—an unhealthy stew of tension, dislike, pretense. . . .

He stood up and stretched. He was getting a little paranoid himself. Time to get his mind on other things and go on down to say hello to the archaeologists in the lounge; did he really know an Arkle, Barkle, or Carbuncle?

When he pushed open the Dutch door of the Tudor room, it was the slender, well-dressed man who rose, smiling.

"Unless I'm very much mistaken," he said in an urbane, slightly nasal drawl, "here is the eminent Professor Oliver now." That would be the sexy Englishman. He even talked like Sherlock Holmes.

The figure in the other chair turned and rose as well. "Hello, Gideon," he said, his voice gloppy with the postnasal drip that had plagued him ever since Gideon had known him. "How are you?"

"Hi, Paul. It's good to see you."

This was not strictly true. It wasn't that he disliked Paul Arbuckle. In fact, he rather liked him in short doses. He'd never heard Paul say a malicious or envious word about a colleague—no common virtue in academe—and he sometimes revealed an exacting intelligence. But there was a dull, dogged, enervating persistence about him. Paul was the kind of researcher who would not let go of an idea until he had smothered it to death, but he seemed to Gideon always to have hold of the wrong idea, always to be drudging away at some arcane, dry-as-dust minutia, while all the provocative, exciting patterns eluded him.

Although he was an archaeologist, he was, like Gideon, an earnest student of Pleistocene man (indeed, if he had other interests, he'd yet to mention them), but the two had never gotten to know one another very well. At anthropo-

logical gatherings they usually managed a scholarly, reasonably agreeable conversation of twenty or thirty minutes,
which sufficed until the next year's meeting. But when two
Americans meet socially on foreign soil, a different level of
cordiality is called for, and Gideon's heart sank at the
prospect of the serious, plodding Arbuckle horning in on his
Dorset evenings with Julie. Having a sexy, interesting
Englishman around didn't seem so hot either.

Nevertheless, Gideon smiled and offered his hand. "What
brings you to Charmouth?"

"Business, naturally," said Paul (naturally), and frowned
behind round, rimless spectacles. As many people do, he
looked like what he was, with his thick glasses, his rumpled
clothes, and his innocuous, vaguely porcine face (Porky-the-
pig-like, really). "I don't know whether you heard, but I'm
not at Michigan anymore. I've been director of field archaeology for the Horizon Foundation since July. I've been
running a terrific dig in France, but I've had to put it aside
and come here on . . . business."

He indicated the other man. "And this is Frederick
Robyn, secretary of the Wessex Antiquarian Society."

When they had all sat down facing the fire, the Englishman
said, "I wonder if you know why we are both in Charmouth."

"I suppose you're here to conduct the Stonebarrow Fell
inquiry Thursday."

Arbuckle looked extremely surprised, Robyn mildly so. It
was Robyn who spoke, raising a cool eyebrow. "And how
do you happen to know that?"

"There was an article about it in the *Times*."

Robyn's suavity faltered. "The *Times!* Good Lord!"

Gideon laughed in spite of himself. "The *West Dorset
Times*, Mr. Robyn, not the *London Times*."

"Still, it's unfortunate that the press should have it at all.
Publicity can do no one any good." He shook his handsome
head. "I suppose it was Marcus himself who told them. The
man is unable to restrain himself." He looked at Gideon and
smiled. "But of course it's precisely that which has necessi-
tated this entire unhappy process."

At that point Andy Hinshore scurried in with a sherry for

Robyn and a lager for Arbuckle. "Oh, hello Dr. Oliver," he said. "Sorry, I didn't know you were here. Can I get you something?"

"A Scotch and soda would be nice, thanks."

As he left, Arbuckle said to Gideon, "This article on Stonebarrow Fell . . . what was the gist of it?"

Gideon had barely begun when Hinshore returned with his drink on a tray. "Perhaps you'd move that thing, sir? I wouldn't want to knock it off the table, God forbid."

Gideon looked down at the ammonite he'd absentmindedly placed on the table near his chair, and put it in his pocket. "It's just a fossil from the beach, Andy."

Hinshore shook his compact head vigorously. "Oh, no, I know the way you scientists are with your fossils. Indeed I do. Last month I almost put a mug of beer down on one of Professor Arbuckle's, and I thought he was going to skin me alive." Chuckling, he put the glass in front of Gideon.

Paul Arbuckle was at times the most literal-minded of men. "Oh," he said, with a wondering, mildly aggrieved air, "I don't think I was going to skin you alive."

"Well," Hinshore said affably, "you could have fooled me."

"You were here last month, Paul?" Gideon asked. "Has this thing with Nate been going on as long as that?"

"Oh, it had nothing to do with the inquiry; just a routine field audit. I visit all our sites quarterly."

"I hadn't realized you'd been here before, either," Robyn said with interest. "How did things look to you then?"

"Everything was fine. Marcus hadn't made any of his strange statements yet—or only a few—and the dig itself was absolutely ship-shape. You know what a fine technician he is."

"More's the pity," Robyn said absently, his eyes on the fire blazing in a metal box in the grand but inefficient Tudor fireplace of vaulted stone. Gideon stole a look at his watch. Not that he was worried, but where the hell was Julie anyway?

Hinshore had remained in the room, listening with open interest. "Oh!" he said suddenly, producing a newspaper from under his arm. "I heard you ask about the *Times* article on Stonebarrow Fell. I keep copies of the paper in the sitting room." He held out the folded paper.

Robyn stretched out an elegant hand. "Thank you. And . . . Andy, is it? . . . I don't think we need anything else."

"Oh—" Hinshore said, his sallow cheeks flushing. "Yes, excuse me. Sorry."

When he had left, Robyn spread the newspaper on the table before him, and he and Arbuckle leaned over it. Robyn was the faster reader of the two, and while he waited for his colleague to finish, he lit a cigarette and puffed languidly, gazing thoughtfully into the fire.

When Arbuckle finally finished, he looked up slowly. "Where did they get all that information? How could they find out about the letter?"

"The irrepressible Professor Marcus, I suspect," Robyn said, "although how he found out I haven't the foggiest notion. In any case, the article is certainly accurate enough, isn't it?"

"Not exactly," Gideon said, putting down his glass. "It implied that I was here as part of your inquiry, and I'm not."

Robyn tapped his cigarette into an ashtray. "I meant as far as the important aspects are concerned."

Gideon, not notably slow to take offense when warranted, wondered if it were warranted now. He looked up sharply, but Robyn's expression was coolly benign.

"Of course," the Englishman went on, "knowing you were coming, they would naturally assume your visit was connected to our inquiry. Don't you think so?"

"I suppose so." Gideon sipped his Scotch. "The question is, how did they know I was coming at all? I barely knew myself."

"I'm sure I have no idea."

"Well, I sure didn't know you were coming," Arbuckle said. He placed his glass on the table and looked doubtfully at Gideon. "Why *are* you here?"

Gideon shook his head and laughed. "Everybody's suspicious of me. Honestly, it's not very mysterious. Mostly because I'm trying to take a peaceful, inconspicuous English honeymoon. As for Stonebarrow Fell, I'd heard that Nate was having difficulties, and I thought I might lend a little moral support, so I went up to see him."

"A sympathetic compatriot in a strange land?" Robyn asked. "That sort of thing?"

"That's about it. And when I was there, Nate asked me if I'd come back when he takes the wraps off that find of his. I'd like to do that, if it's all right with you. I might be of some help."

Gideon caught a small negative shake of Robyn's head and saw him form the words "Well, I . . . ," but Arbuckle spoke up more loudly.

"I think that'd be *great*," he said sincerely. "You're an old friend of his, aren't you? Maybe you could talk some sense into him. Don't you think so, Frederick?"

"Yes," said Robyn, deciding after all not to demur, "I suppose so."

"I've already tried to talk some sense into him," Gideon said, "I wasn't too successful."

"But it isn't too late," Arbuckle said, leaning forward with his typical earnest gravity. "Gideon, this isn't an inquiry in the usual sense. No one's disputing any facts. It's my responsibility, and Frederick's, to simply talk with Marcus and get him to . . . well, to grow up and start acting like the first-rate professional he is." He pulled at his beer, set it down, and frowned with myopic ardor. "However, if he won't do that, we will certainly relieve him and close down the dig. But I just can't believe it'll come to that!"

"Is that true, Paul? The outcome's still open?"

It was Robyn who answered. "My dear Oliver," he said lighting another cigarette, "Arbuckle and I are not a couple of hit men hired to perform a character assassination. We represent, as you well know, two of the most prestigious of archaeological research organizations. Both of us, I should add, were firm supporters, in the face of some rather severe opposition, of Professor Marcus's original application for permission and funding."

He paused to taste his sherry, then pressed his lips together, holding the glass to his temple, as if listening to it. "Quite nice," he said, "although as olorosos go, perhaps the least bit thin."

Gideon doubted that he could taste anything at all. The cigarette in his other hand was his third one.

"But," Robyn went on at his own leisurely pace, "how can we ignore the bizarre nature of his recent statements? . . . Well, you saw what was attributed to him in the newspaper. There are, I assure you, other even more outrageous and offensive examples." He crossed one leg over the other, first arranging an already impeccable trouser crease. "Nevertheless, I think I can speak for both of us in saying we would consider our mission successful if the man would simply give us his promise to restrain his outbursts and stick to the business of pursuing the excavation—which I must admit he does very well. Wouldn't you agree with all that, Arbuckle?"

"What?" Arbuckle asked with a start. He had been staring into the flames. "Sorry, I guess I was thinking about my own dig."

Gideon smiled. When Paul was involved in research, his one-track mind never strayed very far from it.

"Got something interesting going in France?" Gideon asked.

"I do. I sure do." He thrust his stocky body forward, twisting his glass in stubby fingers. All at once, he was more alert, more alive, "It's in Burgundy, near Dijon— Gideon, it's been fluorine-dated at 220,000 B.C.—Middle Pleistocene! Just think, it's as old as Swanscombe or Steinhem! We've got Acheulian handaxes, cleavers . . . What are you laughing at?"

"You," Gideon said, "It's the first time this afternoon I've seen you really come alive. Poor Paul; there you are in the middle of a great dig, with the chance to learn something about the earliest Homo sapiens, and you have to break it off to get involved in a minor squabble over the Bronze Age."

"Really," Robyn murmured in the manner of an actor delivering an aside, "I'd hardly call it a minor squabble."

Arbuckle looked at Gideon, but it was hard to tell what he was thinking. The firelight bouncing opaquely off his thick glasses made his never-too-mobile face look more wooden than ever. Finally he laughed, something he didn't do often.

"You're right. Who cares about the Bronze Age? All I want to do is get this thing over with and get back to Dijon. And don't tell me you wouldn't feel just the same."

"I would," Gideon said, meaning it.

"Now, see here," said Robyn. "I feel I must stand up on behalf of the Bronze Age. For myself, I'd rather deal with jeweled daggers and filigreed breastplates, and pendants of Baltic amber—all neatly tucked away for me in barrows—than go grubbing in muddy riverbeds for vulgar rock choppers and gnawed elephant bones left by coarse and unhygienic man-apes."

Gideon was about to reply when he heard the front door of the hotel open and close, and then the welcome sound of Julie's footsteps in the entry hall. (When had he learned to recognize them?) He half rose, but Robyn was even quicker, springing lightly to his feet.

"Ah, my dear Mrs. Oliver," he said, oozing urbanity, "you are indeed a welcome sight. We've been discussing the most dreary sorts of things for far too long. Now I'd like to propose that you and Professor Oliver join us for dinner. I know a perfectly delightful old coaching inn at Honiton."

He smiled engagingly, the lines around his eyes folding into a fan of handsome crinkles. "I won't take no for an answer."

❑ 6 ❑

THE MEAL WAS as good as Robyn had promised, and they finished two bottles of wine, so the four of them passed a reasonably pleasant evening, during which the subject of Stonebarrow Fell never arose. Robyn was witty and gallant, and Paul made polite, vague conversation. He even managed to come out of his shell in his own blinking, resolute fashion when Robyn said that since the inquiry wasn't until Thursday, why didn't he and Arbuckle motor to Swanscombe the next day and have a look at the famous site where England's oldest human remains had been discovered fifty years before?

When they got back to the hotel, Arbuckle was, in fact, loosened up enough to suggest they have after-dinner drinks in the lounge, where Hinshore had kept the fire going for them. Gideon declined, and he and Julie went up to their room, leaving the two men sprawled (Robyn even managed to sprawl elegantly) in the big chairs, each with a brandy snifter at his elbow.

"Whew!" Julie sighed the moment they'd shut the door. She flung herself into his arms, driving him back against the wall with a thump. "I *love* you," she said, and pulled his face down to kiss him firmly on the lips. "You neat, attractive man!" She put her head against his shoulder and hugged him hard.

"Hey," he said, delighted. "What's all this about?"

"I haven't had you alone almost all *day!* Do you realize this is the first time that's happened since we've been married?"

"Well, the magic has to end sometime," he said lightly, but he hadn't liked it either. He liked this very much better. He put his lips to her hair, fresh-smelling despite Robyn's endless smoking.

Julie slipped her arms under his sport coat and pressed her palms flat against his back, pulling him against her. He could feel how warm her hands were through the thin cloth of his shirt. She was wearing a blouse with a wide, square-cut neckline, and he placed his hands gently along her throat. Under the heavy, dark hair, the nape of her neck was lusciously long and curved. And naked. He let his fingers move to her shoulders under the border of the blouse and felt her flesh respond to his touch.

"Besides, I was worried about you," she murmured, scarcely audible against the tweed of his jacket. "I kept worrying that you'd go climbing on those stupid cliffs and fall off. Or get run over by a car on your way back because you're absentminded and you'd forget they drive on the other side of the street. Isn't that silly?"

"Yes", he said. "Ridiculous." He kissed her hair again and stroked the firm, soft flesh of her shoulders.

"And then," she said, her cheek still against him, "when we were finally able to have dinner together, we had to spend it with those boring people." She began to finger the buttons of his shirt.

"Boring? I thought Robyn was supposed to be sexy and interesting."

She shook her head. "He smokes too much. And his hair's too perfect. He looks like a salesman in a clothing store, or a TV actor. And he doesn't have any hair on his chest. And he's too sure of how fantastically attractive he is."

Gideon laughed. "And just how do you happen to know he doesn't have any hair on his chest?"

Her fingers began to work at his shirt buttons. "Oh," she

said, "you can tell. He's just not the type. Not enough of that hairy male hormone, whatever you call it. He's got a flat, white, hairless chest without those what-do-you-call-them muscles."

"Pectoralis major. And testosterone."

"Yes," she said, and undid a couple of the buttons.

"And you don't like hairless white chests."

"No. I like them like yours. For when my nose itches." She rubbed her nose briskly against his chest. He bent suddenly and lifted her off her feet. It struck him as astonishing that he had never done it before in almost three weeks of marriage.

"Gideon!" she said, caught by surprise. "I'm too heavy!"

"Is that right?" he said, cradling her easily in his arms, showing off, feeling pleasantly powerful and in command. And full of testosterone. When he opened the door and stepped abruptly out into the hall with her, she jerked in his arms.

"Gideon! What are you doing?"

"I thought you wanted to make love on the hearth," he said.

"There are people down there!" she whispered urgently.

"Oh, I asked them about it. They said they wouldn't mind. Paul said he's never seen it done before, and he wants to take notes."

"Gideon, put me down! Somebody might come along. Take me back inside!"

"Turnabout," he muttered. "Spoilsport." He carried her back into the room, shoving the door shut behind them with his shoulder.

"You didn't *really* ask them, did you?"

"You asked me to."

"*Gideon!*"

He laughed and squeezed her. "Of course not, dopey."

"Well, it's just that I really don't know you that well yet. I don't know when you're joking and when you're serious. Are you ever going to put me down?"

"I don't know. You feel awfully good." He hefted her up to kiss her, and the lush, warm curve of her hip rode up against him. His knee jostled accidently against a low table on which sat an electric teapot and flowered china cups and saucers. The saucers rattled. "What would you say," he said, "if I told you that what I'd like most in the world right now was a nice, hot piece of tea? Oops."

They both laughed, and she said, "I'd say you weren't serious."

He carried her to the bed, put her gently down, and knelt at the bedside to run his fingers down her soft throat to the smooth hollow at its base. "I have seen many a handsome fossa jugularis in my day, but yours is by far the sweetest and sexiest." He bent to kiss the fragant flesh and moved back to look at her face. "Julie, I didn't think it was possible to love anyone this much."

"I know that." She lay quietly looking up at him, her hand lightly against his cheek.

Gently, Gideon undid the top button of her blouse. Julie watched his face, her black eyes enormous.

The telephone rang.

"No," Gideon said, "it wouldn't dare."

It rang again. Loudly. It gave the unmistakable impression that it would go on ringing until it was answered.

Gideon grimaced, dipped his face quickly to kiss her, and tramped glumly to the phone.

The voice on the other end of the line was a stranger's; hearty, aggravatingly jovial under the circumstances, and very English.

"Professor Oliver? Wilson Merrill here. Dr. Merrill. Coroner's pathologist, Dorset Constabulary. I'd heard you were in Charmouth, and I know you're on holiday and all, but, well, I wondered if you'd be interested in coming by the mortuary here in Bridport and looking at a body. We'd be most grateful."

The humor of the situation was not lost on Gideon. "You'd like me to look at a body?" he asked, his eyes on Julie, who now knelt on the bed, her hands clasped demurely in her lap.

"Yes, rather. It was found this morning on the shore near Seaton. I've done all I can with it, but I thought, inasmuch as you were nearby, that it might engage your interest. I've read about your work, of course, and it would be a pleasure to meet you.''

"Uh, you'd like me to look at it now? Tonight?''

"Well, yes, unless it isn't convenient.'' The voice hesitated. "It *is* only nine-fifteen, isn't it? Yes, of course it is. The remains are being shipped to the forensic science laboratories in London tomorrow, and I simply thought you might want to have a go at them while they were still here. But if it can't be managed . . .''

"What do you have?''

"Adult male. Greatly advanced state of decomposition, but the skeleton's whole. Husky fellow; Caucasian, I think.''

Gideon hesitated, then looked at Julie again. He shook his head firmly. "I'm afraid it's out of the question this evening, Dr. Merrill. I'm sorry, I'd like to have helped.''

"What about tomorrow morning?''

"Well, yes, I think I could do that . . .''

"I'll be there for you at eight o'clock. Earlier if you like.''

"No, eight's fine. See you then.''

"Righto. Thanks so much. I can't wait to see you in action.''

Gideon put the telephone down and looked up to see Julie getting off the bed.

"Hey,'' he said, moving to her, "where do you think you're going?''

"Well, I thought you weren't interested anymore. Your mind's on other things.''

"Why would you think that?'' he asked, smiling. But he *was* thinking about other things. About Randall Alexander: adult male, husky, Caucasian. And missing from Stonebarrow Fell for two weeks.

"Why would I think that?'' She laughed and gently poked him in the abdomen with a finger. "Because you've been standing there in front of me with your shirt unbuttoned, and you've forgotten to suck in your tummy and stick out your chest.''

"Oh, no!'' he exclaimed, pulling in the one and thrusting

forward the other. "Now you know the awful truth about me. Another flabby-chested, pot-bellied fraud."

"You phony, you're gorgeous and you know it. C'mere." She seized his belt and dragged him down beside her. "Mmm," she said, "I'm interested in bodies myself."

"Me too," he said, shifting his weight so they toppled gently sideways onto the bed, still embracing, their heads on the pillows. "One particular body, anyway. Now, where were we?"

□ 7 □

WILSON MERRILL WAS one of those people who look just the way they sound. Gideon had pictured a squarish, energetic man of forty-five, with a ruddy face and jolly eyes, and so he was. He arrived punctually at eight, just as Gideon and Julie were finishing a gigantic breakfast in the dining room. They were alone, Robyn and Arbuckle having started early on the two-hundred mile round trip to Swanscombe.

Merrill promptly accepted Gideon's invitation to join them for a cup of coffee and plumped himself down at their table. They passed a few minutes in pleasant enough conversation about weather and countryside, and Merrill recommended several country walks they might like, being himself a great walker. (It was not hard to imagine him striding over the downs in knickerbockers and tweed coat, with a shooting stick under his arm, if they still had such things.)

When Julie said, "I hear you've found something in my husband's line," he was off at once, with energy and relish, before he even swallowed the coffee in his mouth.

"Um," he said, and swallowed. "Ah. Yes. Male. Caucasian, I think, but hard to say. An awful lot of putrefaction, and the fish and crustaceans have been having a jolly time with him. Not much face to speak of. They've eaten away most of the soft parts—lips, eyelids, nostrils, that sort of thing. And of course the bloating and hypostasis have produced the most grotesque distortions.''

He put his hands to his face to demonstrate God knows what, but Gideon had noted that Julie was sitting rigidly in her chair, not chewing the toast that had gone into her mouth a moment before. Her eyes caught his in a frantic plea for help.

"Dr. Merrill," Gideon said quickly, "my wife isn't terribly familiar with this sort of thing."

Merrill's hands dropped away from the corners of his mouth, which he had begun to tug outward in a spirited rendition of bloating and hypostasis. "Oh dear, Mrs. Oliver," he said, looking genuinely distressed, "how completely thoughtless of me. Look here, I *am* sorry."

"That's quite all right," Julie said a little thickly, around the toast. She closed her eyes and, with an effort, swallowed. "No problem at all. But it *is* almost eight-thirty," she said brightly, "and I insist on having my husband back in time for one of those walks. So perhaps you'd both better get to your, er, remains."

"I say, I *am* sorry," Merrill said again as he pulled the little Fiat into the light traffic of Charmouth's main street. "My wife doesn't mind in the least when I go on about bodies and things." He chuckled. "Not that I suppose she hears a word of it after all these years. But really, I must remember that many women are rather sensitive about these things."

Not only women, Gideon thought; men, too. Sometimes even physical anthropologists. Julie had not been the only one whose appetite had vanished so suddenly. He was not, after all, a pathologist but an evolutionary theoretician, a student of early man. Naturally, an understanding of what bones could tell was essential, and it was this knowledge that had led him—how, he could hardly remember—into spending a substantial portion of this time with policemen, pathologists, and corpses.

He had never tired of learning about the human skeleton, and to sit down over a fifty-thousand-year-old skull, to tease from it the essence of the long-gone, living man—what he looked like, what he ate, what he did, how he died, sometimes even what he thought—this was the most engrossing activity of his life . . . his work life, anyway. (Julie's arrival on the scene had drastically reordered his priorities, and all to the good.)

Still, an analytical session with an ancient skeleton was something he always looked forward to, "ancient" being the key word. A dry brown skull or a dusty old femur had a clean, curved beauty of its own, apparent to the educated eye or fingertip. But a greasy, decomposing corpse, always pathetic, frequently the victim of a horrendous crime, was another thing. Gideon had never grown used to them.

"Were you able to establish cause of death?" he asked. "Drowning?"

"Assuredly not," Merrill said with emphasis. "No sign of 'drowning lung,' no diatoms in the subpleural tissue or the bone marrow. Definitely not drowning."

"Any other ideas?"

"Well," Merrill said, and looked briefly at Gideon, "yes, I do have some ideas. . . . Would you like to hear them?"

"On second thought, no. I'd be better off coming to my own conclusions. Less chance of bias."

"Quite proper," Merrill said approvingly. "Very professional. Not many are these days, I can tell you."

They drove in silence into the pretty village of Bridport and turned left off A-35 to the very edge of town, where a large hospital and a small police station shared a block of grassy land. They also shared the same mortuary, it seemed. Merrill parked the car in front of the police station, one of those grimly utilitarian Victorian structures of red brick turned by time to the color of dried blood. It consisted of a pair of identical two-story buildings, each with two big brick chimneys crowned with jumbles of sooty chimney pots. On the lawn before the buildings was a small, sad marble column, a memorial to the village dead of the two world wars, with faded artificial flowers at its base.

"Here we are at last," Merrill chirped when he parked,

as if he'd brought them to one of the must-see spots of the British Isles. "In we go."

The entry took them under a gray concrete arch that connected the two dreary buildings and was inscribed with wedge-shaped Roman lettering: COVNTY CONSTABVLARY. On the drab wall of the building on the left was a modern, incongruously bright sign of blue and white: *Dorset Police. South Western Divisional Headquarters*.

"Mortuary's here on the right," Merrill said, then glanced at Gideon. "Something on your mind?"

"Yes. Someone's been missing from the Stonebarrow Fell dig for a couple of weeks; a man named Randy Alexander. Any reason to think it might be him?"

Merrill laughed. "That, my dear fellow, is what we were hoping you'd tell *us*."

Gideon's hope that "mortuary" might signify something a little warmer, a little less dingily depressing than the morgues he'd gotten used to in the United States was quickly extinguished. The Bridport Mortuary might have been a scaled-down replica of the coroner's morgue in San Francisco's gloomy old Hall of Justice.

They entered through a sterile little anteroom, unfurnished but for a solitary couch covered in green plastic, which looked fifteen years old but never sat upon. One wall was of glass, like the viewing room in a maternity ward, but this wall was not for viewing the newly living.

"Observation room," Merrill explained unnecessarily, searching through his pockets for the key that would let them pass through.

It is only in the movies that people who come to identify corpses walk into the morgue and peer into a drawer to see a chilled body with a red tag tied by a string to its big toe. They're there, all right, in their drawers, with tags on their toes, but the insides of morgues are almost never seen by the public. Instead, the body to be viewed, decorously clothed in a sheet pulled up around its neck, is wheeled to the viewing-room window on a gurney. If the head has been damaged, the "better" side is presented to the observer. And if there is no better side, a technician will make whatever cosmetic repairs are possible, more to spare the viewer than to aid in the identification.

Merrill finally found the right key. "At last! Thought I was going to have to disappoint you." He laughed happily, and Gideon smiled unconvincingly back as they entered the morgue proper, a small, white-tiled room with two tables, on the nearer of which was what they'd come to see.

"Whew," Gideon said, steeling himself not to shrink back.

"Pretty bad, eh? Of course, once you get something like this out of the water, decomposition speeds up enormously. Naturally, we've had it in the freezer overnight. By the by"—Merrill gestured at a stainless-steel door in one wall—"we've got a *really* fascinating case in there. Poor old fellow was done in by a high-pressure jet of cellulose spray. Astonishing sight. Never seen anything like it. Perhaps if you have time after you finish here—"

"Thanks very much," Gideon said quickly, "but I think I'd better get back as soon as I'm done. I'm on my honeymoon, you know."

"Honeymoon! No, I didn't know. Congratulations!" Laughing, he led Gideon by the arm toward the corpse. "What's a newlywed like you doing in a place like this, eh?"

"Eh" is right, Gideon thought.

"Well," Merrill said crisply, "we shan't keep you long. Now, let's have a look at this chap."

Gideon made himself look down. He had learned that it was only the first few minutes that were really bad, and that the sooner he got used to it, the better off he'd be. The body, terribly swollen and discolored to a blackish green, lay on its back on a basin-shaped porcelain autopsy table that was tilted slightly so that the pink, transparent fluid that ran sparsely from it dribbled down to a hole at the table's foot and drained through a rubber tube to collect in a thready puddle in a stoppered sink below—for what purpose Gideon didn't know and didn't want to know.

The autopsy had already been performed; the body was

sliced from throat to crotch, its ribs spread open like a pair of cupboard doors. The scalp, with its algaelike cap of mud-colored hair, had been peeled back, the top of the skull sawed off, and the brain removed. The skullcap, neatly cleaned, had been placed near the head, flat side down, like a halved coconut, presumably awaiting Gideon's inspection.

"Well, then," Merrill said, "where shall we begin?" He clapped his hands softly and squeezed his fingers. He might have been a child looking forward to solving a jigsaw puzzle; in a sense he was. "How long would you say he's been in the water?"

"I'll accept your judgment on that, Doctor. Outside of the skeleton, I'm afraid I don't know much about tissue pathology. Besides, the water here is probably colder than what I'm familiar with. That would make a difference, wouldn't it?"

"Oh, yes, all the difference in the world. It would retard the postmortem changes drastically. Now," he said, slipping comfortably into a teacher's role, "this is a typical four-weeker."

"Four-weeker? That rules out Alexander. I was talking to him only two weeks ago."

"I said a *typical* four-weeker. But a body might be caught up in a warm current, for example, or float where there are industrial effluvia that heat the water. Either way, decomposition would be hastened. Or it might run into a particularly voracious school of fish or other flesh-eaters. I grant you, this one seems awfully advanced for two weeks, but let us reserve our conclusions."

At Gideon's nod of agreement, Merrill resumed his lecture where he'd left off. "Now this, as I say, is a typical four-weeker: The face is gone, as well as the flesh of the hands—no fingerprints from this one—and the meat is pretty well eaten away between ankle and calf. And just look at the maceration! Classic washerwoman's skin syndrome." With a finger he pushed gently at one wrinkled foot. The skin slid loosely back and forth. "I could slip the dermis off as easily as if it were a sock."

Merrill looked as if he might demonstrate, and Gideon

interrupted hurriedly. "So he was fully clothed, then?"
Aquatic life, he knew, attacked the uncovered parts of the
body first. On a clothed male it would be the head and
hands, then the area just above the socks, where the trousers
floated free, then the rest.

"Correct, Professor. Leather jacket, jeans, and all the
rest. We've checked, of course, and the clothing *might* be
Alexander's, but there's no positive identification. They'll
be shipped to the Yard today with the body. Now then, does
anything else strike you?"

"Well, there's an odd pattern of lividity. The body fluids
seem to have settled in the arms and legs. Chest, too, it
looks like. As if he'd been draped over a saw horse when he
was killed."

"Ah, very perceptive. Excellent reasoning." Merrill laughed
his jolly laugh. "Erroneous conclusion, however. You must
remember that although a newly dead body sinks for a few
days before floating to the surface, it does not lie upon the
ocean floor. No, it hangs suspended, in a shadowy limbo, as
if were, between surface and bottom." Merrill's gentle eyes
glittered with enthusiasm. And why not, Gideon thought.
Who was he to look askance if Merrill got enthusiastic
about cadavers? There were plenty of people who wondered
what *he* found so absorbing in bones.

"And," Merrill went on, "what with the torso being the
most buoyant part of the body, the corpse naturally turns on
its face, its legs and arms trailing beneath it, its head lolling
forward, more or less like a great jellyfish." He leaned
over, dangled his head and arms, and made a presumably
jellyfishlike face. From this unusual position he continued
to speak.

"Obviously, the lividity—hypostasis is the better term,
really—would therefore be most pronounced in the legs and
arms. Face, too." He stood up straight, smiling charmingly.
"But of course, this fellow doesn't have a face, so it's
moot."

"Interesting," said Gideon, and in spite of himself he
was interested.

"Yes, isn't it?" Merrill responded with sincerity. He

seemed about to elaborate on the subject but caught himself. "See here, you have a beautiful wife waiting for you, so let's get down to our business, which is: What can *you* tell us from the skeleton?" He went to a metal cabinet. "I have sliding and spreading calipers for you, and dissecting tools."

"And if you have a pair of gloves, I'd appreciate them," Gideon said.

"Gloves?" Merrill turned his head. "You mean rubber gloves?"

"Yes, if you have them."

A faint shadow of surprise flitted over the pathologist's face. "I suppose we do, if you really want them. For myself, I find the sense of touch in my bare hands extremely sensitive."

I do too, Gideon thought but did not say. *That's why I want the gloves.* If he'd had the nerve, he would have asked for a surgeon's face mask and a rubber coat.

He slipped on the disposable plastic gloves that Merrill found for him, picked up a probe, and poked gingerly at the gristly tendons and ruined muscles of the face to see the bone underneath. It didn't take much poking. When the head wobbled on the plastic neck rest, he forced himself to steady it with his other hand. It was, he reminded himself, the first touch that was the worst.

"We don't expect any miracles, of course," Merrill said, watching with interest, "but if you can give us anything positive that might be helpful in identification, we'd be most grateful. The race, perhaps . . ."

"You said you thought he was Caucasian?"

"Yes, from the hair. The color's no help after all this time in the water, obviously, but I had a look at some of the head hair under a microscope. It's oval in cross section, and relatively fine, both of which suggest a Caucasian. But even hair gets distorted after a month in the water, so I'm not overly confident."

"Well, you're right. He's Caucasian."

Merrill beamed. "Oh, but I say . . . just like that? But don't you have to measure the breadth of the skull, or index the pelvis, or some such arcane thing?"

"No, there are quite a few indicators visible right here."
Gideon said, and delivered a little lecture of his own. The
skullcap, he pointed out, was dolichocephalic, quite a bit
longer from front to back than from side to side. This was
both a Negroid and Caucasoid trait; Mongoloids, on the
other hand, tended to be round-headed. Moreover, the
malars, or cheekbones, sloped sharply back. In a Mongoloid
skull, the cheekbones would be broad planes that projected
out to the sides, producing the wide, flat face of the Oriental
or the American Indian. Thus, the body was almost certainly
not Mongoloid, and it only remained to determine if it was
that of a white man or a black man. That distinction,
Gideon explained, was not difficult on this particular cranium.

Gideon ticked them off: The brow ridges were undulating,
as opposed to the mesalike ridges more characteristic of
Negroid skulls; the nasal sill—the bottom of the nasal
opening—was marked by a sharp border, and not the "scooped
out" margin of the Negroid skull; the nasal bones themselves were "towered," giving the appearance of having
been pinched together; the shape of the eyesockets tended
toward the triangular, not the rectangular. . . .

Merrill listened, entranced. "Oh, I say, that's marvelous!
I had no idea . . . ! I must say, you're certainly living up to
your reputation."

"Actually, there's more," Gideon said, not above flattery.
"The arch of the palate, for example. You can look at it
from underneath easily enough on this one, what with the
throat muscles and the tongue gone." He tipped the head
back on its neck rest. "The Caucasoid palate is very narrow;
that's why we suffer more from crowding of the teeth. The
Negroid palatine arch, on the other hand—" He stopped
suddenly, staring through the brown tatters of muscle to the
bone and cartilage underneath.

"Ah, you've noticed, have you?" Merrill cried. "I was
sure you would!"

With a probe, Gideon picked at a small U-shaped bone
that lay above the larnyx at the junction of jawline and
throat. "It's murder, isn't it?" he said. "The hyoid's
fractured. He's been strangled."

"Indeed he has. Manually strangulated. And not only the hyoid bone, but the thyroid cartilage as well." With his finger Merrill pushed at the stiff cartilage that formed the prominence of the Adam's apple. "The left horn's cracked. I've been a forensic pathologist for nineteen years and I've yet to see a thyroid broken this way—a single horn fractured—that wasn't caused by manual strangulation. It's the thumbs that do it, you know." Ever ready to demonstrate, he raised his hands, thumbs up. "They press in and . . . pop! Goodbye, thyroid."

The hands came down and he was abruptly grave. "So we have a male Caucasian, strangled from in front—otherwise the thumbs wouldn't have cracked the thyroid horn—killed four weeks ago, perhaps a little less. What else can we infer?"

"Well, we can see he was a big guy, pretty powerfully built."

"I've estimated six feet two, living height; two hundred twenty pounds living weight. Why so thoughtful, Professor?"

"He was strangled from in front," Gideon said, "but how easy would it be to stand in front of a man that big—and presumably strong—and strangle him? I was just wondering if he might not already have been unconscious."

"We *do* think alike. That's precisely my guess. *I* certainly wouldn't have wanted to try it with him awake. I've checked the head, thorax, and abdomen for any sign of a blow or wound that might have knocked him out, but I found nothing. Of course, he might have been drugged, but considering the condition of the internal organs . . ." He waved vaguely at the corpse and shrugged. "Still, the laboratories may find something suggestive."

Gideon nodded. "Well, let's see what we can tell about his age."

"Good." Merrill leaned forward, full of interest. "I've cleaned the skullcap for you so you can look at the sutures."

"I won't need to," Gideon said. "The pubic symphysis is a lot more reliable. That's what I'll want to see."

Merrill threw back his head and laughed. Puzzled, Gideon stared at him.

"No offense, Professor," Merrill said, "but you know what they say: The odontologists go for the mouth, the anthropologists go for the pubis."

No, Gideon didn't know, but he smiled. It was hard not to loosen up with a man who enjoyed his work as much as Merrill did. "Do you mind if I carve up the pelvis a little? If I can use your saw, I'd like to have a look at the symphyseal surface."

Merrill promptly brought out a small battery-operated saw. "I'll do it for you."

"No, that's all right—"

"Wouldn't hear of it." The pathologist elbowed an unprotesting Gideon out of the way, hacked briefly at the soft tissue of the groin with a knife, and set briskly to work on the left pubis with the buzzing saw. "I can see you're not too keen on rooting about in the pelvic cavity, and I don't mind in the least."

Gideon was surprised. He hadn't known it showed. "No, really, I don't mind—"

"Quite all right," Merrill said, now using a scalpel to hack through the tough cartilaginous disk that held the two halves of the pelvis together in front. "You're a dry-bone man, aren't you, and this sort of thing can be pretty revolting if you're not used to it. What? Takes a queer bird like me not to mind it. Ah, here we are, here we are."

He had freed the small section of bone from the body. He scraped it clean with the dull end of the scalpel and rinsed it off at a stainless-steel sink in the corner. "One left pubic symphysis, clean as a whistle."

Gideon took the inch-long, flat-faced piece of bone. The os pubis was that part of the pelvis located exactly at the midline, just above the genitals. For reasons of which anthropologists are unsure, its symphyseal surface—the part that fits against its opposite member—is the skeleton's surest guide to age, growing more fine-grained and pitted, in identifiable stages, from adolescence to late middle age.

Gideon studied it, explaining to an attentive Merrill as he went along. Finally he said, "I'd say he was about thirty-five."

"Marvelous," Merrill said. "Oh, good morning, Inspector."

Gideon looked up to see a big man in shirtsleeves more or less billow to the table, moving in slow, surging strides, like a diver walking on the ocean floor. He was very large, as tall as Gideon and a great deal wider.

"Hullo there, Dr. Merrill," he said. "And this must be the famous Professor Oliver, then." He spoke as he moved, rumbling along with an unhurried, stately rhythm, and he gave the impression of occupying a lot of space, even more than the considerable amount he actually did.

"Dr. Oliver," Merrill said, "this is Detective Inspector Bagshawe of the CID."

"Hello, Inspector."

"A pleasure, I'm sure, sir. You'll forgive me if we don't shake hands?"

Gideon forgave him. His own gloved hands were uninviting in the extreme, and Bagshawe's crisply folded-back white shirtsleeves were scrupulously clean.

"Well," Bagshawe said, affable and placid. "Well, well. Imagine, Professor Gideon Oliver right here in Dorset. Well, now. And how have we been progressing? Does this unfortunate gentleman"—a flick of his head toward the cadaver—"appear to be Mr. Randall Alexander, or does he not?"

Gideon smiled. "That's expecting a lot, Inspector."

"What?" The tufted eyebrows rose in patient incredulity. "Has the skeleton detective finally met his match? Surely not."

"Not at all, Inspector," Merrill interrupted. "We've made some real progress. Professor Oliver's positively identified him as a Caucasian."

"Have you now?" Bagshawe looked at Gideon with something like a sparkle in his eye. "Why then, we've ruled out half the world already, haven't we?"

"Three-quarters," Gideon said.

"Three-quarters?"

"Seventy-five percent of the world is nonwhite, and we can eliminate every one of them. So we really are making progress, you see. We've already narrowed it down to only a billion or so, out of a possible four billion. Half a billion,

really, or even a little less, since we know he's a male."
Now why, Gideon wondered, am I being cute?

"Fancy," Bagshawe said. "Four billion people. Who
would have thought?"

"And that's not all," said Merrill. "We have an idea of
his age now. That is to say, Professor Oliver has: approximately thirty-five years of age."

"Approximately? Would that be, say, thirty to forty?"

"Say thirty-four to thirty-five," Gideon said, drawing it a
bit finer than the evidence warranted. Bagshawe had him
showing off now. There was something about this peaceable,
lumbering policeman that threw one off one's stride. Quite
an advantage for a detective, Gideon imagined.

"Indeed, now? Well, that certainly is something. A
thirty-five-year-old Caucasian; quite helpful, quite helpful."

"I haven't had a thorough look at the skeleton yet,"
Gideon said. "I might be able to turn up something else."

"Do you think you could? I'd be most appreciative. Now,
Dr. Merrill, I was just looking for your report, but I seem to
have misplaced it."

"No, Inspector, I haven't completed it yet. Why don't I
just come along and finish it right now? The file's in your
office. I imagine Professor Oliver would welcome the chance
to work without having me underfoot."

□ 8 □

Working alone suited Gideon, who depended more than most on intuition. To have to explain or defend what he was doing as he went along could throw him off the track or make him lose a glimmer of insight that might flash only once.

Alone, he went quickly over the skeletal system with a probe and gloved fingertips, looking for anything that might catch his attention. He had fought down his initial queasy reaction and was able to work objectively, if not quite with Merrill's zest. The trick was to "unfocus" on the mutilated body that seemed to be rotting before his eyes, and think in terms of a series of bony condyles, fossae, foramina, and diaphyses to be dispassionately examined one at a time.

On the torso the only thing even moderately interesting was the existence of osteophytic growths—the bony excrescences of arthritis—on three of the five lumbar vertebrae, just above the hips. This was not rheumatoid arthritis, which can strike at any time, but the "normal" degeneration of bone surfaces that came to everyone with age. That was what made it odd. You'd expect vertebrae like these in a man of seventy, not one half that age.

Strange, too, that only three vertebrae should be affected. That suggested the growths and lipping were the results of localized trauma—of which he could find no other sign—or of some sort of long-term stress on the lower back. Gideon studied them for a while, finally gave up, and tucked the problem into a corner of his mind.

On the right forearm, masked by swollen, blackened soft tissue, he found something he did understand. Both bones, the ulna and the radius, were shattered, the only signs of antemortem injury other than the fractured hyoid and thyroid. The direction of the splintering and the way the lower parts of the shafts had ridden up over the upper made it clear that they had been broken by a single blow on the outside (the little-finger side) of the forearm. It was precisely the kind of damage done when a victim instinctively flings his arm up over his face to protect it against a club-wielding assailant—the so-called nightstick fracture.

It was also a serviceable explanation of how someone had managed to stand in front of a big, presumably healthy man like this one and choke him to death. Assuming that the blow had come before the strangling (there was no way to be sure, but why would it be afterward?), the big man would have been sick with pain and shock. And he would have had only one useful arm.

Something else had caught Gideon's eye while he was laying back the mess of putrefying muscles and nerves over the forearm fractures: a pierced olecranon fossa. This is a hollow at the elbow end of the humerus—the bone of the upper arm. It serves as a socket in which the top of the ulna rocks back and forth like a hinge when the elbow is opened or closed. Every now and then—about five per cent of the time in Caucasians—the fossa will have a little, smooth, round hole right through it, and this was such a case.

A tiny bell in his mind began to jangle. He wasn't sure why, but he'd heard it enough times to know better than to ignore it. There was something to be learned here. He pushed the probe slowly into and out of the hole.

Think. A pierced olecranon fossa was usually congenital, but some anthropologists believed it might also result from wear and tear. Gideon leaned over the body and opened up the other elbow joint, quickly cutting down to the bone. The fossa was unperforated. Since this kind of congenital condition was usually bilateral, that was a strong indication that the hole in the right fossa had indeed been caused by friction.

All right, assume the bone's been worn through, then. Next question: What might have done it? What kind of movement, endlessly repeated, would grind the end of the ulna slowly through the back of the humerus? Gideon flexed and extended his own arm to feel the pull of tendons, to visualize the play of articulating bone surfaces. Lifting wouldn't do it, no matter how strenuous, nor pulling either. No, what it would take was the full, snapping extension of the elbow joint.

Push-ups? Not unless you did five hundred a day for a year or two. Throwing something, maybe. Throwing hard, over and over again.

Pitching a baseball.

Randy Alexander, the southpaw who had—literally, it would appear—worn out his arm. A perforated olecranon fossa hardly proved it, but it was certainly starting to look that way. By now Gideon's squeamishness had vanished completely. He was totally absorbed, making progress. And he had found something else.

While working on the arms, he had seen that the man had had powerful deltoids, the big shield-shaped muscles that flesh out the shoulder. It was, of course, impossible to tell this from the pulpy, rotted muscle tissue itself, but strong muscles needed strong tendons, and strong tendons sculpted ridges and crests into the bones that anchored them. And those bony ridges and crests didn't rot. On this man's humeri, the deltoid-pull areas were as rough and pro-nounced as mountain ranges on a relief map.

No particular surprise there. What was unusual was that *only* the deltoids had been particularly massive. Again Gideon stood quietly, thinking. What sort of activity would develop the deltoids—which rotate, flex, and raise the arms—yet not enlarge the other muscles of the shoulder girdle? Somewhere, in some recess of his mind, he already had the answer. It wouldn't be the pitching. . . .

Of course. The big deltoids tied right in with those three

arthritic vertebrae. There was just one more thing to check. He turned the stiff, heavy body on its side so that he could get at the back of the thigh, then cut through the hamstring muscles and peeled them away. The femur, the body's longest, strongest bone, lay exposed. Running down the back of its shaft was a well-defined muscle ridge, the linea aspera. "Rough line," it meant in Latin, and on this body it was extremely rough indeed.

It was precisely what Gideon had expected to find, and that settled it. As far as he was concerned, the examination was done. Accentuated linea aspera, enlarged deltoid pull, and premature arthritis of the lumbar vertebrae. He had seen the combination three times before, and he knew of only one thing that caused it—longtime riding of the elongated, low-slung motorcycles called "choppers."

It was the muscle strains brought on by the unnatural posture that did it; that, the bumping, and the increased buffeting by the wind that came from riding while leaning far back. This was Alexander's body all right; coincidence was so improbable as to be out of the question. That "typical four-weeker" business was puzzling, but it would be up to Merrill to figure that out.

So Nate had been wrong after all. Randy was dead—murdered—and Gideon was more disturbed than he should have been. It was utterly irrational for him to feel any responsibility for the death, and he knew it, but there it was all the same. What if he hadn't put Randy off? What if he'd listened to what he'd had to say, there on the hillside. . . .

Abruptly, he stripped off the gloves and went to the sink to scrub his hands twice over with plenty of soap, and water as hot as he could stand it. Putting blame on himself made no sense at all, and he wouldn't let himself do it. Besides, he'd just done a first-rate piece of skeletal detective work, and he had every right to be pleased with it. He sat down at an old steel desk against the wall, his back to the body, and began to write his report.

❑ 9 ❑

INSPECTOR BAGSHAWE'S REACTION was extremely rewarding. "Get away!" he shouted so vehemently that the great, curving cherrywood pipe he was about to light slipped from between his teeth and clattered onto the glass-covered top of his desk, dispersing shreds of toast-brown tobacco through the litter of papers and folders. "*A left-handed baseball pitcher who rode a motorcycle?*"

Merrill's happy laugh rang out. "That's wonderful, Professor! How on earth did you come up with that?"

When Gideon had explained, Bagshawe said, "So you're reasonably certain it's Alexander, are you?" His tone was distinctly more respectful than heretofore.

"I think so. I don't imagine baseball pitchers are too common in England."

"No, but—"

"And a cricket bowler's motion wouldn't have done it. Not enough elbow snap."

Nodding his head, Bagshawe retrieved his pipe, brushed some of the scattered tobacco back into it with a massive, cupped hand, and lit it, drawing deeply. "And it's not only baseball players one doesn't find here. These 'choppers,' as you call them—not very popular here; not yet. And I say, thank the Lord for that. Well, Alexander's background is easily enough verified, and I expect it will support your conclusions." He puffed contentedly and leaned back in his creaking wooden swivel chair. His eyes returned to the report. " 'Radial and ulnar fractures,' " he read aloud. "Those would be arm bones, would they?"

"Forearm, yes."

"Mm-hm, I see." His large hands rummaged awkwardly in a drawer and pulled out another sheet of paper. "Mm, I don't seem to find . . . yes . . . no . . . I don't believe you mentioned that in your report, Dr. Merrill."

Merrill appeared mildly taken aback, and Gideon intervened. "It was hardly noticeable, what with the swelling and distortion. Easy to miss."

Well, not really. He had noticed before how careless pathologists could be, even knowledgeable and enthusiastic ones like Merrill (not that he'd ever known one quite as enthusiastic as Merrill). It was lack of interest in the long bones, he'd concluded years ago. There were all sorts of things to engage pathologist's interest in the head, the trunk, and the internal organs, and they were scrupulously examined. The outlying bones were duller stuff, it appeared, and so they often escaped attention.

"I see." Bagshawe nodded again, clearly not convinced. "Well, then, back to the good professor's report." He puffed at his pipe and read aloud very slowly. " 'Fresh radial and ulnar fractures' "—Gideon almost expected him to begin pushing a bulky forefinger from word to word— " 'which appear to be antemortem . . .' " He put the report on the desk and looked thoughtfully at Gideon.

"Now, what I can't help wondering is, how can you know that? How can you be sure the arm was broken before he died? That's what I ask myself. How do you know he wasn't killed, then pushed off a cliff into the sea so he broke those bones in the fall? Or that they didn't break weeks afterward, when he washed up against a pier or a rock? That's what I'd like to know." Through a rising veil of smoke, he peered keenly at Gideon.

"I don't *know*. Naturally, it's an inferential conclusion."

"Ah, inferential conclusions," Bagshawe said sadly. "Now, speaking for myself, I admire inferential conclusions tremendously. However, courts of law don't always share my admiration.''

Gideon laughed. "I've noticed the same thing myself." He had, as a matter of fact, spent some harrowing moments of his own on the stand as an expert witness. ("Now, *Doctor* Oliver, do you *really* mean to imply that you can, ah, 'infer' from a *single*, tiny bone, a *finger* bone . . .")

"Really, Inspector," Merrill said stuffily, taking offense on Gideon's behalf, "I can assure you that if Gideon Oliver says those fractures were antemortem, they were. You may rely on his opinion without reservation."

Low in his throat, Bagshawe made a good-humored sound. "Well, I'll just tell them you said that, Doctor, and I'm sure we won't have any problem." He turned smiling to Gideon. "Still . . ."

"All right," Gideon said, "I have three reasons for thinking the bones were broken before death." Lists of three, he had found, as had many a professor before him, were almost mystically persuasive, especially if counted on the fingers.

"One"—he ticked it off with his forefinger—"there are no other fractures, aside from the bone and cartilage in the throat, and no signs of the kind of injuries that bouncing down a cliff face or being tossed against a pier might produce. Two"—two fingers rapped Bagshawe's desk—"the existence of an antemortem nightstick fracture fits in with the probable facts, because it explains how someone might have stood in front of a husky, healthy Randy Alexander and strangled him. And three"—both of the other men watched Gideon's hand to see him tick it off, which he did—"three, the upper and lower segments of the broken bones overlap in exactly the way they would be expected to if jerked out of position by a spasm of the flexor digitorum profundis, the flexor pollicis longus, and the pronator quadratus."

He might have said "forearm muscles," but he had shifted into a sort of pedantic high gear for the moment, and he let it pass. "Had he been dead already, the muscles would have lacked tonus, and they wouldn't have pulled the bones out of place." Gideon paused to catch his breath.

"Excellent," Merrill said. "Clear thinking."

Bagshawe pulled ruminatively at his pipe and said, "Umm, umm."

"Of course," Gideon went on, "we can't absolutely exclude the possibility that the bones *could* have been broken later and somehow gotten shifted into those positions, but it's pretty unlikely. I think the fractures occurred before death—just before death—and the arm must have swelled quickly and been wedged into position inside his sleeve. He was wearing a leather jacket, wasn't he?"

"Yes, a leather jacket," Bagshawe murmured. "Well, well, that tells us quite a lot about our victim. Now all we need to do is to find out about our murderer."

"For starters," Gideon said, "we know that he was left-handed—like Randy."

"Why, that's right," Merrill interjected. "The fractures. I see. Of course."

"Well, I don't see," Bagshawe rumbled.

"The nightstick fractures," Gideon said. "They were in his right arm. And if he threw up his right hand to protect his head, then almost certainly he was warding off a blow delivered with his assailant's left hand."

"Ah, I see," said Bagshawe. "Yes, that could be. Unless, of course, the assailant delivered a *back*-handed blow—with his right arm. Or unless Alexander was attacked from behind, say, and just happened to twist to his own left to look around when he heard someone behind him. Then, of course, it would be his own left hand that was flung up in any event, would it not?"

"No, Inspector," Merrill said. "I'll have to support Professor Oliver on this. I do see your point, but I'd say that nine out of ten times—I speak from my own experience, you understand—a nightstick fracture of the right arm indicates a left-handed attacker, and vice versa."

"Well," Bagshawe muttered, "I expect you're right. Still, in my opinion, it's a bit premature to rule out other possibilities." He cocked his head slowly to one side. "Something's just occurred to me . . . Do you suppose there's any merit in this? Since he was wearing a leather jacket, I wonder if there might not be some sign of the weapon on his sleeve: an imbedded fragment of wood or metal, perhaps, or an indentation that shows the shape of the object. What do you think?''

"It's been in the water for weeks," Gideon said. "Would there be anything after all that time?"

"Probably not," Bagshawe said with a sigh. "Still, I think I'll suggest the forensic lads have a look. No stone unturned, you know. Well, well." He put his pipe down and stood up. "Thank you, Professor, it's been most enlightening. I'll go up to the excavation this afternoon and tell them about poor Alexander. Until then, I'd appreciate it if you'd keep all this to yourself."

Gideon nodded and got up too, and was afforded the novel sensation of seeing his own sizable hand engulfed in an even larger one.

"May I send you back?" Bagshawe asked.

"No, no," Merrill said, jumping up. "My pleasure."

"Fine," Bagshawe said. "Fine. Oh, Professor, while you're here . . . I understand from Sergeant Fryer that Mr. Alexander made an appointment to tell you something but that he never kept it. Would you mind going over the particulars once more?"

Head down, arms folded, leaning against his desk, he listened closely while Gideon described the incident. "And," he said, "did anyone overhear him make this appointment with you?"

"I don't think so. We were out in the open, and no one was around. Well, Nate Marcus saw us talking—he came looking for Randy—but he couldn't have heard what we were saying. At least I don't think so."

"And what was his reaction.?"

"None, as far as I remember. Or, on second thought, maybe he seemed a little irritated. He asked if it was a private discussion."

"Ah. And did anyone else overhear you?"

Gideon thought for a moment. "We walked by the trench together. I suppose that any of the three of them—Sandra, Barry, Leon—could have seen us, or maybe heard us. But we were just chatting at that point. Randy waited until we were out of sight before he got serious."

"As if he didn't want anyone else to hear?"

"That was the impression I got."

"And Professor Frawley? Where was he during all this?"

"We left him in the shed. He couldn't have heard us."

"Ah," Bagshawe said again, with more relish. "So of them all, only Professor Marcus might have overheard, and he seemed . . . irritated, I believe you said?"

"Wait a minute, Inspector. Nate sounds irritated most of the time. You're not implying that he killed Randy to keep him from telling me something, are you?"

"Implying?" Bagshawe pointed incredulously to himself with the stem of his pipe. "Me? No, no, just collecting data. Implications come later. As in anthropology, no doubt." He smiled. "By the way, you wouldn't happen to remember if Professor Marcus is left-handed, I suppose?"

Was he? Were any of them? Gideon couldn't remember.

"No matter," Bagshawe said kindly. "I'll just have to look into it myself."

"Look, Inspector Bagshawe, I'm not trying to protect Nate. I don't think for a minute he did it, but whoever did, I'm as interested in seeing him caught as you are. I guess I feel, well . . ."

Responsible was what he felt, like it or not. And guilty. He had self-righteously put Randy off with conditions that were no more than ploys to keep himself out of the Stonebarrow mess, and now Randy was dead, killed that very day, it appeared.

"Well, personally involved," he concluded weakly. "But are you saying that Nate is a serious suspect?"

Bagshawe stopped in the process of relighting his pipe. He took it from his mouth, tipped his big head, and grinned, showing square, complacent teeth. "Now what sort of copper would I be if I answered that?"

The resolutely amicable Andy Hinshore served Julie and Gideon a plentiful late lunch of roast chicken and fried potatoes while Gideon gave Julie a nongraphic summary of

his morning's experiences at the mortuary, having decided
that Bagshawe's proscription did not apply in her case.

He was just concluding when the telephone in the reception hall rang. After a few seconds they heard Hinshore
shouting into it. "I'm sorry, I didn't understand you. . . . Could
you speak a little slower? Sir . . . ?"

The conversation continued in this vein, and then, as
Gideon was pouring more tea from the pot on the table,
Hinshore's voice caught his attention more sharply.

"*Skeleton detective*, did you say? Did you say *skeleton
detective?* Sir, this is a hotel. . . ."

"Oh-oh," Gideon said, the pot poised above Julie's cup,
"maybe we should make a break for it before Andy figures
out who that's for."

Julie smiled wryly at him, a what-have-I-gotten-myself-
into grin. "Gideon, dear, is this the way it's always going to
be? Are you really in this much demand? When do you find
time to teach?"

"Honestly, I only work on a few cases a year. I don't
usually get calls every day."

"Except in Charmouth, England, incognito."

"A puzzlement." He went ahead and poured the tea just
as Hinshore came in, frowning.

"Professor, I've got a bloke on the telephone; some kind
of foreigner. Seems to want to speak with you. If you want
me to—"

"No, Andy, I'll take it, thanks. Did he say who he is?"

Hinshore spread his hands. "I think he said his name's
Ebb."

Ebb. No one he knew. "I promise," he said to Julie, "no
new cases." He tossed back a quick gulp of tea and went to
the telephone. As he picked it up, he heard Hinshore's awed
whisper to Julie: "They call him the skeleton detective?"

"Hello," Gideon said into the receiver. "This is Gideon
Oliver."

"Hello, Gideon! This is Ebb!" The voice was elderly,
excited, happy.

"Ebb?"

"Ebb, Ebb. How many Ebb's do you know?"

"Abe!" Gideon shouted. "Abe Goldstein!"

"Finally, the dawn breaks. That's not what I said? Abe?"

"Abe . . . where are you calling from?"

"London. I just got here. I'm coming right away to Charmouth." The old man's thin voice was so recognizable, so full of its familiar, creaky zip and sparkle, that Gideon couldn't understand how he had been even momentarily confused.

"I'll come and get you. I can be there in a few hours."

"Come and get me? What am I, breakable? I can't take a train? I love a train ride."

"Okay, let me check on the schedules, find out which station you leave from. Give me your number and I'll call you right back."

There was a cheerfully exasperated sigh over the telephone. "Listen to him. I can't find this out myself? I leave from Waterloo, but, for your information, there's no train station in Charmouth. The nearest one is Axminster, a few miles away, you know where? I'll be on the . . ." Gideon heard paper rattle. "The train that gets in at five-fifty-eight."

"Fine, I'll book you a room here and I'll meet you at the station."

"That I'll accept with pleasure."

"Abe, is everything all right? This is kind of a surprise, isn't it?"

"With me, all right? Of course, why shouldn't it be all right? No, I'm coming because of this thing with Nathan. You know I'm on the Horizon board of directors? So I'm coming, but unofficially, just to talk a little with him. Maybe I can help him see straight. The man knows how to run a dig, believe me, but he doesn't know when to stop talking. Still, it's ridiculous what's happening. Who wants an inquiry? Listen, have you been up there yet, to Stonebarrow?"

"Yes. Things are pretty messy."

"Messy? What messy?"

"Well, it's not just the inquiry. One of the students has been murdered—"

"Murdered? God in heaven, you're telling me that—" Abe's voice was drowned in a squeal of telephonic pip-pip-

pips. "Gideon, I got no more coins for this telephone. They make you crazy the way they eat up the money in front of your eyes. I'll see you at five-fifty-eight. Give my love to Julie—"

The line pipped again, gave one imperious, terminal cluck, and went dead.

□ 10 □

GIDEON AND JULIE had the afternoon to themselves, and they spent it walking east over the deserted, rocky beach from Charmouth toward Golden Cap, along the base of the blue lias cliffs. It was the kind of time they had dreamed of when they planned the trip: mesmerized into a tranquil stupor by the sound of the surf, they wandered aimlessly along the shore in the thin November sunlight, talking now of one subject, now of another—all of it desultory and haphazard, and lost as soon as the next thundering wave washed their minds clean. Now and then they kissed gently or simply embraced without a word. They held hands most of the time and paused frequently to look at the sea, or so that one of them could show the other some small, perfect spiral of a petrified sea creature embedded in the rocks at their feet.

"Gideon, is that Stonebarrow Fell up there?" Julie said suddenly.

"Where?"

"Up there, where you've been staring for the last five minutes."

"Have I? Yes, I guess Stonebarrow would be up there, just about straight above us."

She squeezed his hand. "Don't think unpleasant thoughts; it's too lovely here." She moved closer to him and made a little motion with her shoulders. He was barely conscious of it, and couldn't have described it, but he knew what it meant: Hug me.

He put his arm around her and squeezed. "I'm not thinking unpleasant thoughts."

"Yes, you are. You're worried about poor Nate Marcus and what's going to happen to him tomorrow."

He smiled. "Yes, you're right. Pretty close, anyway. Okay, no more unpleasant thoughts." He squeezed her once more, and they began to walk again, with his arm over her shoulder and his fingers resting lightly on the cool nape of her neck.

Pretty close, but not quite on the mark. What he was thinking about was Randy Alexander. If—just if—Alexander had been flung from the top of Stonebarrow Fell, he would have landed immediately in front of where they were. And immediately in front of them was a semicircular basin of cloudy, stagnant-looking sea water, about two hundred feet in diameter, formed by a great, curving reef that spread seaward from the base of the cliff. In it was a lot of algae and some floating debris. As Gideon watched, the tide, which had been flooding for some hours, began to retreat, flowing out of the lagoon and taking with it a large, rotten log, presumably to be carried out to sea.

As he walked, he looked more closely at the basin. It seemed to be fifteen or twenty feet deep at its center. More than deep enough. Kneeling, he touched his fingers to the water. Warm, far warmer than the ocean, as was to be expected.

He flicked the water from his fingers and stood up. He had solved Merrill's little mystery. Assuming that Alexander's body had fallen from Stonebarrow Fell, it would have landed smack in the middle of this stagnant, warm pond, in which decomposition would have proceeded far more quickly than in the colder open sea. The body might easily have lain there in the lagoon for two weeks before being floated— just like the log, already fifty feet offshore—out into the Atlantic, to be beached by the current at Seaton . . . looking just like one of Merrill's typical four-weekers.

* * *

*Immigrant pushcart peddler metamorphosed into world-
renowned anthropologist* was the way one of television's
more literate interviewers had once introduced Professor
Abraham Irving Goldstein, and the phrase, literally true,
was as good a nutshell description of Abe as Gideon knew.
In 1924, a seventeen-year-old freshly arrived from Russia,
speaking nothing but Yiddish, he was hawking thread and
ribbons from a pushcart on Brooklyn's Pitkin Avenue. A
decade later he had his Ph.D. from Columbia and was
embarking on a career that would make him one of the
world's foremost cultural anthropologists, first at Columbia,
then at the University of Wisconsin—where he'd been
Gideon's professor, and Nate Marcus's as well—and finally
at the University of Washington.

Through it all he'd managed to keep his immigrant
pushcart peddler's speech patterns. Whether these still came
naturally sixty years later, or were part of his "delightful
panoply of studied eccentricities" (as the same interviewer
had called them) was a moot question. Abe himself pro-
fessed innocence. ("Accent? What kind accent?")

Gideon hadn't seen him for a few months now, and he
watched with a trace of anxiety as the deep-blue train from
London drew smoothly to the platform at Axminster. His
old friend and mentor, now long-retired, was getting along
in years, to the point at which one always wondered whether
even a short space of time might not produce some sad and
irreversible change, some awful omen of approaching
decrepitude.

He needn't have worried. In the lit interior of the car that
stopped directly in front of him he saw Abe get to his feet,
sprightly and cheerful, ruffle the hair of a patently enchanted
five-year-old boy in the seat opposite, and deliver a courtly
bow to a blond, pretty woman, obviously the boy's mother.
When he shuffled down the aisle with his bag, Gideon could
see that his eyes had all their usual sparkle, or maybe just a
little more than usual; that would be the pretty young
mother.

Abe was a thin, active man—Gideon had once made the

mistake of calling him "spry" within his hearing—whose nervous energy and shock of frizzy white hair gave him a distinct resemblance to Artur Rubinstein. Years ago, when Gideon had been walking with him during an anthropological conference in Boston, they had been approached by a teenager who shyly asked for Abe's autograph. Abe, who had been the subject of magazine articles and television programs, complied with a flourish, and the boy watched him with adulation in his eyes. But when he looked at the signature, his face fell; he had thought, he stammered, that Abe was the great pianist. Abe had responded in character: He had put his arm around the boy's shoulder, drawn his head close, and said, in a conspiratorial whisper, "Ah, but Abraham Irving Goldstein is my *real* name."

When he clambered down to the Axminster platform, he did it with painful slowness—he was increasingly troubled with arthritis—and when Gideon embraced him, he was keenly aware of just how frail the old man's body was.

"Abe, you *are* all right, aren't you?" he asked, then suddenly laughed.

"So what's so funny?"

"I'm laughing because I know exactly what you're going to say."

"What am I going to say?"

"You're going to say, 'So why shouldn't I be all right?' "

Abe smiled. "So why shouldn't I say it?"

They talked of other things on the short drive to Charmouth, and it was not until they joined Julie that Gideon told him about his visit to Stonebarrow Fell, about the murder of Randy Alexander, about his lagoon hypothesis, and, in passing, about the disappearance of the Poundbury calvarium.

He had talked through a round of predinner sherries in front of the fire in the Tudor Room, and then a second round, to which Andy Hinshore contributed an accompaniment of pâté and bread.

When they thanked him, he grinned. "It does my heart good to see people enjoying themselves in this room. Just think, people have been sitting before this fireplace in comradeship and warmth—this very fireplace—for five hundred years. Five centuries ago, someone stood here, sheltered from the night, just as I stand here, with his hand on this stone, just as mine is. It's almost as if . . . as if I'm communicating with him, like.''

"Mr. Hinshore," Abe said, smiling, "did anyone ever tell you you got the soul of an anthropologist?"

Hinshore seemed genuinely pleased. "Why, thank you, Professor. I take that as a real compliment. Well," he said, and cleared his throat, "here I am, chattering away, with you trying to talk business. Is it all right if I serve dinner in ten minutes?"

Gideon continued talking, and Abe and Julie continued listening through the sherry and pâté, and then through bowls of oxtail soup in the dining room, where they were the sole diners, Robyn and Arbuckle not yet having returned from Swanscombe. Hinshore had already served their main course of roast lamb with mint jelly before Abe said anything.

"So what do you think, Gideon? This is too tall an order for me, bringing Nathan to his right mind?"

Gideon shook his head slowly as he dipped a slice of lamb in Mrs. Hinshore's homemade mint jelly. "I don't know, Abe. I don't think Nate's about to listen to reason. He's really gone overboard on this theory of his."

Abe rolled his eyes. "This cockamamy Mycenaean theory."

"That's the one. I really think he's gotten obsessive about it. Nate's not his old self, Abe. All the old nastiness is there, but none of the healthy skepticism about his own ideas. You'll find him changed." Gideon grimaced. Hadn't Jack Frawley used just those words?

Abe swallowed the bread he'd been chewing. "Changed, obsessive . . ." He exhaled a long, noisy sigh. "I made a big trip for nothing, you think?" He seemed suddenly tired, drained. As he ought to be, Gideon thought; he had been traveling for at least fourteen hours, and according to his Sequim-based biological clock, it was now about 4:00 A.M.

The same thought apparently occurred to Julie. With a small crease of concern on her brow, she said. "We probably ought to get you to bed early, Abe. You've had a long day, with an important one coming up tomorrow."

Ordinarily he would have rounded good-humoredly on her at the nursely "we," but instead he shrugged wearily. "I was going to go yet tonight and have a talk with Nathan, but maybe you're right. Anyway, I wouldn't want Arbuckle and the Dorset man, what's his name, Robyn, should think I was fraternizing with the enemy."

"I'd never met Robyn before last night," Gideon said. "Do you know him?"

"Yeah, I know him a little."

"What do you think of him?"

Abe chewed his lamb and pondered. "A very clean person," he said finally. "A nice dresser. You got to give him that."

Gideon laughed. "I gather you don't think too much of his professional abilities."

"I got nothing against him. A *doppes*, a dilettante. He plays at archaeology, like in the nineteenth century rich people did."

"Will he be fair at the inquiry?"

"Sure," Abe said, "I think so. Why not? So will the other one, the one from Horizon, Arbuckle. Not the most brilliant person in the world, but he does his job. In the words of Dr. Johnson, 'a harmless drudge.' "

Hinshore came to clear the table. "Everything to your liking, Professor Goldstein?" Since Gideon had explained to him who Abe was, he had treated him with solicitous respect.

"Fine," Abe said. *"Delicious."*

Hinshore's narrow face lit up with pleasure. "I'll tell the missus. And now perhaps a little cheese? We have a fine old Brie and some first-class Gorgonzola. A little more St. Emilion to go with it, perhaps?"

They had the cheese but not the wine. Julie's brows knitted. "Gideon," she said, spreading the pungent, runny Brie on a slice of bread, "this student you think was murdered—"

"There's no 'think' about it. The broken ulna and radius, the fractured hyoid, the crushed larynx—"

She shut her eyes and waved the bread at him. "All right, I believe you."

Gideon grinned as he cut some blue-veined Gorgonzola. "I'm starting to sound like Merrill."

"Heaven forbid. We'd have to get a divorce." She popped the bread into her mouth and licked her finger. "From what you said, Inspector Bagshawe thinks the killer is someone at the dig, maybe Nate himself. Is that right?"

"He didn't say it in so many words, but that was the impression I got, yes. With Nate at the head of the list."

"But why? Why not somebody from outside the dig?"

"Well, I think Bagshawe's just beginning with known factors. Where else could he start?"

"Didn't Alexander belong to some kind of motorcycle gang in Missouri? Couldn't there have been some sort of grudge, and they bumped him off?"

Abe looked accusingly at Gideon. "Bumped him off? This is what comes of being married to a skeleton detective? And such a nice girl she was."

"She certainly was," Gideon said. "But no, I don't think a motorcycle gang is too likely. Why come all the way to nice, quiet Dorset to do it, when he could have been just as easily bumped off the road in nice, quiet Missouri?"

He turned suddenly to Abe. "Do you remember if Nate is left-handed?"

"No," Abe said promptly.

"No you don't remember, or no he's not left-handed?"

"No he's not left-handed."

Gideon heaved a relieved sigh, then looked up. "How can you be that sure? You haven't seen him in years."

"Because," Abe explained. "I remember. Julie, you're thinking something?"

"Uh-huh, I am," she said slowly, reaching for another piece of bread. "Let me ask this. Now don't you two jump down my throat—remember, I don't know the man—but is there a possibility that Nate Marcus actually did kill him— to keep him from telling whatever it was?"

Gideon was hardly about to jump down her throat. His protests to Bagshawe notwithstanding, the idea ranged uncomfortably about the perimeters of his mind. "I don't think so, but I'm not as sure as I'd like to be. What do you think, Abe? You probably know him better than I do."

Abe still had a little dinner wine left. He swirled it thoughtfully. "You know how you read in the paper when there's some terrible murder and the mother says, 'No, it couldn't be my son who did it, such a darling boy, always so polite'? Well, this is how I feel about Nathan. Maybe not always so polite, but a murderer? Impossible." He drained the wine, tilted his head, lifted a white eyebrow. "Still, who knows? All the time the criminologists are telling us anybody could be a murderer with the right motivation."

"I don't really believe that, though," Gideon said.

"Me neither," said Julie.

"Me neither," said Abe. "*Nu,* so much for the criminologists."

Gideon paused in the act of slicing a chunk of Gorgonzola and snapped his fingers softly. "Something just occurred to me. I need to make a telephone call. Be right back."

He found Barry Fusco on his first attempt, at the Coach and Horses, and waited impatiently while the landlord called him to the telephone.

"Barry, when I was up at the dig a couple of weeks ago, you came down to the gate to let me in. Are you responsible for letting people in, or were you just being helpful?"

"Huh?" Barry sounded as if he'd been asleep. "No, I'm on gate duty this month."

That was what Gideon had hoped. "So you'd know about any visitors?"

"Uh-huh," Barry said through a yawn. "I mean, we all have our own keys, but if it's a visitor, someone who doesn't have one, I'm supposed to let him in."

"Do you remember if there were any other visitors the day I was there?"

"There were some school kids—"

"No, they left before I did. Was there anybody there after me?"

"Uh-uh. Nope."

"Why so sure?"

"Because the whole time I've been on, I only had to let visitors in twice, and that was on the same day—you and that school group. That was it."

"You're positive?"

"Sure. Nobody else. We used to get some people in the summer, but not now. What's the difference, Dr. Oliver?"

From the way he was talking, Gideon knew he hadn't heard about Randy. Evidently, Bagshawe hadn't yet made his trip up the hill. "Barry," he said casually, "are you right-handed?"

"Am I . . ." He laughed, as if Gideon had asked him a riddle. "All right, I'm right-handed. Why?"

"What about the others? Leon, Sandra, Dr. Frawley?"

"I don't know. I think everyone's right-handed, but I'm not sure. Wait a minute, Randy's a lefty. He used to pitch Class-A ball. Did you know that?"

"I think I did hear something about it. Thanks a lot, Barry."

"Things are shaping up," Gideon said as he returned to the dining room. "It looks like it must have been somebody from the dig who killed him. If not Nate, then one of the others: Frawley, Leon, Sandra . . . who am I forgetting? Oh, Barry. Five suspects."

"How come?" Abe asked. "Why?"

"Let's assume I'm right about Randy's body being tossed into that lagoon from the top of Stonebarrow Fell itself, okay? Well there haven't been any outsiders up to the fell since *before* Randy was killed—I was the last one, in fact. . . . So an insider must have done it. Simple."

"How do you know this?" Abe asked. "About no outsiders." The fatigue seemed to have left him; there was color in his cheeks and a liveliness in his eyes; he sensed a mystery, an adventure.

Gideon told him about the call to Barry. "I suppose someone could have climbed over the fence, and Barry might not have seen him, but that's pretty doubtful. It's a pretty small dig."

"Gideon," Julie said, "you'll need to tell Inspector Bagshawe about this, won't you?"

Gideon nodded. "I was going to call him in the morning anyway—about the lagoon."

On Hinshore's suggestion, they took their coffee in the Tudor Room, where the fire had been renewed for them. For a few lazy minutes they sipped quietly, gazing into the orange flames.

"I got a question," Abe said, still looking into the fire, his cup at his lips, the saucer held just below it. "This theft of the Poundbury skull in Dorchester; where do you think it fits in?"

"Fits in with what?" Gideon asked.

"With what?" Abe repeated, waggling the saucer impatiently. "With everything—the whole *mish-mosh*."

"Why should it fit in at all?"

Over the rim of his cup, Abe looked at him as if Gideon had asked why one and one should be two. The old man put the cup down and wiped his lips with a napkin. "Listen, how far from Dorchester to Charmouth?"

"Thirty miles, maybe."

"Fine. Now, let me ask you: In your whole career, did you ever run into a . . . what are they calling it . . . an inquiry into a dig?"

"Not personally, no."

"No," Abe said. "What about a murder on a dig?"

"No."

"No. And stealing a calvarium from a museum? This, did you ever see?"

Gideon shook his head.

Abe nodded his. "No, no, and no. Three things that never happen, and they all happen inside of a few weeks of each other, and inside of thirty miles of each other. And you think they're just three separate pieces of monkey business, nothing to do with each other?" He looked at Julie and jerked a thumb at Gideon. "Some detective!"

Gideon grumbled in mock annoyance. "In the first place, Dr. Goldstein, I'm *not* a detective—"

"Hoo, boy, you're telling me."

They all laughed then, and Gideon poured more coffee for them from the silver pot. "Maybe you have a point, Abe," he said.

"Of course. And here's another connection between all three things: you."

"Me?"

"You. You just happen to discover Poundbury's missing; you just happen to arrive here the next day; you just happen to be the one Alexander wants to tell a secret—and you just happen to be the one that winds up analyzing the poor guy's bones."

"But it's true: I *did* just happen—"

"Of course." He put down his half-empty cup and rose. "I think I'll go ahead to bed now." He clasped Gideon's shoulder and spoke to Julie. "This husband of yours; sometimes his fancy-dancy anthropological theories get a little *ungepotchket*—you know *ungepotchket*?"

Julie shook her head.

"Screwed up," Gideon murmured. His years of friendship with Abe had taught him a great many Yiddish expressions—by osmosis, as it were.

Abe narrowed his eyes, considering. "Screwed up? No, this I wouldn't say. *Ungepotchket* is more, well . . . unnecessarily rococo."

Julie laughed. "Does it really mean that?"

"Sure," Abe said. "But about Gideon, this I got to say. Wherever he is . . . always it gets interesting. Good night, folks."

His papery face suddenly crinkled in a laugh, and on the spur of the moment Gideon got up and gently embraced the frail figure. "Good night, Abe. Sleep well. I'm glad you're here."

When he had left, Gideon said to Julie, "He really could have a point, you know."

"Of course I got a point!" floated down the hall, followed by the closing of a door.

"Well," Julie said, "you *do* seem in the thick of things for a man who was going to be uninvolved."

"I know. It's funny, isn't it? But none of it was my doing, and once I give Bagshawe a call in the morning—and go up to the site at ten—I'm out of it."

Julie smiled and leaned back comfortably in her chair. In the firelight her cheeks were peach-colored and transparent-looking, as smooth and soft as the petals of a rose; she might have been a candlelit Madonna of Geertgen or La Tour. "Sure you are," she said. "All the same . . ."

"All the same you just have a feeling."

"Uh-huh."

"Me, too. And to tell the truth, I wish there *was* something I could do."

"Well," she said, and leaned forward to stroke the line of his jaw, "Abe's certainly right about one thing. Life with you isn't dull."

□ 11 □

THE NEXT MORNING Gideon called police headquarters. Inspector Bagshawe wasn't in, but Wilson Merrill was. The pathologist began to talk excitedly as soon as he picked up the telephone; the remains had definitely been identified as those of Randy Alexander.

"How?" Gideon asked, "Dental records?"

"Yes, the forensic people telephoned the police in Missouri —or is it Missoula? Or are they the same place?—and were put in touch with the young man's dentist. Indeed, Alexander's dental records matched exactly what we'd found in the cadaver. The charts are on their way, but there's no doubt about it. The only mildly disturbing element, of course, is the state of decomposition of the body after only two weeks, but I suppose we just have to attribute that to—"

Gideon quickly outlined his hypothesis about Alexander's body having lain in the warm lagoon at the base of Stonebarrow Fell for two weeks before it drifted out to sea.

"Why, yes, that would account for it, of course!" Merrill was delighted. "In summer, no doubt, someone would have discovered it the next day, but in winter there'd be no one on the beach to find it. Splendid work! I'll go and have a look at that lagoon myself." There was a pause. "Oh, I say. That would mean—unless there are similar lagoons in the area—

that he might very well have been thrown from Stonebarrow
Fell itself, wouldn't it?''

"I'm afraid so. Highly likely, I'd say. And what's more,
it appears that there haven't been any visitors to the dig for a
month, so . . . ''

"Oh, dear. The murderer would have to be a member of
the expedition, wouldn't he? Unpleasant.''

"It looks that way, yes. But of course I might be off-base.
I'm afraid the inspector will think it's all pretty speculative.''

"I'm afraid it's a better guess than you think. The
instrument that broke Alexander's arm has been quite positively identified as a mallet from the tool chest of the
excavation.''

"But how is that possible? How could you make such an
identification?''

"Not I, but our forensic scientists in London once again,
and a first-rate piece of sleuthing it was too. Do you
remember Inspector Bagshawe's idea about the sleeve of
Alexander's leather jacket providing some clue as to the
weapon?''

"Yes, of course.''

"Well, it provided more than a clue. In the first place,
there was an indentation in the leather, indicating that the
weapon had a flat striking surface with a well-defined
circular margin—like that of a hammer or a mallet. Now,
adhering to the leather itself—embedded in it, actually—
they found a ragged scrap of paper.''

"Paper? But it'd been in the water for two weeks.
Wouldn't it rot?''

"So I should have thought. But, I am instructed, that
doesn't always occur. In this case, the sizing had indeed
rotted away, but the paper fiber itself was still there, as was
some cement on the back of it, and there was even a ghost
of printing on it which, under analysis, turned out to be the
lowercase letters *a* and *s*. Intriguing, isn't it? Now what
would you guess this mysterious shred of paper to be?''

Gideon was silent. Even if he'd had any idea, he'd hardly
have wanted to spoil Merrill's enjoyment.

"Ha.'' Merrill cleared his throat. "Well, to make a long

story short, the paper was an adhesive label of the sort put
on objects to identify and price them. What had happened
was that the tag had apparently been placed on the mallet
carelessly, so that it was draped over an edge of the striking
surface, partly on that surface itself, partly on the side of the
mallet's head, where it belonged. Moreover, the part that
was on the striking surface had not adhered thoroughly—
one corner had gotten folded over, so that the adhesive side
of it was facing up. Do you follow me?''

''I think so, yes. When Randy was hit with the mallet,
the glued side of the paper—which was uppermost—must
have stuck to his sleeve.''

''That's it precisely.''

''That would mean, wouldn't it, that it was the very first
time the mallet had been used? The glued paper would
surely stick to the first object the mallet struck.''

''Exactly. A brand-new mallet with the price tag still on
it.''

''Dr. Merrill, Alexander came in with a brand-new mallet
the day I was there. I think he'd just been sent to buy it.''

''Indeed he had, and it turns out to be the very one. But
let me tell the story. Our lads did some quick detective work
and identified the tag: It was a 'Texas' sticker—the 'as' was
the last part of the name. Texas Homecare, as you may
know, is a chain of DIY stores—''

''DIY?''

''Do It Yourself. Don't you use the term on the other side
of the Pond?''

''Oh, yes. Right.''

''Well, they have a branch in Bridport, where they do in
fact sell mallets, and did in fact sell one the very day
Alexander was last seen. This information was passed on to
Inspector Bagshawe—''

''Who immediately went to Stonebarrow Fell to see if he
could find a fairly new 'Texas' mallet with part of the price
tag torn off.''

''He did indeed, and readily found what he was looking
for. Useless for fingerprints, of course, inasmuch as it's
been in use for two weeks. But—and this was confirmed

only this morning—the torn edge of the tag on the mallet matched exactly the torn margin of the tag on poor Alexander's sleeve. A triumph of detection, what? And all done in less than twenty-four hours.''

It was true then. Randy Alexander had been killed by a fellow member of the dig. Until that moment it hadn't truly sunk in; it had simply been a piece of a jigsaw puzzle that fitted neatly into place. Now it was real. One of them was a murderer: Frawley . . . Sandra . . . Barry . . . Leon. Maybe even Nate. Why not Nate, really? Did *any* of them seem like a killer? He couldn't honestly say he liked all of them, but murderers . . . ?

''Professor,'' Merrill was saying, ''Detective Inspector Bagshawe is here now. Would you like to speak with him?''

Gideon told Bagshawe briefly about the lagoon and about what Barry had told him. ''And since there weren't any visitors—''

''The murderer would have to be a member of the Stonebarrow party, wouldn't he? So it would seem.''

There was a long pause during which Bagshawe's heavy, unhurried breathing sounded in Gideon's ear.

''How is the investigation coming along, Inspector?''

''Tolerably well, Professor, tolerably well.''

Obviously, information was not going to be readily volunteered from the other end of the line. Gideon made another try.

''I understand you haven't told them about Randy yet?''

''No, that's true. Thought it would be best to pursue a few other inquiries before I gave them the news, but I'm on my way there now.'' He paused, seeming to turn something over in his mind. ''You know, this makes things a bit problematical.''

''What does?''

''The mallet . . . the piece of business about the lagoon . . . all of it pointing to an inside job.''

''Why problematical?''

''Because, Professor, among the several interesting facts I gathered on Stonebarrow Fell was this: They're right-handed to a man—to a woman, when you include Miss Mazur. Not a left-hander among them.''

"You're sure? Whoever it is may have been trying to hide it." He realized with a small shock of surprise that at least a little part of him had been hoping that Frawley was going to turn out to be a southpaw.

"Yes, Professor," Bagshawe said patiently. "I'm quite sure. If he was killed by a dig worker, he was killed by a right-hander. It looks like this is one of those one-out-of-ten cases the good doctor was talking about."

Gideon didn't quite believe it. His experience had apparently been different from Merrill's. From what he'd seen, a nightstick fracture could *always* be used to predict the handedness of an attacker. People didn't go around wielding bone-smashing clubs—a mallet in this case—backhanded or in their weaker hand. "Either that, or we're wrong about assuming the killer's one of the crew."

"And do you think we are?"

"No," Gideon said after a moment. "I think we're right."

"Well," Bagshawe said, "that's that, then, isn't it? I assure you, they're all dyed-in-the-wool right-handers. My guess is that there was a scuffle sometime that afternoon—Alexander was last seen at three o'clock—right there in the fog, near the edge of the cliff, and the killer grabbed the mallet any way he could—perhaps it had already been knocked out of his right hand—and wound up picking it up with his left hand. You see," he said generously, "I don't doubt your conclusions about a left-handed blow—only about a left-handed attacker."

"I guess you're right," Gideon allowed, but it still didn't sit right. "Anyway, where does the identification of the hammer lead us?"

The "us" was an accidental admission; Gideon was more involved than he thought.

Bagshawe, possibly realizing this, effectively ended the conversation. "A very good question, sir," he said pleasantly, "and I'm most grateful to you for all the help you've given us. I'm sure you understand, by the way, that all our little hypotheses and findings are between us; to be kept in the family, so to speak.''

"Of course,"

"Well, that's all right then. A very good day to you, Professor."

Gideon replaced the receiver and leaned back in the armchair, hands behind his head, staring absently out the window. Their room, one flight up, overlooked the ancient, rock-walled back garden of the Queen's Armes. In the distance, about half a mile away, was the profile of the hillside that swept smoothly up to Stonebarrow Fell, lush and pearly green against a threatening, shifting sky of blacks and grays.

He and Julie had breakfasted early with Abe, Robyn, and Arbuckle. Afterward, Robyn and Arbuckle had retired to the sitting room and Abe had whispered to Gideon that he was going to the Cormorant to try to talk some sense into Nate.

Now Gideon heard a soft tap at the door behind him, and then the sounds of Abe and Julie talking. He got up and went to them.

"How'd you do with Nate?"

"No luck. Everything he said, he stands by." Abe shook his head disgustedly. "Every foolish thing. Already he's planning a press conference after the inquiry—so the whole world can learn his wonderful secret from his own lips." More slowly this time, he shook his head again. "It's not the way a scholar should act. It's not what I taught him, Gideon."

"What did he say about Randy?" Julie asked.

"What about his mysterious find?" asked Gideon. "Would he tell you what it is?"

"Not a word. Only that it's going to 'blow my mind.' *Feh*, where did he learn to talk like this?"

"Abe," Gideon said, "do you suppose it's possible that he's really got something—"

"To prove what?" Abe flared up peevishly. "That Agamemnon invaded Charmouth? In what, a wooden horse? Don't be ridiculous. What did they teach you in archaeology?"

"All right, all right," Gideon said hastily. "I'm not an archaeologist, remember?"

"That you don't got to tell me," Abe snapped. Then he patted the back of Gideon's hand. "So why am I mad at you? Nathan's the one who's making a fool of himself." He looked at his watch. "Come on, it's after nine. Let's get the others and go. It's a big hill, and my arthritis is bothering me. Nathan will meet us there. Good-bye, Julie," he said, and turned dejectedly to leave. "I wish I wasn't here. Who asked me to come?"

Gideon raised his eyes bleakly to Julie as he began to follow Abe out the door.

She stood on tiptoe to place a quick kiss on his cheek. "Be careful. Both of you seem to keep forgetting there's a murderer up there."

□ 12 □

A MURDERER? TRY five. He'd been telling himself none of them looked like killers, but now the whole crew looked guilty as hell.

Gideon and Abe, flanked by Robyn and Arbuckle, had found Nate Marcus in the shed, seated at the cleaned-off worktable with his staff. All the dig members looked up, blinking into the daylight when the door was opened, and Gideon was afforded a frozen, snapshot glance. They might have been a cast assembled by a film director and told to look as edgy and disreputable as they possibly could.

Sandra Mazur was posturing exaggeratedly as she smoked a cigarette, holding it out in front of her between two rigidly stiffened fingers and theatrically sucking in her gaunt cheeks as she pulled in great lungfuls of smoke.

Next to her, Leon Hillyer picked nervously at his golden beard and smiled an unconvincing welcome to Gideon.

Jack Frawley's face looked like soggy, gray plaster of Paris, sunken in on itself and flabby-jowled. His basset's eyes slid and shifted like beads of mercury, from the blank tabletop to Nate, to the newcomers, and back to the tabletop.

Even the ingenuous Barry Fusco, with all his farm-boy freshness, looked shifty, his all-American grin a nervous parody. And Nate was the most blatantly agitated of all. He was literally chewing on the knuckles of his left hand, and

when the door opened, he jumped to his feet, wiping his
hand on the side of his pants. His face was greenish, and his
eyes were sunken, as glazed as a couple of four-minute
eggs.

It was obvious that Bagshawe had indeed come and told
them about the murder, and Nate's first words confirmed it.
"Sorry, meant to meet you at the gate," he said, sounding
short of breath, "but the police just left, and we've been
talking about . . . what they told us. It looks like they've
found my missing student. He's been, uh . . . killed."

Gideon could feel him flinch away from the word *murdered,*
but the archaeologist recovered himself as he spoke. Brusque-
ly brushing aside Robyn's and Arbuckle's startled ejacula-
tions and Abe's cluck of sympathy, he continued more
firmly, even aggressively; Nate never went very long without taking the offensive. "The cops are down on the beach
poking around, but they're coming back, so let's get on
with it."

As Gideon trooped back out with the others into the gray
morning, he found Stonebarrow Fell, which had seemed so
lovely two weeks before, ugly and sinister. The hacked-out
trenches with their stark, vertical sides and their dew-
concealed piles of gray dirt looked raw and naked, and
somehow shocking, like open graves. Far below, beyond the
fell's sharp edge, the sea was mole gray, the same color as
the sky, and sullen-looking whitecaps scudded on the water's
surface. As they walked in a solemn file over the broad
crown of the hill, the wind lowed forlornly around them,
driving long, shuddering ripples through the dense grass.

He really was depressed. Since when did digs remind him
of graves? He realized as he plodded on that it was more
than the weather, more than even the murder, that was
making him so gloomy and apprehensive . . . something entirely different. For an idea was taking unwelcome root, an
unsettling idea that he knew exactly what Nate's "astonishing
and sensational" discovery was. And he wished to hell it
had popped up before this, when he might have done
something about it.

They stopped at a small rectangular canvas-draped pit a

hundred feet from the main trenches, in a rough area of bushes, vines, and chalky rock. Nate began at once.

"As all of you know," he said in a shrill, rapid monotone, "the Wessex culture has long been viewed as a manifestation of the pan-European trade and travel of the Bronze Age, and is believed to have arrived in Britain in slow stages from Britany—this notwithstanding the three-hundred-year difference in radiocarbon dates between Breton and Wessex graves. But be that as it may..."

It was evident that Nate had prepared this speech—he didn't talk like this naturally—and that he was hardly listening to himself. Gideon studied him; unless he was shamming—and his brash, outspoken personality didn't lend itself to pretense—he was genuinely upset. Although he'd spoken rather harshly of Randy's lackadaisical ways, it was apparent that the news of his death had stunned him.

"It is also well known that the Bretons were and are a race of round-heads," Nate droned on. "Of brachycephals, as Dr. Oliver would say." At the sound of his name, Gideon snapped to attention. "And for that matter, the immediate predecessors of the Wessex people, the Beakers, were also notably brachycephalic. Thus, we have always assumed the Wessex also to be round-headed. Also so they are, in the later Wessex sites.

"But here," Nate said, and now the old, challenging electricity crackled in his speech; his eyes came up from the canvas-covered pit to engage those of the others. "Here at Stonebarrow Fell we've got the earliest known Wessex site—maybe the very first. What would you say if we found someone here who wasn't brachycephalic at all, but *long*-headed—*dolichocephalic*—just like the Mycenaeans of 1700 B.C.?"

Gideon's heart seemed to flop and plummet. Now there wasn't any question about where Nate was leading, incredible as it seemed. The excavation crew fidgeted in subdued excitement. All, that was, except Frawley, who, with his head down and his hands clasped very much like a graveside mourner's, chewed somberly on his cheek. Abe and Arbuckle stood there looking stoic and patient, and Robyn's sole reaction appeared to be the raising by one millimeter of his left eyebrow.

"What would you say," Nate went on, seemingly made more contentious by the lack of response, "if the guy buried here wasn't just long-headed, but was *so* long-headed that was outside the range of every—*every*—known Beaker or Breton skull, but easily *within* the range of the Mycenaeans?"

Without waiting for a reply, he reached down, pulled up the canvas, and flung it away from him. It sailed directly into Barry, who grabbed it, snickered nervously, blushed, and stood there holding it.

"There," Nate said throatily.

Everyone's eyes were riveted on the two-by-three-foot pit. Nate, seemingly unable to stand the momentary silence, burst into a low, agitated babble. "Would you believe that was sticking right out of the ground—part of it anyway? Huh? Abe? Gideon? Englishmen have been walking over it for a hundred years, probably, and nobody ever noticed it!" Here there was a lancing, triumphant glance at Robyn. "The ground around it was weathered away, and you could barely see it. I almost didn't see it myself; I just stumbled onto it. . . ."

The skull fragment was in the precise middle of the rectangle. The rounded eminence of the right parietal, Gideon could see, would indeed have projected a fraction of an inch above the surface of the ground, but no one—except perhaps a particularly alert anthropologist—would have taken it for anything but a rock. It had been dug—dissected out, really—with the scrupulous care typical of Nate Marcus, so that it lay partially embedded in a two-inch-high shelf of earth, like the museum exhibit it had once been.

It was Pummy, all right.

Gideon couldn't think of any way to say it other than to say it. "Nate, that's the Poundbury calvarium . . . the skull fragment missing from the Dorchester Museum."

Nate's expression went from self-satisfied to blank to furious in two seconds. The flesh around his lips grayed and seemed to sink into his face. Gideon observed this transparently genuine reaction of astonishment and indignation with relief. Nate was as honestly surprised as everyone else.

"Bullshit!" he shouted, as soon as he could speak. "You don't know what the hell you're talking about!" He turned on Gideon, his fists clenched at his side, his body tightened as if he was going to spring at him. Gideon, used to Nate's irritating habit of automatically hitting out when challenged, didn't take offense.

"It's Poundbury, without a doubt—" Gideon began.

"Bullshit, bullshit—"

Abe reached over and patted Nate on the shoulder. "Now, Nathan," he said mildly.

Robyn's voice cut icily through. "Professor Marcus, will you kindly keep your observations, cogent as they are, to yourself for just a few moments? Oliver, are you quite positive?"

"Completely."

Nevertheless, Gideon stepped into the trench and knelt to look more closely at the fragment. He blew away a thin layer of chalky dust. "You can see that it's been placed here recently," he said. "Look at the color: that same amber tone all over. If a part of it had actually been sticking out, exposed to the elements, it would have been darker than the rest, wouldn't it? More weathered, too."

"You're nuts," Nate said. "What are you talking about? I don't believe this."

Abe shushed him gently, his hand on his arm, and Nate subsided with a strained laugh.

Carefully, with his forefinger, Gideon brushed at the earth around the bone. "And it wouldn't have mineralized to this brownish color in such a chalky, white soil. Besides that, if it had really been here for over three thousand years, the soil would fit around it like a plaster mold, which it obviously doesn't." He brought his face even closer to it. "And look, the earth's compacted here—and here—from digging a hole and then forcing the bone into it. And I think . . . yes, I can see where the identification number's been scraped away and the bone's been stained to make it look—"

"That," said Robyn, "is ample, and quite instructive.

Obviously, Professor Marcus was so intent on proving his fantastic theory that he disregarded the signs that point so unequivocally to this object's being a fraud.''

Arbuckle, who had been blinking and frowning behind the thick, none-too-clean lenses of his glasses, appeared to suddenly understand. "Unless," he murmured in a shocked whisper to Nate, "you buried it there in the first place." He took a backward step away from Nate, as if afraid of catching something.

"Buried it?" Nate repeated blankly. "Why would . . . You mean *planted* it? Me? You're out of your mind!''

Arbuckle held up both hands. "All right, Nate," he said quickly, "I didn't mean to accuse you." He lowered his chin and went doggedly on. "But *somebody* must have, er, planted it.''

Nate stared hard at the shrinking Arbuckle, then at Gideon, and spoke through compressed lips. "Okay. All right. I blew it. You're right, I should have seen the signs. Somebody must have buried . . . No," he said slowly, "that's impossible. What would be the point? How could they know anyone would find it? I could have missed it easy . . . It could have lain there a hundred years. It wasn't even near the trenches . . . ''

"First things first," Robyn interjected. "We're here today to look into whether Professor Marcus has been conducting his research in a sufficiently professional manner." In an undertone he added, "As for myself, frankly, I consider that this latest . . . happening . . . makes the question moot.''

Nate's dark face turned a mottled red, but before he could respond, Abe stepped in, with a quick glance toward the enthralled students. "And I think," he said mildly, but in a tone that encouraged no argument, "this discussion should be continued in private, with only the parties concerned." He grasped Nate's arm and steered him in the direction of the shed. Nate went unresistingly, and Arbuckle and Robyn, after an exchange of grim looks, moved to follow, as did Frawley.

"Gideon," Abe called over his shoulder, "maybe you'll

finish up with the skull so we can send it back to where it belongs?''

An embarrassed silence descended as soon as the others left, until Gideon spoke.

"I'll need some tools."

"I'll get them," Sandra said hastily. "We keep a toolbox at the excavation." She trotted elegantly off.

"I can get a packing crate," Leon offered.

"I'll go with you," Barry jumped in. All of them were eager to get away from the scene of disaster, and no wonder.

When Sandra returned, Gideon, also wishing himself elsewhere, took an angled dental pick, a toothbrush, and a small paintbrush, and quickly worked loose the dirt around the bone. By the time the crate arrived, he was done. He lifted the calvarium with both hands, settled it among the Styrofoam peanuts, and closed the lid.

"Will you see that this goes to Dr. Arbuckle?"

"You bet, Gideon," Leon said.

There was another awkward silence until Barry literally shook himself into speech. "Mr. Robyn gave me his keys for you to use to get out of the gate," he said, producing a leather key case. "He said you could leave them with the guy at the Queen's Armes."

Gideon's mood was gloomier than ever as he crested the hill and started down. At the fence he found a slender young man in a fawn-colored suit delicately rattling the lock.

"I've been calling out for half an hour," he said when Gideon got within speaking distance. "I was beginning to fear I'd have to scale the thing." He smiled genteely, the English sort of smile that raises the inside corners of the eyebrows and wrinkles the forehead charmingly. "It would have been hard on the suit."

"It would also have been trespassing," Gideon said, not disposed to banter.

Unabashed, the young man announced, "Curtis Honett. I'm with the *West Dorset Times*."

The *West Dorset Times*. The newspaper that seemed to know so much. "Sorry to disappoint you," Gideon said, slipping out and relocking the gate behind him, "but I think Professor Marcus will be canceling his press conference."

"What press conference?" Honett moved closer. "I understand that the bone missing from the Dorchester Museum turned up here today. Is that true?"

Gideon barely managed to hide his astonishment. "Where did you hear that?"

The reporter drew his motile, auburn eyebrows together. "It isn't true? Mr. Chantry was certain—"

"Mr. Chantry?"

"My boss, the editor. He's been working personally on the Stonebarrow story."

"And just where does Mr. Chantry get his information?"

"You wouldn't want me to divulge our sources, would you?" He grinned brightly. "So it *is* true then?"

"Sorry," Gideon said, "I'm afraid 'no comment' is the most you're going to get from me." He turned to head down the path. "And don't quote me on that." Then, relenting slightly, he added. "You'll want to talk to Dr. Arbuckle of Horizon or Mr. Robyn of the WAS on this. But I think they're going to be tied up for a while."

"The *West Dorset Times*," said a cultivated voice, "at your service."

"Good morning. May I speak with Mr. Chantry, please?"

"One moment. What name shall I say?"

"Gideon Oliver."

In a few seconds another voice came on, whispery and apologetic. No, Mr. Ralph Chantry was not in his office at the moment. No, no one else was familiar with the Stonebarrow matter. No, no one was sure just when he would return, but tomorrow was likely. Could Mr. Oliver try again tomorrow? Gideon replaced the receiver and leaned back in the leather armchair, staring out unseeingly at the ragged fog that obscured the hillside he'd come down half an hour before.

He wondered moodily about the inquiry still going on in the bleak little shed on the fell. Whatever the explanation for the amazing "happening," as Robyn had called it, Nate's career was finished. Even Abe's ability to smooth rough waters was unlikely to do much good, given the cold look in Robyn's eye and the equally dark, if less penetrating, one in Arbuckle's. Whether or not Nate had planted the skull himself—and Gideon couldn't believe that he had—was immaterial. Nate was in charge of the dig and had to bear responsibility for everything that occurred on it. And, of course, he had personally done all the work on the calvarium himself, and had been braying about it in his usual obnoxious manner for weeks. There was no way he could ever possibly live it down.

"Gideon," Julie said, "I think it's time for you to forget about Stonebarrow Fell. How about a hike in the country? I've got a booklet that shows some local walks."

"Looks like rain."

"So we'll take our ponchos. You know, you can still hike along some of those old right-of-way footpaths that have been there for centuries."

"It's been a wet winter; they'll be awfully muddy."

She laughed and plopped herself into his lap. Her arms went about his neck. "My, you're feeling adventurous, aren't you?"

He smiled and clasped his hands around her waist. "I guess I'm a little mopey. I don't like thinking about what's going to happen to Nate, even if he brought it on himself. And the murder..."

"You need a hike," she said firmly, "and you are going to get one."

He had continued to stare out the window, but now he put his hands on her shoulders, set her straighter on his knees, and looked at her face. She was smiling down at him, her black, luminous eyes so lit with love that his breath caught unexpectedly in his chest. How had he ever done without her? If she were to leave, the hole in his life would be so vast. . . .

"Yes, ma'am," he said. "Where will we hike to?"

"'Wootton Fitzpaine, a tiny village a few miles from Charmouth,'" she said, reading from a booklet, "'and one of the vicinity's most popular rural walks.'"

"And why Wootton Fitzpaine in particular?"

"Because," she said, "it has such a nice name."

He rose from the chair, lifting her in his arms as he did so, pleased with the solid weight of her. "I can't imagine a better reason."

The walk to Wootton Fitzpaine began, according to *Scenic Dorset Walks,* only a block from The Queen's Armes, at the opening to a rough and muddy track—two wheel ruts, actually—laughably signposted *Barr's Lane.* The track ran for about an eighth of a mile, forming a narrow alley bounded on either side by crude, head-high stone walls of some antiquity. At the end of this lane a stile led into open meadows, but just before this stile the wall on the left side gave way to a sturdy, seven-foot-high chain-link fence that enclosed an extensive dog run at the back of a neat, thatch-roofed house.

As they were about to push through the stile to get into the countryside, they were astounded by a roar so loud that Gideon at first thought it must be a caged and furious lion inside the house. Momentarily petrified, they stood with their hands frozen on the stile.

When he saw it, Gideon thought at first it *was* a lion—a long-legged nightmare lion—but it wasn't. It was a dog. Huge, malevolent, and bellowing—"barking" wasn't the word for it—it came tearing around the side of the house, racing toward them with death in its red eyes.

Instinctively, Gideon stepped in front of Julie as the thing bounded wildly against the fence. The animal, which must have known from experience that it couldn't get at them, gave it its best nonetheless. Raging and slavering, it leaped again and again at the shuddering fence, its forelegs as high as Gideon's head, its thick chest on a level with his own.

"Is that a *dog?*" Julie asked in a small voice, peeking around his shoulder, and making a move to get out from behind him. He could see fingers of color returning to her cheeks and had no doubt that his own face was also on the pale side.

"I don't know what else. The Hound of the Baskervilles, maybe."

From the house behind the dog came a petulant call. "For heaven's sake, Bowser, be quiet!"

Gideon and Julie looked at each other. *Bowser?*

A stocky man in late middle age, with a military bearing, a gray, bristling military mustache, and a sandy toupee, came grumbling from the back door.

"Be quiet, I said!" The dog, with bad grace, reluctantly stopped trying to devour them and instead satisfied itself with ferocious glaring and panting.

The man approached the animal and grasped it firmly by its wide collar. Its head, Gideon noted, was not far below the man's shoulders, its neck almost as thick as his waist.

"Hullo," the man said, smiling crisply. "I'm Colonel Conley. I hope the Beast didn't frighten you."

"Frighten us?" Gideon said. "Not at all. He was just being friendly."

The colonel laughed. "Hardly. He'd as soon eat you as look at you. Americans, are you? Out on a walk to Wootton Fitzpaine?"

"Yes," Julie said. "That's quite an animal. What in the world is he?"

"Crossbreed," Colonel Conley said. "I went into dog breeding after the war, you see, and Bowser is my prize. Proper name, Pyecombe Sable of Hempstead. Half mastiff, half staghound, with perhaps a little werewolf thrown in. Magnificent creature, don't you think? Ran in the Count de Vergie's pack, you know?" Gideon and Julie looked mutely at him. "At Château Touffon? Near Vienne? You really haven't heard of it? Famous for its stag hunts, and the count's pack is disputably the best in the world. Unfortunately, Bowser tends toward overenthusiasm, and he tore the throat out of a horse." He dug his knuckles fondly into the root of a huge, tawny ear. "And," he whispered respectfully, "came as near as dammit to doing in a man. I'm afraid he has a bit of a mean streak in him."

"Does he really?" Gideon said, eyeing Bowser, who was quivering and twitching with convincing blood lust.

Again the colonel laughed. "I'm sure you've noticed. Don't worry, though. There isn't any way he can get through." He shook the gate in the fence, jangling a sturdy padlock on a heavy chain. "I take extreme precautions. It's perfectly safe. Enjoy your walk, and don't pay any attention to him on your way back. He gets accustomed to you after a time or two."

As they twisted their way through the stile to enter the open country, Bowser thundered again, deprived of his rightful prey, but Colonel Conley tugged on his collar and said, "Bad show, Bowser," and the dog sat down, mumbling and drooling. Julie and Gideon walked a few hundred yards into the meadow, out of sight and sound of the dog, and then Julie sat suddenly on a log and started thumbing through *Scenic Dorset Walks*.

"Are we lost already?" Gideon asked.

"No, I'm looking for an alternate way back."

"And disappoint Bowser?"

"You better believe it." She chewed the corner of her lip and wrinkled her nose. Strange. Gideon had always thought nose-wrinkling ridiculous and unsightly; on Julie it devastated him.

"No," she said, "we have to come back through Barr's Lane unless we want to go way out of our way and walk along A-35." She closed the booklet. "Uh-uh. What kind of country walk would that be?"

"Right. Besides, don't worry about Bowser. I had him in the palm of my hand." He sat down next to her on the log. "Hey, just look at where we are. Can the world be all bad if there are still places like this?"

"This is Dyne Meadow, according to the book. It *is* nice, isn't it?"

They were in a green and gently undulating grassy field bordered on one side by a dark copse of pines, and on another by a sparkling, tree-lined stream. To the west they could see a ruined stone barn around which grazed a few placid cattle; and to the north, half a mile off, a farmer plowed his field near a stark, whitewashed farmhouse. The noise of his tractor was like the far-off, lazy buzzing of a bee. It might have been 1940 or 1920. If not for the tractor, it could have been 1720.

"How lovely," Julie sighed. "Let's just stay here forever."

They stayed, in fact, half an hour, just drinking in the peace, and then, pacified themselves, proceeded hand in hand.

As Gideon had predicted, it was extremely muddy, especially near the stiles, where the ground had been churned into glue by cattle hooves. But it was Dorset mud, of which the locals were justly proud. Gray and gloopy as it looked and felt, it was solid enough so that it hardly wet their feet, yet liquid enough to slide from their shoes without caking. The lowering sky, while it threatened to burst with rain at any moment, held off, and the moisture-heavy air was fragrant with Dorset's grassy smell.

Rights of way in rural England are not quite what Americans imagine them to be. They are unlikely to be posted, and they frequently do not consist of paths visible to the naked eye. Following a guidebook, one simply skirts the western flank of this coppice of larches, bears slightly right, and walks through the northern end of that beech spinney, then crosses the gravel road, bearing north-northeast at a spot one hundred yards west of the signposts to Knickers-on-Tyne, just beyond a lightning-shattered pine tree. Even with a map, one is likely to spend a lot of time lost and trespassing. After a while Julie and Gideon settled for following the instructions in *Scenic Dorset Walks* in only the most approximate fashion, taking care to give plenty of room to the bulls they occasionally saw, and to avoid walking over worked fields that weren't supposed to be there.

They never managed to find Wootton Fitzpaine, but they walked through quiet woods and over grassy hills from which there were misty views of rolling, impossibly green countryside quilted into squares and trapezoids by trim, winter-brown hedgerows, and dotted by scattered groups of two or three thatch-roofed old buildings. They climbed over wooden stiles and walked through little white picket gates (who kept them all so spruce and freshly painted?) with gateposts set neatly in the middles of hedges, and they crossed little burbling brooks on footbridges consisting of a single plank. And always there was the fragrance of rain-wet grass. They saw no other people except farmers, and those at great distances, but there were cows and sheep and great black birds that squawked overhead.

"Are those crows?" Gideon asked. "Or ravens?" His voice startled them both; they had been walking in easy, companionable silence for almost an hour.

"Let me know if one lands on a ruler, and I'll tell you."

"Come again?"

"The crows are a few inches smaller. Otherwise I can't tell; at least not from here. There's something about the tails, I think."

"Some park ranger you are. I thought you knew all about birds."

"But I'm not a park ranger anymore. I got married, remember? And, being a good, old-fashioned wife, I left my lovely job in lovely Olympic National Park to go where my husband went."

"Yea," Gideon said, "even unto San Mateo, California." He said it lightly, but it was something that worried them both. When they had met, she had been senior ranger at the park in Washington and he'd been teaching at Northern California University, where he'd been made full professor the year before. They ran into trouble at once. There had been no ranger jobs for Julie anywhere near San Francisco Bay, and the newly opened Port Angeles campus of the University of Washington—the first university on the Olympic Peninsula—did not yet have a graduate anthropology department to which Gideon might apply. Somebody's career had to be interrupted for a while.

There had been a lot of discussions, but no arguments. To both of them, the idea of Gideon doing anything but teaching anthropology was absurd, so Julie had resigned her position—or rather, taken a leave of absence, just to be on the safe side. They had justified the decision on the grounds that Gideon's salary was the greater of the two, but Gideon suspected that underneath, she really was an old-fashioned wife for whom the husband's career came first. And underneath, Gideon knew very well that he liked it that way, closet chauvinist that he was. At any rate, when they got back from Europe, Julie would face the unenviable prospect of job-hunting; she wasn't old-fashioned enough to want to stay home and take care of him.

That he liked too, so maybe there was hope for him. On the other hand, what was there he *didn't* like about her?

"I'm glad I quit," she said a little timidly. "Being with you is everything to me. You know that, don't you?"

"Yes. I know." He squeezed her hand, trying to put everything into it.

"Good." She squeezed back. "Now tell me what that telephone call to the *Times* was about. And about what happened at Stonebarrow Fell this morning."

While they walked with loosely linked fingers in a dimly lit wood of mixed beech and pine, he told her.

"That's crazy," she said. "Why would a reputable archaeologist like Nate Marcus do something as stupid as that? You said he's a little odd, but you never said anything to suggest he wasn't ethical."

"I think he is ethical, even if his judgment is off sometimes and his mouth is a couple of sizes too big. To tell the truth, I don't think he did plant the thing. But Robyn thinks so; I could see it in his face, and I can't blame him. Paul probably thinks so too, but who can tell with him?"

"Gideon," she said, "can I ask you something? If your friend Nate is a good archaeologist, the way you keep saying he is in spite of everything, how could he have been fooled? You recognized Poundbury Man right away. Why didn't he?"

"Good question, but you have to remember that I'm a physical anthropologist and he's an archaeologist. He'd heard of Pummy, sure, but he wouldn't know it from any other skull you put in front of him—just the way I might not recognize some famous piece of pottery that he'd spot from a hundred yards away. It's worse for him, really, because all skulls look pretty much alike if they're not your business."

"But why didn't he recognize the other things—the compaction of the earth, those things. . . ."

"That's harder to explain away. I guess he was so intent

on proving his theory, so overjoyed at what he thought was evidence, that he ignored all the signs—refused to let himself see them. It wouldn't be the first time it's happened.''

''I suppose so,'' she said doubtfully. It was a while before she spoke again. ''But I'm still mixed up. If Nate didn't put it there, who did?''

That was the question, all right. If not Nate, who? Frawley? What could he possibly gain from it? It was Nate's dig, not his, and Frawley didn't go along with the Mycenaean theory anyway. One of the students? For what possible reason? No, the only person who could conceivably benefit from the bogus find was Nate. And Nate, as wacky as he could be sometimes, would never try to pull off something like this. No matter how much he might have changed. Or would be?

They emerged from the trees near the crown of a long green hill that sloped gently away below them, idyllic and inviting, toward another holly-green copse at its base. A soft, cold mist had begun to drift around them—under the trees, they had failed to notice it—and they slipped into their hooded ponchos before continuing.

''You know what I keep wondering?'' Gideon asked. ''Where the heck is the *Times* getting its information? They knew about the inquiry, they knew about the skull—''

''Obviously from someone on the dig.''

''No, not so obviously. How could anyone on the dig know I was going to visit the site? Except for you, Abe was the only one who had any idea I was coming, and he certainly didn't call the *Times* from Sequim, Washington.''

''Are you sure? Have you asked him about it?''

''Of course not.'' Then he smiled. ''Never mind 'of course not.' With Abe, you never know, do you? I'll ask him, but how could he? And why?''

They had gone a third of the way down the hill when the mist congealed into a pelting, freezing downpour as abruptly as if someone had turned on an ice-cold, needle-spray shower.

''Time to go back,'' Gideon said unnecessarily. He could

hardly hear himself with the hammering of the rain on his hood.

Julie nodded, her face running with water. "Maybe Bowser will be off sleeping in his doghouse in weather like this, and we can sneak by."

"Doghouse?" Gideon shouted over the rain. "He probably lives in a cave strewn with bloody bones."

□ 13 □

WHEREVER BOWSER HAD been, his gigantic nose told him when they'd reached the foot of Barr's Lane, and he came charging viciously through the rain, throwing his heavy body against the wire fence again and again. Gideon had been expecting it this time, but even so, the hairs on the back of his neck went up, and he and Julie moved by the monstrous animal with all due speed.

Chilled through, and with their feet soaked, they had hoped for a hot lunch at the Queen's Armes. Too late they remembered that Hinshore and his wife went to Bridport on Thursdays to do their weekly shopping, so the hotel was deserted.

They had, however, noticed an old, attractive pub, the George, across the street. More in need of hot food than warm footwear, they went there without changing from their wet clothes. Inside, happily, the George was a rustic pub at its best—a small, barely modernized seventeenth-century coaching inn with oaken beams and flagged floors, smelling of beer and fried fish. Half of one wall was a fireplace so capacious that there were two small tables with benches within it, one at each end. Between them, in the old fireplace's center, was a small wood stove with a metal hood and chimney, in which burned a cozy little blaze of scrap lumber. Although the pub was crowded and full of cheerful noise, one of the tables inside the fireplace was vacant, and Gideon and Julie made for it, gratefully basking in the dry warmth.

They sat with the steam rising from their wet shoes until the blood seemed to move through their bodies again and they were able to take off their ponchos and think about ordering. On the bar was a placard listing the luncheon menu: Ploughman's lunch, £1.20; shepherd's pie, £1.20; haddock and chips, 90p; steak-and-kidney pie (with peas and chips), £1.20.

"Steak-and-kidney pie for me," Julie said, not surprisingly. In a few brief weeks she had developed a near-addiction to the pungent stew. "And a gallon of hot tea."

"And I'll have the shepherd's pie." He worked his way through a crowd at the little bar to order from a barmaid, as harassed as English barmaids always seemed to be, and as friendly, then came back to the table carrying two brandies. "To help us thaw out."

Gideon swirled his brandy, sniffed it, took a good-sized swallow. "Ah," he sighed, "that's better. Hey, that trudge through the rain was fun. I speak retrospectively, of course."

"It *was* fun, and you know it." She watched him take a second, thoughful sip from the snifter. "You're wondering what happened at the hearing, aren't you?"

Gideon smiled. Pretty soon they wouldn't have to use words at all. "Yes—"

From across the room a high voice cut through the noise. "What's the matter, you can't even say hello?"

"Abe!" Gideon cried. "We didn't know you were here. Come join us!"

At the far end of the bar, Abe disengaged himself from the group of English men and women he had been conversing with. There were hearty, teasing good-byes, and someone even clapped him on the shoulder. A young woman offered to carry his plate and glass for him, an offer Abe declined. Holding a nearly empty half pint of beer in one hand and a plate of fish and chips in the other, he threaded his way toward them.

Gideon marveled at him, not for the first time. How could

anyone be more out of place in an English country pub?
And how could anyone seem more at home? As tenaciously
as Abe had clung to his old speech and mannerisms, he was
at the same time the most adaptable of men, fitting himself
to local custom—whether in a university faculty club, a
Bantu kraal, or a Dorset pub—with a willing ease that was
unmistakably genuine and enthusiastically reciprocated.

"So," he said as he sat down and arranged his food
fussily before him, "you had a nice walk? You didn't get
wet?" He corrected himself with a smile. "Wet you didn't
get?"

"Wet we got," Gideon said, "but it was a nice walk all
the same."

The barmaid came with their tea and food, and Gideon
ordered another glass of beer for Abe. For a few minutes
they busied themselves with their meals. Gideon's shepherd's pie was substantial and fortifying, an earthenware pot
filled with spiced ground meat and overflowing with a thick
covering of steaming, brown-crusted mashed potatoes. After
a few minutes, as if by agreement, they sat back a little,
ready to talk.

"Well," Abe said, "it didn't go so good at the hearing.
Nathan's got troubles. They're closing down the dig."

"You weren't able to say anything that helped?" Gideon
asked.

Abe pushed a golden shred of haddock back and forth on
his plate. "I said, and they listened, but what do they care
what a wonderful dissertation he wrote in 1969, or that he
ran a beautiful dig on Baffin Island in 1977? This they
already knew. With *now* they're concerned." He shrugged
and let his fork fall to the plate. "It was a fair decision; I
can't complain. As for Nathan, I could talk myself blue in
the face and he wouldn't know how to say, 'I'm sorry, I
made a mistake.' "

"Poor guy," Gideon said quietly.

"Yeah, the poor guy, but what could they do? For this he
has only himself to thank."

"Abe," Gideon said, "you don't think it's possible that

he did it, do you? Stole the skull from Dorchester, buried it here, and pretended to discover it?''

Abe shrugged elaborately. "Who knows? First he swears up and down he didn't do it, and then he swears up and down it's impossible that anybody else should do it."

"I don't understand," Julie said. "Why is it impossible?"

"Because," Gideon said, "the fragment was a couple of hundred feet from the dig, and barely visible. It could have gone unnoticed forever. Anybody who'd planted it would have made it more noticeable and put it near the trenches, where it would have been sure to be found."

"Well, if it was so impossible to find, how did Nate find it?"

"He . . . I don't really know." Gideon turned inquiringly to Abe. "Did he say?"

"He found it because he's a perfectionist who can't stand it if one little pebble is out of place on his dig. He says he's taking a walk, he sees a piece of paper on the ground, he bends down to pick it up, and out of the corner of his eye, bingo, he sees the bone. Just luck, that's all. But," he said, addressing Julie, "the thing is, whether he put it there himself or not, he's the director and he's got to be responsible— and Stonebarrow Fell is now completely *farpotshket*. You know *farpotshket?*"

"That," Gideon said, "is screwed up, plain and simple."

Abe nodded. "Screwed up. You said it, buddy."

Like the others, Julie was toying with her food. "I suppose it's a silly idea," she said, "but isn't it possible that Nate is just as much the victim of a hoax as Horizon Foundation or anyone else?"

Gideon replied. "But as Abe said, it's Nate's dig; he'd get all the credit for anything found there. Who else would have anything to gain?"

"Wait a minute," Abe said, brightening. "Maybe that's the wrong question. Maybe the question should be: Who had anything to lose?"

"And the answer," Julie said excitedly, "would be Nate Marcus. Couldn't somebody have sabotaged him? Duped him into thinking he had a legitimate find that proved his

theory, so that in the end he'd be ruined because the thing
would eventually be shown to be a fraud?"

"That," Gideon said admiringly, "is absolutely labyrin-
thine. But I don't know if it holds up. If someone was doing
it to discredit Nate, how could he know for sure the fraud
would even be discovered? Sure, I recognized it as Pummy
when I saw it, but a lot of anthropologists might not, and for
all anyone knew, the substitution in the Dorchester Museum
might have gone unnoticed for years—and Nate would have
been a hero."

"Unless," Abe said, "Julie's secret hoaxer made sure the
word got out; for example, a little word to the *West Dorset
Times?* There was a reporter waiting at the gate for us, you
know."

"Yes, I know," Gideon said. "And that reminds me...Abe,
you never told the *Times* I was coming to Stonebarrow Fell,
did you? Or anyone on the dig?"

Abe looked blankly at him. "What for?"

"That's what I thought," Gideon said. "Now, back to
this theory you two are cooking up—this unnecessarily
rococo theory, to borrow a phrase—I think it falls down on
one crucial point; from what you said, Abe, Nate's maintaining
that *he* discovered the thing personally, without any little
hints from anyone else. So how could anyone be duping
him?"

"That's true," Abe mused. "Even when he saw it, he
almost didn't see it."

"That's what he *says*," Julie said vigorously. "Maybe
he's protecting someone."

"Protecting the one who sabotaged him?" Gideon asked.

"Well . . ." Julie laughed suddenly. "I think you're right.
This theory's started to sound a little unga...umpki..."

"*Ungepotchket*," Abe said, a smile on his face. "Very
good. You learn quick. But *ungepotchket* or not, I think
maybe you got something. Only what, I don't know."

Gideon thought so too. Something wasn't quite right in
her rationale, but the basic idea was starting to make sense.
Nate had the most to lose, all right, and plenty of well-
earned enemies who would love to see him lose it. Was it

possible that he'd been set up? But how? They were silent for a moment, and then Julie asked, "Abe, what will happen to him now? What will they do to him?"

"Nothing will happen to him," Abe said with a shrug. "They'll just close down the dig, that's all. And Professor Hall-Waddington doesn't want to press any charges; he just wants his skull back. But Nathan's reputation is finished. He'll never lead another dig, and if he ever gets out of that little college in Missouri, I'll be surprised. It's a pity; a sad ending for a boy with a lot of promise."

"It sure is," Gideon said. "And you wasted a lot of time and money coming all the way out here."

"Not wasted," Abe said, and as the old man looked up, Gideon saw a telltale gleam in his eye. "You don't close down a dig overnight, even a little one. It takes a few days to wind it down, right? You got to backfill, clean up, straighten out the catalog, write a site report. . . . They asked Nathan to do it—which was a kindness, in my opinion—but he said no. Your Inspector Bagshawe told him he has to stay in Charmouth awhile, but if he never sees Stonebarrow Fell again, it will be too soon. So I said I would do it."

"You? You're going to personally supervise closing it down?"

"Sure, what's the big surprise? Who else, Frawley? Why not me?"

"For one thing, because you're a cultural anthropologist, not an archaeologist."

"In *my* day," Abe said, "anthropology wasn't split into a hundred little pigeonholes—microethnology, paleolinguistics—you were an anthropologist, that's all, and you had to learn everything."

"All right, but still—why you? Why aren't Robyn and Arbuckle doing it? They're the ones who say it has to be shut down."

"It's not their job," Abe said, showing a little impatience. "Robyn left already for Bournemouth, and Arbuckle went back to his dig in France for a couple of days. They'll come back and check and see that I closed it down right, and that's that."

"Robyn and Arbuckle are going to check on *you?*"

"Why not? They have to sign the final papers. Look, Gideon, what's all this arguing? Don't make a big *tzimiss* out of it. I'm glad to get the chance to do something . . . better than watch the rain fall down in Washington."

"What about your arthritis, Abe?" Gideon said more gently. "It's a four-hundred-foot climb."

Abe waved his hand grandly. "I walked it today, didn't I? Did I complain? Did I slow anybody up? . . . Well, maybe a little, but what's the hurry? Gideon, it'll be fun for me, something for an old man to do."

"Abe," Gideon said slowly, "closing down a dig isn't fun. You're doing it because this whole thing doesn't sit right with you, and you think you can do a little poking around up there. Am I right?"

"Did I say you were wrong? And what's more, it doesn't sit right with you, either. There's somewhere a little monkey business, something rotten in Denmark, no?"

"Well—"

Julie put down her teacup with a rattle. "Now wait a minute, you two. In the first place, from what you tell us, Gideon, Inspector Bagshawe is more than capable of handling any monkey business. And in the second place, if one of those people up there really is a murderer, then . . . Abe, are you sure you want to be up there on that lonely hill, alone with them?"

"Eh," Abe said. "If one of them really killed that boy, already he's shaking with fright. To kill someone else right in the same place is the last thing he'll do. Besides, the police will be over the place for a few days. And anyway, what do I know about murders? That's your husband's department. But I'll tell you the truth." He poked his own chest with a bony, elegant forefinger. "Me, I'm interested in skulls that disappear from museums and turn up in the ground, instead of the other way around. If Hall-Waddington wants to drop it, that's his business, but me, I'm still interested. And for this kind of interest, believe me, nobody's going to kill me."

Abe put a chip in his mouth and chewed it slowly. "Listen, Gideon, I was thinking . . ."

"Oh-oh," Gideon muttered.

Abe looked up in innocent surprise. " 'Oh-oh'? What, 'oh-oh'?"

"Oh-oh, whenever you tell me you've 'been thinking,' in that particular tone of voice, it means you've cooked up something for me that's going to get me in trouble."

"Me?" The old man's moist eyes opened wider. "Julie, listen how he talks to me, his old professor, who taught him everything he knows," He turned back to Gideon and spread his hands. "What did I cook up? Nothing. I was only thinking you might like to help me with the shut-down, spend a little time up there—maybe two days, maybe three days. I could use somebody I can trust. Frawley and the others . . . frankly, I'm not too impressed."

Ordinarily, Abe would have applied a good deal of embellishment to such a request: He was an old man, his powers were failing, he needed an alert, bright young man beside him, someone he could lean on in his infirmity, et cetera. This time, however, he seemed to think that coaxing was unnecessary.

And of course he was right. Gideon was just as curious, just as interested in poking around Stonebarrow Fell as Abe was. But Gideon had more than buried skulls on his mind. The uncomfortable feeling of being responsible—albeit unknowingly and unwillingly—for Randy's death had not subsided, and a couple of days up on the dig, mixing naturally with the crew, might provide answers that Bagshawe, in his official capacity, would have difficulty finding. Just how much the inspector would appreciate his assistance Gideon didn't know, but that was the inspector's problem.

Julie made a resigned but reasonably cheerful sound. "Okay, I've been wanting to see some of the Hardy things we never got around to, anyway—the cottage at Bockhampton, things like that. Maybe I'll do a little touring on my own while you two do your Sherlock Holmes thing up there." Her hand found Gideon's knee under the table. "But you're going to have to promise to be careful."

He covered her hand with his. "Of course we'll be careful, but Abe's right. There's nothing to be careful about."

"And remember, you're not a detective."

"She's right," Abe put in.

Gideon shook his head despairingly. "Why does everyone find it so necessary to keep reminding me of that? When did I ever claim to be a detective?"

The barmaid cleared away the dishes, and Gideon refilled the flowered teapot from the metal pitcher of hot water that had been served along with it, pouring the water directly onto the two gigantic, soggy teabags—each one big enough for three pots of American tea. "There is one thing, Abe," he said. "I hope it's okay with you if I don't start until Saturday. Tomorrow Julie and I are going over to Lyme Regis. I want to see if I can hunt down the omniscient editor of the *West Dorset Times*."

Abe spread his hands and appealed to Julie. "You see the way it is? One minute you give them a job, and the next minute they're asking for time off."

□ 14 □

THE "MYCENEAN MAN of Stonebarrow Fell" was revealed yesterday to be a hoax that has left the anthropological establishment reeling with embarrassment. The much-heralded Bronze Age relic had in fact been stolen from the Greater Dorchester Museum of History and Archaeology and secretly implanted at Stonebarrow Fell, where it was subsequently "discovered" by expedition director Nathan G. Marcus.

In a tense scene at the dramatically isolated site high above Charmouth Beach, American physical antropologist Gideon P. Oliver denounced his countryman's find as a fraud, and was immediately supported by representatives of the Wessex Antiquarian Society and the Horizon Foundation, the expedition's joint sponsors. The abducted skull, actually some 27,000 years older than the British Bronze Age, has since been restored to its place of honor in Dorchester.

Professor Marcus has refused comment, but the *Times* has learned that he has been suspended and recommended for censure by the two sponsoring organizations. In his stead, Dr. Abraham I. Goldstein, Pro-

fessor Emeritus, Columbia University, assisted by
Professor Oliver . . .

With a sigh, Gideon put the word-processed draft on the
desk. "This will be in today's edition?"

"Yes," Ralph Chantry said, elbows on the desk, chubby
fingers steepled in front of his lips. "I trust you have no
objections?" Despite the overheating in his office, he was
burrowed into a thick woolen sweater-vest.

Gideon shook his head. "No, I have no objections."
What difference did it make? It would soon enough be
front-page news in the small world of anthropology anyway,
and that was the only world that would matter for Nate.
"Well, maybe one. I don't know that I exactly 'denounced'
the thing."

Chantry took the paper, turned it toward himself, looked
down his short, wide nose at it, and sniffed. "What would
you say to 'condemned'?"

"How about 'indicated'?"

Chantry made a face. "Not enough drama. 'Revealed'?"

They settled on "demonstrated." Chantry changed the
word with a heavy blue pencil, made the required grammati-
cal adjustments, and placed the sheet in a smudged, dog-
eared folder, which he flung lightly into a wooden box
labeled *Egress* in Gothic lettering.

"Now exactly what is it I can do for you?"

He peered sharply at Gideon over the tops of a pair of
crescent-shaped reading glasses that sat precariously low on
his nose, and out from under raised, meager eyebrows. The
effect was at once shrewd and humorously sleepy, benign
and obliquely malicious; W. C. Fields playing Benjamin
Franklin. His head, bald except for a few strands lovingly
combed from left to right across the top, was tilted alertly
forward. Ralph Chantry looked as froglike as any man
Gideon had ever seen. It would have been only faintly
surprising to see him part his wide, dry lips, uncoil a ribbon
of tongue, and haul in a fly.

"What I'd like to know, Mr. Chantry, is where you get
your information on the Stonebarrow dig."

"I'm afraid that's privileged. It's accurate, is it not?"

"Yes, it's accurate, but I'd still like to know."

"Afraid not, dear man. Isn't done. The press in America has the same convention, I understand." He smiled amiably. "Would you care for some tea? Takes the chill out of one."

"No, thanks. Look, Mr. Chantry, a hardworking and dedicated"—Gideon couldn't quite bring himself to say "brilliant"—"anthropologist has just had his reputation ruined up there—"

"As well it should have been!" Chantry cried with vigor. He lifted a dripping tea bag from his cup with a spoon and dashed it into an ashtray. "The man was given a scientific responsibility of no mean proportions, and he violated his trust. He perpetrated theft and fraud and God knows what else, all to aggrandize himself and support his vile theory. Mycenaeans indeed!" He pushed his *Egress* box crossly forward and back to show his indignation.

"I'm not so sure about all that," Gideon said. "I'm starting to wonder if he wasn't victimized himself."

"Really? How very unpleasant. But see here; if you're implying. . . . Just what is it you're implying?"

"I'm not really sure," Gideon said truthfully. "But something's wrong." He leaned forward, his elbow on Chantry's desk. "For one thing, you knew I was going to be at the site—and printed it—almost before I did. I hadn't thought *anyone* knew."

Chantry waggled his eyebrows and smiled again. His teeth were tiny, pearly little nubbins like two neat and gleaming rows of pygmy corn. "Superior journalism, dear boy."

Gideon laughed in spite of himself. "Maybe so, but there's more than journalism involved, I think. Let me ask you this: When you sent your reporter up there yesterday, did you tell him exactly what time to go, or was that just an accident?"

Chantry considered, tapping his teacup gently against his upper teeth. "My informant told me that ten o'clock Thursday morning would be a propitious time to call."

"Propitious," Gideon said. "Yes, if what you're trying

to do is ruin Nate Marcus." He wasn't sure just when he'd swung over wholeheartedly to Julie's theory that Nate had been set up, but he had.

"Really!" Chantry said pleasantly. "Do let's be reasonable, shall we? I'm sure I don't know what you're going on about. Whyever should I wish to ruin Professor Marcus?"

"I don't think you do, but I think someone could be using you." That had a foolishly theatrical ring to it, but he plowed on. "Don't you think it's awfully coincidental that your informant told you to send a reporter at the precise moment when everything was happening at once? If he'd gotten through the gate, he would have been right at the critical point, the . . ."

"Denouement?" Chantry offered.

"Exactly. Amazingly propitious, wouldn't you say?"

"No, I wouldn't." Chantry was firm. "I'd go as far as 'serendipitous'—in the sense of turning up unanticipated consequences—but certainly not as far as 'amazingly' propitious. This sort of thing happens all the time in journalism. You fish for pilchard and you catch a sole."

"Mr. Chantry," Gideon said, "I suppose you know about Randy Alexander by now?"

"You mean that he was murdered? Yes. I was terribly, terribly sorry to learn that." He sounded as if he meant it. "And I assure you that if there is any way I can help in that matter, I certainly shall."

"Well, I think the skull and the murder may be related."

Chantry sat very still. "You think? Is there some reason for so thinking?"

"No, not really; not yet. But they have to be. It's too wild a combination of events for them to be unrelated."

The editor studied him for a long time. "I'm afraid I don't agree with you. I've seen stranger combinations of events, quite unrelated." He put his cup on his desk and leaned over. "Really, I am sorry," he said civilly, "but unless you come up with more convincing evidence, I simply cannot at this point reveal my informant, and that must be my final world. I'm sure you understand. Now, do let's have a drink. I have some excellent sherry. And are you free for lunch?''

The interview was over. "No, sorry," Gideon said, standing up. "I'm meeting my wife. Thanks for your time." Then he added, a little grudgingly, "And I do understand your position."

"I'm so glad," Chantry said with a serene and froggy smile.

"Even if you didn't learn anything from Mr. Chantry, it was worth coming to Lyme Regis for this!" Julie said between mouthfuls. "Yum!"

Gideon laughed. "I always liked a girl with a healthy appetite."

"Well, you've got one." She eyed the little jam pot, empty for a second time. "Do we dare ask for another refill?"

They were in the Goose House, a tiny, white, storybook cottage near the bottom of the crooked, climbing main street. They sat at a window looking down on the quiet beach, where fossil hunters took advantage of the mild weather to wander desultorily along the sand, turning over rocks with their toes. On the table between them was what was left of a hearty Dorset cream tea: Dorset dumplings filled with a rum-and-apple mixture and flavored with ginger, a pile of butter-drenched scones, jam, tea, and of course a bowl of heaped, clotted cream, as sweet and thick as ice cream. They had not breakfasted that morning, and they had done extremely well by the rich meal.

"Do you really want some more jam?" Gideon asked.

"You don't have to sound so incredulous." She pushed away her plate and smiled contentedly. "No, I've had more than enough. I feel as if I'm made of clotted cream."

Gideon refilled the teapot with hot water and settled comfortably back. "Clotted cream looks terrific on you."

"I'm just lucky you like your women Rubenesque."

"Rubenesque? You've got a long way to go to Rubenesque. On the other hand, it's a good thing I don't like Modigliani."

Julie raised a single eyebrow at him but didn't reply. As

she poured the tea she said, "So you're still down to four possible informants, right? Frawley or one of the three students."

"Five. Nate, too."

"Nate? Do you really think it could be Nate?"

"No, but you said 'possible.' He'd certainly be in a position to forward most of the information Chantry got." He put down his cup. "And what about Robyn? Or Arbuckle?"

"Robyn," Julie said, "or Arbuckle. Now there's an interesting thought."

"Well, I'm just covering all the bases. I'm not really serious." Or was he? He considered. "You know, when you come down to it, Frederick Robyn is no friend of Nate's, what with the way Nate's been lambasting the Society. I suppose it's possible—barely possible—that he'd want to get even."

"And Arbuckle?"

"No, I don't think Paul has anything against Nate. He didn't even want to be here. The poor guy just wants to get back to Pleistocene man in France. But Robyn, now—"

"You don't actually think he had anything to do with the murder, do you?"

"Well . . ." He shook his head sharply. "No, we're being ridiculous. Unfair, too. Just because Nate, in his inimitable fashion, has been a little ungracious to *him* is hardly a reason to suspect him of fraud and murder."

"Still, it's a possible motive."

"For the hoax, maybe, not for the murder. And anyway, there weren't any visitors to the site the day Randy was killed, remember? That lets off both Robyn and Arbuckle. So we're back to the original Suspects Four: Jack Frawley, Barry Fusco, Leon Something, and Sandra Something."

"And Nathan Something. As an outside possibility."

"Okay, right. Come on, let's go see the town and walk off some clotted cream."

Lyme Regis had everything the guidebooks said it did: steep, narrow, winding streets; charming old pubs and inns bedecked with their original open-beam woodwork; quaint, clean shops; ancient cottages painted in soft pastels; a pretty

harbor. Postcards, posters, and bookets celebrated the film-
ing of *The French Lieutenant's Woman* there, as if the
village dated its true genesis from Meryl Streep's arrival,
but there were also signs—harder to find—of Jane Austen's
visits, of Louisa Musgrove's dramatic fall in *Persuasison,* of
the Duke of Monmouth's ill-fated landing in 1685.

Yet, with it all, the village was vaguely unsatisfying;
perhaps it was the insistent Olde Englande atmosphere,
cloying after Charmouth's simple, homespun ambience.
They walked down Marine Parade to take the obligatory
tourist's hike along the tilting top of the Cobb, the serpen-
tine breakwater of gray stone blocks, but even this seemed
tame. There were no waves or wind, and the tide was out,
so that the boats moored within the crook of the Cobb lay
sprawled clumsily on their sides in the gray mud.

But standing at the very end of the Cobb, facing east,
they looked across smooth, open water at the fresh, green,
billowing coast of Dorset. The rounded dome of Stonebarrow
Fell was easily identifiable and looked, from here, peaceful
and lovely. They gazed out, Gideon's arm about Julie's
shoulder, her arm around his waist under his jacket, her hand
resting in his far hip pocket.

She straightened suddenly. "I just had a thought. What
Barry told you was that there weren't any visitors, right?"

"Right," Gideon said dreamily, continuing to stare over
the water.

"Well, would Frederick Robyn be a *visitor?* Or Paul?
They must have their own keys. Barry wouldn't have had to
let them in. When Barry said there weren't any visitors—"

"He wouldn't necessarily have meant them," Gideon
said, snapping alert. "Damn, that's right. Robyn lent me his
key yesterday. He *might* have been there! Now that's something I want to look into."

"No, it isn't," Julie said firmly.

"It isn't?"

"No. It's something for you to tell Inspector Bagshawe,
and for him to look into."

He smiled. "I keep forgetting; I'm not a detective." He
glanced at is watch. "What I am is an anthropologist, and

inasmuch as it's only two o'clock, maybe I ought to go up to the dig this afternoon, after all, and see if I can help Abe out.''

"Absolutely not. You told him tomorrow. Anyway, by the time you got back to Charmouth, changed into working clothes, and climbed the hill, it'd practically be dark. How about a drive in the country instead? To Cricket St. Thomas.''

"Because you like the name?''

"Of course.''

"Fine. I had such a good time not finding Wootton Fitzpaine, I bet not finding Cricket St. Thomas would be just as much fun.''

"If we can't, there's always Burton Bradstock or Whitechurch Canonicorum. Or, in a pinch, Sleech Wood.''

"It's only a little thing,'' Abe muttered, "but still I don't like it.'' He was staring at a three-by-five-inch index card in his hand. With his other hand he tugged gently at his lower lip. "Something funny, something funny.''

Gideon had arrived at Stonebarrow Fell at 8:30 A.M., expecting to be the first one there, but Barry, Leon, and Sandra were already at the trench, working under Frawley's direction, and observed by a yawning police constable. Abe had been in the shed, poring over the expedition records spread on the table in front of him. The heater had thoroughly warmed the building, indicating he'd been there for some time, and the coffeepot was already halfway down.

Gideon poured himself a cup. "What's funny?''

"There's no milk for the coffee,'' Abe said, still looking at the card, "only powdered stuff. Tomorrow I'll bring some real milk, from cows. Partially hydrogenated coconut oil who needs?''

"I'll bring it,'' Gideon said. "What's funny?'' he asked again.

Abe handed him the card. "Have a look at this.''

"It was a "find card,'' a device that is commonly used on archaeological digs. Its purpose is to make an immediate, on-the-spot record of every object discovered the moment it was found. The dirt smudges on this one suggested that it had been used as intended.

The card was made up as a printed form with blank spaces for written entries. Gideon scanned it quickly. *Site:* CHA 2-2; *Date:* 11-1; *Loc:* Q1-5; *Depth:* 21" (12" had been written in before it, but had been crossed out); *Descr:* Human femur, left, partial. Proximal 100 mm.

There was illegible information scribbled after *Matrix, Orientation,* and *Remarks;* and finally, at the bottom, after *Recorded by,* Leon Hillyer's name had been scrawled.

It was strange, Gideon thought, that he hadn't heard anyone mention the earlier finding of a human bone. The femur, of course, was the thigh bone, and the "Proximal 100 mm." would consist of not the shaft itself but of the ball that inserts into the hip socket, along with an inch or two of femoral "neck"—the small, diagonal column of bone that joins the all to the shaft.

When he looked up, Abe said, "So? What do you see?"

Gideon shrugged. "Well, I hadn't known they'd found any human remains—that is, before Pummy came up—and yet this was discovered a month ago. Aside from that, I don't see anything strange."

"Okay, now look at this." He slid an open bound notebook across the table. "This is the field catalog. Look at November first."

Gideon looked and blinked with surprise. "There's only one entry: 'Number one-forty-nine: Four faience beads.' There's no bone listed."

"That's right, and that's what's funny. Nathan is a little *fartootst,* but he knows how to run a dig, and when a dig is run right, *every* night you take the find cards and you enter the information in the permanent field catalog. You don't miss a night. Otherwise, numbers get mixed up, things get lost. . . . You know this; what am I telling you?"

"You're right," Gideon said. "It was probably Frawley's job to maintain the catalog."

"It was definitely Frawley's job." Abe took back the notebook and placed his thin hands on it, one on top of the others. "I looked through the whole thing, and nowhere is a mention of a human bone; not a peep." He closed the book and finished his coffee with a gulp. "So the big question is: Why not? Why didn't Frawley write it down in the permanent catalog? And where *is* this mysterious human femur, left, partial? It's not in with the other finds."

Gideon looked at the card he still held in his hand. "Isn't it possible that when Frawley had a look at it he concluded that it wasn't really a bone? That Leon had misidentified it? It happens all the time. That's one reason a worker doesn't enter it directly into the catalog himself, isn't it?"

Abe looked at him quizzically. "It happens all the time that you find four faience beads and you think they're a leg bone?"

Gideon laughed. "Maybe you're onto something, Abe— although I'm not sure what. I don't see how this can have anything to do with the Poundbury skull—"

"Poundbury? Of course not. This was a month ago. Besides, this one is a femur. Pummy is . . . what was it?"

"Left parieto-occipital; hard to confuse the two, even for an archaeologist. It'll be interesting to hear what Jack Frawley has to say."

"That I'm very interested in myself." He put the card into a file box and closed it. "Well, Inspector Bagshawe will be here in a few minutes, so why don't we go outside and get to work?"

"Bagshawe's coming here?"

"He was here yesterday, too, interviewing everyone, picking up tools, looking under potsherds. It makes everybody nervous, but I guess it's got to be done."

"Good, there's something I wanted to mention to him."

"*Good* morning, gentleman!" Detective Inspector Bagshawe's booming, peaceful voice reverberated in the shed. He closed the door behind him, hung his vast checked overcoat on a peg, and ambulated majestically to the table, where he sank confidently down onto a metal folding chair that looked alarmingly flimsy for the job. "I shouldn't be very long today, and I'll try my best not to get in the way of your scientific pursuits."

"It's no trouble, Inspector," Abe said. "I'm just going.

Make yourself at home. Have some coffee. Gideon, when you're finished talking, you'll come join us at the dig?''

When Abe had left, Bagshawe looked at Gideon across the table with placid expectation, his big, curving cherrywood pipe between his teeth, and his huge hands clasped loosely on the table.

"Well, I don't think I really have anything important," Gideon said, suddenly diffident, "but I wanted to mention that the day Randy was killed there may have been some outsiders at Stonebarrow Fell after all. It's just possible that Frederick Robyn or Paul Arbuckle might have been here. They had their own keys, and Barry wouldn't be likely to consider them 'visitors.' Anyway, if it's okay with you, I thought I could discreetly check around—''

Bagshawe grinned. "In this case, lad, the CID, ever alert, are far ahead of you. Dr. Arbuckle was here before, all right, on an audit, but that was weeks ago, when Mr. Alexander was demonstrably alive and well. As for the afternoon of November thirteen, when he presumably ceased being either, Dr. Arbuckle was provably in Dijon, and Mr. Robyn in London. Of course, either of them might have nipped away for a few hours and slipped into Stonebarrow Fell—seen by no one—but in all honesty I don't think so. And as for your prowling about, why, if I were you I wouldn't do anything about it. Why not leave that sort of thing to us?''

A fragment of remembered conversation leaped into Gideon's mind. His eyes widened. "What did you say?''

"I said, 'Why not leave that sort of thing to us?' And what's wrong with that?''

"No, the sentence before that.''

Bagshawe took the pipe out of his mouth and looked oddly at Gideon. "The sentence before that? I said I wouldn't do anything about it if I were you. Merely a turn of phrase, Professor, nothing more.''

"Inspector, when Randy tried to tell me whatever it was, and I suggested he tell Frawley instead, he said, quote: 'He wouldn't do anything about it.' ''

Bagshawe stuck the pipe back between his teeth. "He

wouldn't do anything about it," he repeated, frowning, and sat a moment longer. "So?"

"What would that mean to you?"

"That even if he told Frawley, Frawley wouldn't do anything about it, that's what it would mean." The inspector's patience was wearing a little thin.

"Sure, that's what I thought at the time. But let's say Randy already *had* told Frawley—before he ever talked to me—and Frawley just refused to do anything about it. What would Randy have said to me in that case?"

"He would have said . . . why, he might have said the very same thing: 'He wouldn't do anything about it.' " He lowered his chin to his chest and looked at Gideon with dawning appreciation. "Professor Frawley just might know what the young man was trying to tell you, mightn't he? Well, now, that's worth exploring. Do you know, I've already asked him—as I've asked everyone—if he had any idea what it might be."

"And he said he didn't?"

"As did they all. But with Professor Frawley—ah, I had my suspicions. There was a sort of hitch, a holding back, a sidling away of the eyes, if you know what I mean."

Gideon nodded. He knew very well.

"Well then," Bagshawe said, "let's try again. Why don't we just go and chat Mr. Frawley up right now?"

"We?"

Bagshawe looked squarely at Gideon, not unkindly. "Professor, since it's all too apparent that you're going to be sniffing and poking about up here in any event, why, I'd be a great deal more comfortable having you doing it where I can see you. I've got enough trouble here already, and it wouldn't do to have Gideon Oliver done in under my very nose while pursuing inquiries of his own." He huffed on the bowl of his pipe and rubbed it on his sleeve. "Think of the paperwork."

□ 15 □

THEY FOUND JACK Frawley at the dig, completing some cross-sectional diagrams of the pits on a sheet of quadrille paper attached to a clipboard. He was wearing a shapeless, colorless canvas fisherman's hat, a decrepit old windbreaker, worn cotton jeans, and old tennis shoes. His stubby, metal-stemmed pipe, unlit, was clenched in his teeth, the bowl upside down. He was, Gideon thought, working at looking like an archaeologist. What he looked like was Monsieur Hulot.

When Bagshawe had said, "We would like a word with you, Professor Frawley," his face had paled, and pale it remained. Bagshawe had led them—not by accident, Gideon was sure—to a flat, rocky area near the cliff edge: just about the spot from which Randy must have plummeted into the rock-encircled lagoon. Far below, the tide was in. It boomed and gurgled hollowly, as it must have done that day.

"Now, Professor," Bagshawe began without preface, "when I asked you yesterday if you had any idea of what Mr. Alexander had wanted to tell Professor Oliver, you said you did not."

Frawley nodded. "I, uh, I believe I did say something to the effect that I couldn't think of anything right offhand."

From the twitchy wobble of Frawley's eyes, Gideon knew

instantly that he was lying. And he sure was that Bagshawe knew it, and that Frawley knew they knew.

Bagshawe fixed Frawley with a steely eye. "I won't quibble about that. I shall simply ask you whether you have, on further reflection, remembered something."

"Well, you know, actually, I might have had a word or two with Randy that morning, now that I think about it," Frawley said, and accompanied it with a weak laugh. "But it was just one of those little technical things that crop up; nothing important."

Bagshawe shifted easily into a more soothing manner. "Now, Professor," he said slowly, "if there's anything you're reluctant to say, I can assure you that Professor Oliver and I—"

"It's only that it's nothing relevant to Randy's . . . to the case you're working on."

"One never knows," Bagshawe said reassuringly. "Often, it's the little things that provide the critical clues."

"Well . . ." Frawley's soft, doggy eyes fixed on the inspector in melancholy appeal. "I'm just afraid you'll get the wrong idea . . . about a certain party. . . ."

"Well, now, Professor, why don't you just trust me to be the judge of that?" The big teeth showed in a peaceable, bovine smile.

Gideon admired the inspector's patience. For himself, he was ready to kick the oleaginously reluctant Frawley in the shins if this went on much longer. "For Christ's sake, Jack," he said.

Frawley started. "Okay. All right." But still he couldn't get himself going. He put his unlit pipe in his mouth and frowned in thought, going *puh, puh, puh* softly around the pipe stem with moist lips. Bagshawe smiled encouragingly at him. Gideon looked impatiently out to sea.

"I think you can already guess what he told me," Frawley said, his eyes on his shoes. "He told me that the skull Nate was so excited about was a fake; somehow he'd found out that Nate himself had stolen it from Dorchester and secretly buried it here. He wanted me to stop Nate before he actually dug it out and announced it."

"And why," Bagshawe asked, all policeman again, "didn't you tell us this before?"

Frawley pursed his lips and made the pecking, chin-thursting motion that some men make when their collars are too tight, although his own sat loosely on his neck. "In all frankness, I was afraid that you'd jump to the conclusion that Nate had killed Randy to protect himself. And I didn't want that to happen."

Gideon cut in. "If you knew Nate had planted the skull, why didn't you stop him before he dug it up with all that fanfare?"

The question seemed to catch Frawley by surprise. "Why? Why didn't I stop him? Well ... speaking candidly ... it wasn't my place. ... I'm only ... and how could I be sure Randy was telling the truth? Maybe he was lying."

"Wouldn't that be all the more reason to go to Nate, or just to check it out yourself?"

"And why, Professor," asked Bagshawe, "did you not go to the authorities?"

"Authorities?" Frawley's eyes were beginning to take on a hunted look.

"The Horizon Foundation, the Wessex Antiquarian Society ... the police?"

"Well, gosh, I hope you fellows don't think I'm some sort of criminal." He managed a gummy little giggle. "I was just trying to do my job. There are times," he said sanctimoniously, "when fidelity outweighs adherence to scientific research. Nate is my ... my superior, and I believe I owe him my support and my loyalty."

And may no one ever be that loyal to me, Gideon thought, *or that supportive.*

"No, Professor," Bagshawe tolled," I don't think that's the way it was."

"I beg your pardon?" Frawley said.

"Shall I tell you how I think it was?"

Frawley looked mutely at him and licked his lips. His cheeks glistened unhealthily.

"I think," the inspector said at his slowest, "that when you heard that Professor Marcus planned a hoax, you were only too delighted with the news, and the last thing you wanted to do was to stop him. You *wanted* him to bring off this dirty great fraud of his.''

Frawley made incredulous noises.

''If you had stopped him in time,'' Bagshawe continued, ''it would have been no more than an embarrassment, with no one the wiser, except for you, him, and the young man. All in the family, you might say. But . . . if he was allowed to bring it off—and was then exposed—ah, *then* there would be hell to pay. His career would be finished. As indeed it is—as indeed you wanted.''

''Wanted? That's ridiculous! Why would I want such a thing?''

''Jealousy. Envy.''

''Me jealous of *Nate?*'' From somewhere he summoned a sort of soggy dignity. ''I don't think I should have to stand for this.''

''Jack,'' Gideon said, ''are you the one who gave Ralph Chantry his information?''

''What?'' Frawley stared at him with convincing blankness. ''Who?''

Barely pausing for this uninformative exchange, Bagshawe continued in his inexorable way. ''I've looked into your background, Professor Frawley, and I know that Professor Marcus was made head of a department of which you are the senior and eldest member. I know that he, a much younger man, was made a full professor while you remained an associate. I know that you advised in faculty council against his hiring.''

Shielding his eyes against the sun, Frawley looked up at the massive policeman. ''Just who do you think you are?''

Bagshawe went on remorselessly. ''Now then, I ask myself: Might there not be another reason why you haven't told us this before? And why, when you finally did tell us, you so carefully implied that Professor Marcus might be not only a hoaxer but a murderer as well?''

''I don't know what you're talking about,'' Frawley practically squeaked. ''Why don't you say what you mean?''

''I'm talking about the fact,'' Bagshawe intoned, ''that

by so very indirectly accusing Professor Marcus you were hoping that we would overlook your own motive for killing Mr. Alexander." His voice was like the doomful knell of justice. In it Gideon could hear the clank of chains, the bleak, muffled *kerchunk* of iron dungeon doors slammed home.

Frawley heard them too. This time he did squeak. "Me? Why would I want to kill Randy?"

"Will you deny that Mr. Alexander, who liked his little joke, played one on you? Didn't he convince a group of equally playful Indians in Missouri to tell you that they were soon to hold a once-every-hundred-years secret dance during which they would dig up a sacred vulture egg that had been buried at the *last* ceremony? And to solemnly inform you that you were the only anthropologist they trusted enough to be present?"

"Christ," Gideon said. "And you bought it, Jack?"

Frawley made a motion with his head that was part denial, part assent, part frustration.

"He not only bought it," Bagshawe said, "he presented a paper on it to the Eastern Missouri Anthropological Society and was thereby made—so my informants advise me—an object of some ridicule."

Gideon felt a brief wave of compassion for the visibly sagging Frawley. That kind of joke was every anthropologist's nightmare, and if Randy was in the habit of playing merry little pranks like that, it was a wonder he'd lived as long as he had.

"All right, Inspector, you're right," Frawley said, seeming to drag the words out of himself. "I was jealous of Nate. I've behaved like a fool—but I *didn't* kill Randy! As God is my witness, I never thought in my wildest dreams that Nate . . . that anybody . . . would murder Randy." As if he didn't already look sufficiently abject, Frawley had taken off his hat and was crushing it in both hands. "I'll try to make amends. Please believe me when I say you'll have my complete cooperation in any way you want."

Bagshawe sucked his teeth and studied him. "I think it goes without saying, Professor Frawley, that I'd take a very dim view of it if you attempted to leave the vicinity of Charmouth without my permission.''

''Yes, of course, Inspector. I wouldn't think of it. I want to do everything I can to help solve this terrible tragedy.''

Gideon felt like going away and washing his hands somewhere, but he asked another question. ''Jack, before you go—we've found a discrepancy in the excavation records from November one. There's a find care on a partial human femur, but it was never entered in the field catalog.''

Frawley looked uncomprehendingly at him. ''What?''

''You make the entries in the field catalog, don't you?''

''Yes, every night; sometimes the next morning. A femur, did you say? That's impossible. We've never found a human bone—not until Poundbury Man. We thought we had some ribs, but you straightened us out on that.''

''You're positive?''

''Of course I'm positive. I'd know about it if we had, wouldn't I? No, we never found one. Ask anybody.''

Gideon remembered the scrawled signature in the lower righthand corner of the card: Leon Hillyer. He would indeed ask somebody.

Gideon and Bagshawe remained near the edge of the cliff, looking out toward the water. The sea was a flat, summery blue, and a white, picture-book passenger liner steamed eastward from Plymouth, riding the horizon toward France.

Bagshawe took out his pipe and lit it with a wooden match, using his wide body to block the breeze. Then he sat down on a chair-high boulder, first arranging the skirts of his coat like the tails of a cutaway.

''Nasty piece of goods, our man Frawley,'' he said cheerfully. ''Do you think he told us the truth about what Alexander said to him?''

''I don't know,'' Gideon said, ''but I don't see Jack Frawley as a font of veracity.''

Unexpectedly, Bagshawe guffawed. ''No, you're right there. Still, if it's true, it provides us, doesn't it, with a plausible motive for your friend Professor Marcus—who, by the way, continues to proclaim himself innocent of both murder and fraud.''

''I take it Nate's still your prime suspect?''

''Prime suspect? Oh no, I wouldn't say that. There's Professor Frawley, isn't there, and then the others as well. Five in all, and all prime.''

''Five? You mean all the people on the dig?''

''Just so, Professor. A single day's work—interviews with the lot, and a few calls across the Pond—and we've turned up, I'm sorry to say, credible motives for every man-jack of them, and Miss Mazur, too. And none of them took much digging. Young Barry Fusco, for instance, owed Randy some three thousand dollars, which he was having a hard time repaying. Randy, so it's said, had been making nasty noises at Barry, threatening to go to the lad's father when they go back home.''

''His father? Why would he go to his father?''

''Well, you see, Barry borrowed it in the first place to keep his father from finding out he'd wrecked a new car that had been a present. Apparently, the father's a stern old gent of whom Barry lives in considerable awe.''

''And so Barry might have killed Randy to keep his father from finding out?''

''Exactly, Professor, but I can see you're not taken with the idea. Well, neither am I, but there it is. Now, Sandra Mazur and Leon Hillyer each present a bit more potential; two points of a steamy little triangle, with Randy being the third.'' He smiled with the metaphor.

''Do you mean Sandra was having affairs with both of them?'' This surprised Gideon. The brittle Sandra hardly seemed the sort of woman to stir up male instincts of violence or passion—not his at any rate.

''I know what you're thinking,'' Bagshawe said, ''but there's more involved than the young lady's charms; there's a tidy sum of money. Miss Mazur, you see, will come into a sizable inheritance on her thirtieth birthday. Both men were in grim pursuit, and each, I gather, had been unaware he had a rival. Sufficient reason for homicide, I should say, should one of them find out.''

Gideon thought it over. Leon, ambitious and bright, did seem the kind of man who wouldn't be at all averse to marrying for money. And although it might appear that Randy, coming from a wealthy family himself, had less to gain, his position had been insecure. From what Nate had said, his father had been threatening to disinherit him. It was obvious to Gideon, knowing what he knew about Randy's style of living, that Randy would have welcomed the advantages of a rich wife.

"You're saying," he said, "that Leon might have found out about Randy and killed him?"

"Yes; without premeditation, I should think. Leon's a clever young man. If he'd planned to do Randy in, he'd choose someplace removed from the dig to do it. But I don't rule out an argument and a hot-blooded murder."

"But where's the motive for Sandra in all that? And do you really think she could have killed Randy, even armed with a mallet? She can't weigh much more than a hundred pounds."

Bagshawe waved dismissively. "Given the proper incentive, women have been known to kill men a great deal larger than themselves, as I'm sure you know very well. And she had an incentive. It seems she'd become disenchanted with the ways of our Randy and had, in fact, settled on the lucky Leon as her man. This, she claims, she finally told Randy, but he seems to have taken exception. He threatened to make their affair public—and a few little tidbits about certain of Miss Mazur's, ah, unusual proclivities as well." He lowered his eyes and coughed delicately. "Well, then, Leon, you see, with his eye on a rising academic career in the Ivy League, if that's the right term, might very well bow out and find himself a more socially acceptable wife. You see?"

"I think I do, and I guess that Sandra might have a motive, all right. But why would she tell you all this?"

"She didn't, but a chambermaid at the Jug and Sceptre, where Randy was putting up, heard them shouting at each other early one morning, and told all to Sergeant Fryer—remarkable memory for details, that woman has—and with what Miss Mazur *did* tell me, it wasn't hard to piece it all together.''

He leaned over, tapped his pipe against a rock, blew through the stem, and put it in his pocket. ''So you see, Professor, the investigation progresses satisfactorily, and there's no reason at all for you not to return to your bones.''

''I think I've just been fired,'' Gideon said with a grin as Bagshawe got to his feet. ''And speaking of bones, I have some questions to ask Leon about still another bone that's turned up, or rather, that hasn't turned up.''

''That's the ticket,'' Bagshawe said with an amicable lack of interest.

''It's a piece of a femur that seems to have been found and then lost again. You're welcome to sit in if you like.''

Bagshawe let his expression answer for him, and very eloquent it was.

When Gideon went to the dig, he stood for a while, watching the crew work at backfilling under Abe's efficient direction. With newly informed eyes he took a good, long look at them, but Sandra seemed as drawn and hard-edged as ever, not his idea of a seductress—no matter how rich— and a pretty unlikely murderess, too, although she was a better bet for that. The rosy-cheeked Barry looked no less wholesome than ever, and Frawley no less ineffectual. And Leon, who was coolly lecturing Abe on some stratigraphic complexities, hardly fit the mold of Bagshawe's hot-blooded murderer. Cold-blooded, however . . . that might be another thing.

But when it came down to it, there was something unsatisfying, something inescapably spurious about every one of the hypotheses Bagshawe had advanced. And what about the left-handed mallet blow? None of them, after all, were left-handed. How could he fit that inescapable fact into even the few shadowy patterns that had emerged thus far? Or was he offbase in his continuing certainty that the killer was left-handed? Bagshawe disagreed with him, and Bagshawe was a pretty fair cop.

When Abe called a halt for lunch, Gideon took him aside. ''Frawley says Leon never reported finding any bone.''

"Is that so?" Abe said thoughtfully. "Maybe we should have a little brown-bag talk with Leon."

Most of the staff were taking advantage of the fine weather to eat their sack lunches on the bluff, but Leon had made for the shed. He was at the table writing a postcard, a cup of coffee beside him, when Abe and Gideon came in. He looked up, smiling.

"Hi, Abe. Hiya, Gideon."

"Leon," Abe said, "you wouldn't mind if we had a little talk? It shouldn't take long."

"Not at all, Abe. Just let me finish this card or I'll never get back to it."

Gideon went to the table in the corner to make coffee for himself and Abe. Above the hot plate, a small mirror was taped to the wall. In it he could see Leon bent over the postcard, writing slowly. There was something . . .

He put down the coffee jar and whirled around. "You're writing left-handed!"

There was a long, frozen moment during which Leon stared speechlessly back at Gideon, and Abe stared from one to the other. At last Leon mutely lifted the hand in which he held his pen.

It was his right hand, inarguably his right hand.

"I . . . sorry," Gideon said lamely. "My mistake."

"You were looking in the mirror," Abe said. "You saw it backwards."

"I guess so. Sorry," he said again, feeling idiotic. "I don't know what I was thinking of." But he knew very well; he had a case of left-handed mallet murderers on the brain.

"What's the big deal anyway?" Leon asked.

"No big deal," Abe said. "So, let's have some lunch, and we'll have our little talk."

He tore open a brown paper bag, removed its waxed-paper-wrapped contents, and spread it out as a make-do tablecloth. He and Leon had their meals with them, but Gideon was empty-handed; he had promised to meet Julie at the George for a late lunch. Still somewhat disconcerted, he peeked once again at Leon in the mirror—right-handed, definitely right-handed—and brought back the coffee mugs.

"Jesus Christ," Leon said. "Fish paste." He was peering into one of the two sandwiches packed for him by his landlady. He groaned and shook his head in waggish despair. "The English."

Abe smiled tolerantly. As well he could, Gideon thought. Mrs. Hinshore had provided a thick, aromatic roast-beef-and-horseradish sandwich for him.

"Wow," Leon said, watching him unwrap it. "I think I'm staying at the wrong place." He was relaxed and smiling, his elbow over the back of his chair.

"Leon," Gideon said, "do you remember coming up with a fragment of a human femur a few weeks ago?"

"Uh-uh."

"November one, it would have been. It was never entered in the field catalog."

"Maybe," Leon said absently, chewing slowly, "but I don't think so."

"You don't *think* so?" Abe looked up sharply from his sandwich. "A human bone isn't important enough to remember?"

"Well, sure it's important, Abe," Leon replied with some edge, "and I guess I'd remember it if I dug it up. So I guess I didn't."

Abe put the sandwich down on the paper sack and reached inside his cardigan sweater. His hand emerged with the find card, which he extended to Leon.

Leon wiped his fingers, took the card, and frowned. "Huh," he said, " 'human femur, left, partial.' That's my handwriting, all right. . . . Boy, it's hard to remember. You're talking about a month ago; we've dug up a lot of stuff since." He shook his head at the card and handed it back. "I don't know what to say, Abe."

He took another dreamy bite of his sandwich. "Wait a minute; maybe I do remember." He swallowed, his eyes rolled upward. Gideon was struck with the distinct impression that some quick fabrication was underway. "Yeah, that's right—I found *something* I thought might be a human bone, and I wrote it on the find card. I remember, I got all excited about it." He laughed merrily at himself. "And then when Jack looked at it, he said it was just a piece of a steatite carving.'' Again he chuckled at himself.

"That's hard to buy, Leon,'' Gideon said. "A couple of weeks ago you recognized the difference—a damn subtle one—between the ribs of a deer and those of a human being. Now you're saying you couldn't tell the difference between a stone carving and a femur?''

Leon hunched his shoulders and spread his hands humorously. "What can I say? I'm human too.''

Abe looked at him, running a finger over his chin. "In the field catalog on November first, there is only one entry: four faience beads. No steatite carving.''

Thoughtfully, Leon reached into his paper sack, ignoring a second sandwich and bringing out a roll of mints. He offered it around. "Polos. They're like Lifesavers.'' Gideon and Abe declined, and Leon popped one into his mouth and dropped the roll into a shirt pocket. "Well,'' he said at last, "I sure don't know how to account for it. Maybe I got the date wrong on the card.''

"That's possible,'' Abe said pleasantly, "but in the whole catalog there's no steatite carving.''

Again Leon spread his hands.

"There was something else, Leon,'' Gideon said. "Originally, you put down the depth as twenty-one inches, then crossed it out and changed it to twelve. What was that about?''

"I did?'' Leon asked for the card back from Abe and made a show of studying it intently. "Oh,'' he said with a smile, "I see what you mean. No big mystery. I just transposed the numbers by mistake. Do it all the time. I'd make a hell of a meter-reader, huh?'' Still smiling, he handed the card back to Abe. "Boy, you guys are *picky!* And I thought Nate gave me a hard time.''

"Was Nate giving you a hard time?'' Gideon asked.

"Well, no, not exactly a hard time.'' Was it Gideon's imagination or did Leon seem a little uneasy? "But we've been spending a couple of evenings a week over beers, having some good old-fashioned arguments about my dissertation.''

"He's chairing your committee, isn't he?"

"Yeah, and he keeps wanting me to do the thing like a technician—which is just what *he* is, when you come down to it—but I just can't do it. You know, that's exactly what's wrong with archaeology: The emphasis is all on data, on digging up *things* and recording them." He leaned forward intently. "If we spent half as much time thinking about what it all means as we do photographing and drawing and recording every crummy, dog-biscuit potsherd we dig up, maybe we'd *know* something."

"I think you have a point," Gideon said, as willing as ever to take up an academic argument, but not unaware that Leon had rather skillfully changed the subject, "but you have to remember that archaeology is a funny science. Even at its best, it obliterates evidence as it discovers it. If you have poor scholarship in the field, you destroy future knowledge. Look at the nineteenth-century archaeologists. Look at Schliemann; if he had known how to properly record and catalog what he found at Troy—"

"There, that's just what I mean. We think in terms of catalogs, lists of *things*. We shouldn't be writing catalog entries; we should be writing chapters on the social history of mankind. We're supposed to be humanists, aren't we? —not compilers of minutiae that nobody gives a damn about, and that don't matter a damn when it comes down to it."

Gideon was experiencing something close to déjà vu. This was another installment of the discussions *he* had had with Nate over those beers so long ago. Only Gideon had been on Leon's side of the fence then. Leon put his argument very well, better than Gideon had at the time, and Gideon sympathized with his impatience even if he no longer quite agreed.

"You got to remember," Abe put in, "sure, we're humanists, but also we're scientists, not philosophers. We got to depend on empirical data for our conclusions. If you start with lousy data, you get rotten conclusions."

Leon laughed good-naturedly. "The two of you sound like Nate. I can see where he gets his ideas. You ought to join us at the George one night; you'd enjoy it. But I still say the proper aim of archaeology is to learn about the people who came before us, not about inanimate artifacts."

" 'You are not wood,' " said Abe, " 'you are not stones, but men.' " He shrugged. "Shakespeare," he said apologetically. "Mark Antony."

Leon laughed again. "You guys are really something." He closed his paper sack. "Well, I guess I'll get back out to the dig. I really enjoyed talking to you."

"I don't think we're quite finished yet," Abe said. "I'm still not so clear on this bone you didn't find."

Leon looked at both of them, his youthful, trimly bearded face showing its first indication of strain. "Look, if you're accusing me of something, how about telling me what it is?"

"Nobody's accusing you, Leon," Gideon said. "We've found a pretty peculiar discrepancy, and we're just trying—"

"Well, why the hell don't you talk to Frawley?" Leon stood abruptly and pointed at the find card. "If I said I found something, I found it. That card was in the file, wasn't it? Why don't you ask Frawley why he didn't put it in the catalog?"

"We did ask him," Gideon said. "He says he never heard about a femur, and you never turned in a card."

"Well, he's lying."

"Hold it a minute," Abe said. "Let me get this straight. Now you're saying you *did* find it and you told him about it?"

Leon made a jerky, exasperated gesture with his hand. "I'm saying I don't remember—but if I wrote it on the card, then obviously I did. Jesus Christ, that's why we *have* the cards; so if we forget something, it's down on paper." He breathed deep, closed his eyes for a moment, and smiled at them. "I'm sorry, I guess I'm a little jumpy. Who isn't? I think I need a walk, if it's okay with you." He made for the door without waiting for an answer.

"Sure, why not?" Abe said, and then held up the sack Leon had left behind. "Don't forget your fish paste."

* * *

"There's an old story," Abe said, as Leon, clutching his paper bag, shut the door none too gently behind him. "Skolnick borrows a kettle from Mandlebaum, and when he brings it back, Mandlebaum says, 'Look, there's a big hole in this kettle; how am I supposed to use it anymore? You got to give me another one.' Skolnick says no he won't, so they argue about it, and finally they agree to go in front of the rabbi to settle it. You know this story?"

"Does a horse in a bathtub come into it?"

"No, that's a different story. In this one, they go in front of the rabbi, and here's what Skolnick tells him: 'In the first place, Rabbi, it's a lie that I borrowed a kettle from Mandlebaum. Never did I borrow anything from him. In the second place, the kettle had a hole in it already when he lent it to me. And in the third place, it was in perfect condition when I gave it back to him. So you can see I'm completely innocent. Don't blame me.'"

Gideon laughed as he finished his coffee. He went to a sink in the corner to rinse both cups. "It sounds like Leon's story all right: In the first place I never found a femur; in the second place, if I did, I don't remember; and in the third place, I only *thought* I found it—it was really a steatite carving."

"And in the fourth place," Abe said, stretching, his hands clasped behind his neck, "it must be Frawley who made the mistake in the first place, so don't blame me."

The find card was lying on the table. Gideon picked it up, read it once more, and waved it gently back and forth. "You know, Abe, I'm not sure what this is about, but something tells me it's important."

"Me, too. I agree with you a hundred percent. There's funny business, all right, only what it is I don't know."

Gideon looked at his watch. "Almost one o'clock. I'm going to go down the hill and have lunch with Julie. And I think I ought to drop by the Cormorant and talk to Nate about this."

"Nate? I wish you luck. Twice I tried to talk to him yesterday, just to cheer him up, and he wouldn't even come to the door." He shook his head worriedly. "All day long he sits in his room and sulks. They bring him his meals, which he doesn't eat."

"Well, it's easy to understand."

"Sure, but healthy it's not. Nathan's got a depressive side to him, you know that? Maybe even melancholic. Healthy," he repeated darkly, "it's not."

□ 16 □

BUT NATE, IF he didn't look precisely healthy, was far from melancholic when Gideon saw him next, and he was certainly not sulking in his room or refusing to eat. He was, in fact, at a table in the George, with the scant remains of a wedge of pork pie in front of him, while the barmaid was exchanging the empty, foam-webbed pint glass on his table for a second one brimming with dark, creamy stout. There was also a nearly empty highball glass before him. Flushed and disheveled, he leered and mumbled at the waitress, who gave him the blind smile reserved for unwelcome attentions from such patrons and hurried away.

This was all startlingly un-Natelike behavior. As often as the two them had huddled over mugs of weak beer in their graduate-student days, Gideon had never seen him drink enough to get sloppy. For a moment, Gideon, coming through the door with Julie, stared. Nate stared blearily back.

"Hey, Gid! Come on over. Buy you a drink. Bring the foxy lady."

Gideon hesitated, and then began to steer Julie toward his table. "That's Nate Marcus. I'd like to talk to him."

"That's Nate Marcus? The intense, dogged scientist I've been hearing about?"

"In the flesh, and stewed to the gills."

The closer they came, the tighter he seemed. Sweating and red-eyed, he wavered as he leaned forward to push out a chair for Julie, and he moved with a drunk's exaggerated slow motion, as if his own chair was balanced precariously on a tightrope instead of sitting firmly on the sturdy old floor of the George.

"What are you drinking?" His speech was slow too, and overly precise. He'd been drinking, it appeared, for quite a while.

"Nothing, thanks. We just came in for some lunch. Julie, this is Nate Marcus. Nate, this is my wife, Julie."

"What do you mean, nothing? How often do you get offered a drink by an old buddy you just helped crucify?" He made an ugly, rattling, laughing sound.

Gideon sighed. It didn't seem too promising. "I think maybe we'd better talk another time." He began to get up.

"Wait, hold it . . . please." Nate's hand pawed flabbily at his arm. "I'm sorry," he said. "Not mad at you." His reddened eyes focused more or less on Julie. "How do you do, Mrs. Oliver? I seem" he explained graciously, "to be a little drunk." To Gideon he said, "Stay, please." Gideon lowered himself back into his chair.

When the barmaid came for their order, he and Julie both asked for Ploughman's lunches. Nate ordered pints of stout for them as well. "Put it," he declaimed, "on my bill. If you please."

"Nate," Gideon said, "there's no reason—"

Nate closed his eyes and held up his hand. "No, no, no, no. Nope." His head rotated gingerly back and forth. "No. Insist. Want you to know there aren't any hard feelings. Just trying to do your job, that's all. Should have listened to you in first place. But . . . but . . ." His voice trailed away while he stared glumly at his pork pie. Then, as if drawing inspiration from it he went on. "But . . . God—damn—it," he said with labored precision, "how could you possibly think that I would . . . that I could fake a . . ."

"I never thought you did, Nate. Somebody did, but not you."

Nate shook his head and blinked. "But that's what I can't

understand. How could ... I'm telling you, I found it *myself!*" His hand jumped convulsively and knocked over the highball glass. The amber dregs ran over the wooden table, releasing a fog of Scotch fumes. Nate seemed not to notice. He stared earnestly at Gideon.

"What Gideon means," Julie said soothingly, "is that someone tricked you somehow."

"Tricked me?" He weighed this while he took another pull at his stout. "No, impossible. I found it by accident. It could easily have laid ... lain there another three thousand years. It was under a bush, between the roots, with only a little bit sticking up. You could hardly see it when you looked right at it; just a tiny, teeny, weeny—"

"Then how did you see it?" Gideon asked.

"I thought," Nate said grandly, "that you believed me."

"I do," said Gideon, not a hundred percent sure that he did, "but just how *did* you see it?"

"Well." Nate appeared to be conducting a boozy search of his mind. "I was coming back from a walk at lunch, right? Okay. There was this scrap of paper on the ground, caught in the brush. I just happened to see it shine in the sun. Just a shiny blue scrap of paper. Naturally, I bent down to pick it up." He turned to Julie and explained primly, "Good housekeeping is essential during any excavation. That's what good archaeology comes down to: good housekeeping." He raised his glass, toasting good housekeeping, good archaeology, or both, then drank and put the glass carefully down again, leaving a foamy mustache on his lip. He looked blankly at both of them, and Gideon thought he might be wondering who they were and where he was. But surprisingly, he found his thread again.

"I bent down to pick it up," he repeated, "and there, just a few inches away, I saw it. It was curved," he said, with sad intensity. "I knew it was part of a skull right away. ..." His eyes had begun to brighten, as if he'd momentarily forgotten what had happened since, but he checked himself, shivered, and stopped speaking.

The barmaid arrived with Julie's and Gideon's pints and wiped up Nate's spilled drink, keeping well clear of him.

Tonelessly, Nate said, "Cheers," but did not lift his glass when they drank.

Gideon put down his glass. "Nate, forget about that part of it for a while. I want to ask you—"

"Forget about it!" he said in a strangled voice. With an effort he composed himself. "Want to ask me what?" he said calmly, then stifled a burp. "Pardon me," he said to Julie.

"Was another bone ever found up there on Stonebarrow? A femur?"

"No. No other bones. No femurs, no nothing. Why, what's it to you?" He snickered vapidly, cleared his throat, and put on a serious expression again. "Who says there was a bone?"

"Leon Hillyer wrote up a find card on a partial femur."

"Leon Hillyer," Nate muttered with disgust, and then mumbled some more.

"Pardon?"

"I said," Nate enunciated loudly, "that he is too damn incompetent to fill in a find card correctly."

Gideon let that sink in for a few seconds. Then he said, "He strikes me as kind of bright. Didn't he win a Gabow Award a few years ago?"

"Gabow Award," Nate grumbled. "He's glick and he's slib, that's all he is."

"Pardon?" Gideon said again.

"I *said*," Nate practically shouted, "that he is gl . . . slick and glib, that's all. Wants to jump to grand conclusions without going through all the grubwork." He swallowed a long draught of the stout and studied the glass somberly. "Hell, who doesn't? But that's what archaeology is: recording and counting and sorting. And," he added with a fierce look at Julie, "housekeeping."

"I'm sure it is," Julie said politely.

"Damn right." Nate closed his eyes and seemed to doze.

The barmaid brought their Ploughman's lunches: warm rolls, butter, big crumbly, blue-veined wedges of Stilton, pickled onions, tomato, and chutney. " 'Kew," she said.

"You don't suppose the gentleman wants another glass of stout?"

"I don't think so," said Gideon.

"That's good," she responded sensibly, and went away.

"What do we do now?" Julie asked.

"Eat, I guess, and let Nate enjoy his snooze. I'll get him back to the Cormorant when we're done. It's only a couple of blocks."

Julie thoughtfully sliced into a large pickled onion. "Poor, poor man. Do you still believe he didn't do it himself? Plant the skull, I mean?"

"Yes, I do. Even though Frawley says he did."

Nate had begun to snore softly. Gideon turned his own chair slightly away from him and cut off a section of cheese. He was extremely hungry. "The Stilton's good, isn't it?"

"Mmm, fabulous. I suppose you're going back up to Stonebarrow Fell after lunch? No country walks today?"

"I think I'd better." He smiled and caressed the back of her hand with his fingertips. "Poor Julie. I've been ignoring you, haven't I?"

"Oh, that's okay; I know Abe needs you. You know what I'd really like to do, though?"

"Speak," Gideon managed, with his mouth full of roll and chutney, "and it's yours."

"Do you remember that beautiful meadow on the way to Wootton Fitzpaine, where we sat on a log for a while?"

Gideon nodded. "Dyne Meadow."

"Uh-huh. Well, there's a full moon tonight. I looked it up; it comes up at seven-oh-four. Wouldn't it be lovely to go back there, sit on that log, and watch the moonrise? The sky's clear and it's not very cold. Am I being silly?"

"I think," Gideon said, "it sounds like a great idea. We'll have dinner early and take along some brandy with us."

Julie smiled and fell happily to her chutney.

"Grubwork," Nate announced startlingly, "and Hillyer thinks he's too damn brilliant to be bothered with it. *That's* his problem. Archaeology is ninety percent grubwork and ten percent brainwork." He inhaled noisily. "And fifty percent housework. Leon thinks it's a hundred percent intell . . . intellectualization.''

"Yes," Gideon said. "he told me that the two of you have had a few friendly arguments about that.''

"*Friendly arguments?*" Astonished, Nate stared woozily at Julie. "You hear that? Friendly arguments! Ha, ha.''

"They weren't friendly?" Gideon asked.

"*Un*friendly arguments, that's what they were. I told him last summer, back at Gelden, I told him all right.'' He looked accusingly at his glass. "You bet I did.''

"Told him what, Nate?''

"Told him," Nate said, "that unless he showed me on this dig that he was at least *trying* to learn how to do the grubwork, I wasn't going to approve his dissertation, and I was going to recommend that he be fulnk . . . flunked out. And . . . and he hasn't made one goddamn effort—not one. So's gonna be goom-bye, Leon. Ho, ho, ho.''

"Wait a minute, Nate. You're telling me Leon is *flunking?*''

"Damn right. I don't give a damn how many Gabows he wins. Archaeology is ninety percent grubwork, eighty percent—''

"And he *knows* you're flunking him?''

"Well . . . sure. . . .''

"Leon Hillyer!'' Gideon whispered fiercely. Why hadn't it occurred to him before? Nate had practically leveled an accusing finger at Leon ten minutes ago—without knowing it, of course—and it had gone right by Gideon. He jumped up and went to the bar.

"Do you have any candy?''

The man behind the bar gestured to a rack of packaged candies near the cash register. "What'll it be?''

Gideon pointed. "Those.''

He handed over seven pence, took the candy, and went back to the table. Nate was hectoring Julie.

"Grubwork! Grubwork, grubwork, grubwork—''

"Nate," Gideon interrupted, slipping back into his seat, "you found the skull when you were on a walk during the lunch break, right?''

" 'S right.''

"Do you usually take the same walk?"

"Sure, why shouldn't I?" He glared truculently at Gideon. "Eat a sandwich, then circle the fell. Takes ten minutes. So what?"

"And a scrap of paper caught your attention, and then you saw the fragment?"

Nate made a vexed sound deep in his throat. He was getting sleepy. "Already tol' you, din' I?"

"And what color was the paper?"

"How the hell would I know? Who gives a—" He turned to Julie. "Par'n me."

"You already told me once," Gideon said. "I just want to hear it again."

Nate squeezed his eyes shut and puffed out his cheeks. "Boo," he said.

"Blue?"

"Buh-loo." One eye opened stickily, and then the other. "Or was it gheen?"

"Or both?" Gideon asked. "Like this?" He opened his hand to show the roll of Polos lying on his palm; green and white lettering on a blue background.

Nate stared for so long that Gideon began to think he'd gone to sleep again, this time with his eyes open, but at last, with amazement in his voice, he said, " 'S right. 'S what it was—Polos. How the hell you know tha'?"

Very far gone now, he fell back in his chair, made a swipe at his empty glass of stout, and knocked that over too. "Don' feel too great," he said. "Wan' go home." Then he started snoring again, a little less softly and a lot more wetly.

Julie, who had continued to make progress with her lunch, wrinkled her nose and pushed away her plate. "I guess I've had enough. Now will you tell me what this is all about? What's so important about Polos?"

"If you had a project director," Gideon said, "who took a predictable walk every day, and who was a bug on housekeeping, and you wanted him to 'accidentally' find a half-buried skull fragment, what would be easier than planting it in his path and then leaving a crumpled-up, bright-blue candy wrapper right there where it would be sure to catch his eye?''

"And you think that's what this Leon Hillyer did?"

"Well, he's popping one of these mints every time you look at him, so he'd sure have a supply of wrappers. And a reason."

"To make Nate look bad, you mean? Maybe get him fired?"

"That's the idea. Leon might easily do better with another major prof who saw things more his way."

Julie shook her head doubtfully. "It sounds pretty far-fetched."

"This whole affair is far-fetched. Anyway, it worked; Nate's in disrepute, isn't he? And he's damn likely to lose his job at Gelden."

"But wait a minute now. Didn't you tell me that Jack Frawley said that Randy said... whew, I'm getting mixed up... that Randy told him that Nate had planted the skull himself?"

"That's what he said, all right, and you're not the only one who's confused." Gideon pushed his chair back from the table. "I think I ought to go back up the hill and talk with a few people, starting with Leon."

"And leave me," Julie said, her voice rising, "with this"—she pointed at the rhythmically oinking archaeologist—"this *body?*"

"No, I'll get him back to his place first. You stay and finish your Guinness. See you later, honey." He tapped Nate on the arm. "Ready?"

"Hoo," Nate said, "I feel lousy."

With Gideon's considerable help, he got to his feet and managed a reasonably steady gait to the door. Once in the street, the fresh air seemed to revive him a little, and they proceeded in stately silence to the Cormorant, a graciously moldering old inn with some elderly potted plants on the sidewalk in front and a proprietorial ale sign swinging gently over the entrance. *Courage*, it said, as if offering solace or guidance.

Unlocking the door to Nate's room presented certain

difficulties, inasmuch as Nate insisted on doing it himself, but finally it was accomplished, and he looked gravely across the threshold at Gideon.

"Who . . . whom . . . you think murdered Randy?"

"It beats me, Nate."

"Me, too,. You b'lieve I did it?"

"No."

Nate nodded with satisfaction and beckoned Gideon closer with a crooked finger. "Me neither," he whispered. Then he burped, yawned, and gently closed the door.

□ 17 □

IT WAS APPARENT that Leon sensed something was wrong the moment Gideon told him he wanted to speak with him. Quietly, he stepped away from the group at the dig and trailed Gideon to the workroom with the anxious air of an eight-year-old following his father out to the woodshed.

"I want to ask you something about the Poundbury skull," Gideon said as soon as they sat down at the table, "and I think you'd better consider very carefully before you answer it."

Leon's hand darted to his short golden beard, tugging at it under his chin. "The P-P-Poundbury Skull?"

Gideon was finally onto something real. It was the first time he'd seen Leon genuinely ruffled. "Did you take the Poundbury calvarium from the Dorchester Museum," he said, sounding to himself very much like Inspector Bagshawe at his most orotund, "bury it here at Stonebarrow Fell, and then lead Nate to it?"

"Lead him to it? What do you m-mean, lead him to it?"

Gideon took the roll of Polos from his jacket pocket and slapped it onto the table. Leon's left eyelid twitched and then began to quiver, and the color drained from his face as suddenly as if someone had pulled a plug. A muscle leaped at the side of his throat. It was extremely quiet in the shed. The metal walls creaked gently, expanding in the afternoon sunlight. Someone had been gluing pottery not long ago, and the air was sharp with acetone.

"Yes," Leon said, so faintly that the whispered, sibilant *s* was all that could be heard.

Gideon was surprised. He didn't quite know what he had been expecting, but it wasn't a flat admission.

"To make Nate look bad?" he asked quietly. "To get him out of your hair?"

"Yes," Leon said again, more audibly this time. His eyelid still trembled slightly, and now it drooped stubbornly halfway over the eye. He tilted his head slightly back to look out from under it. "W-what are you going to do?"

"Leon, there's only one thing to do. Everyone concerned in this has to be told."

Leon lunged forward in his chair, his clenched fists coming down hard on the table. "Gideon, *please!* I n-n-never meant to go this far—I'm begging you . . . !"

"It's got to be done, Leon."

"But what w-will happen to me?"

"I don't know. When we're done here, I'm going to go down and see Nate. I want him to know first, and we'll see where he wants to take it from there." Assuming, of course, that he was sober enough to make any sense of it.

Leon dropped his head and massaged his eyes hard. "Oh, God," he whispered, "I can't believe this is happening."

Paradoxically, Gideon was sorry for this intelligent, articulate, advantaged young man, now reduced to twitching and stuttering, who had cold-bloodedly and deceitfully tried to ruin his gullible professor. Nate's career, it now seemed, might be salvaged, but Leon, with all his bright promise, was through in anthropology. An episode like this would never be forgiven. Nor should it, Gideon reminded himself sternly.

"Who else was in on this?" he asked on a hunch. Professor Hall-Waddington had mentioned an American student "slouching about" Pummy's case, and that didn't sound like the quick, graceful Leon.

"What?" Leon asked dully, his face still pale, his eyelid still drooping.

"Was anyone else involved?"

Leon sighed again. "Uh, no." There was a scarcely noticeable pause between the two syllables.

"I understand the 'no.' What does the 'uh' mean?"

Leon said nothing.

"Come on, Leon. Who else?"

Leon finally had his eyelid under control. "Randy Alexander," he said, not looking at Gideon.

Randy. Gideon didn't know if he was surprised or not, or if it made sense or not. On the whole, he thought it did. If nothing else, it forged that missing link, that connection Abe had foreseen, between the Poundbury affair and the murder. But beyond that, Gideon was almost as much in the dark as ever. Just what *was* the connection? Had Randy been killed because he'd threatened to expose the hoax? *Had* he in fact threatened to expose it? Had he gotten cold feet, and then tried to lie his way out of it before he got into trouble, first with Frawley and then with Gideon?

Gideon made a slight head-shaking motion. The more he found out, the less clear—if that were possible—everything became. "Why was Randy in on it?" he asked. "The same reason you were?"

"Randy? No, he just did it for a lark, for the fun of it. I talked him into it. It was easy."

That fit in with what Gideon knew about Randy. "Leon," he said, "this throws a new light on Randy's murder."

"His *murder!* I don't—you don't th-th-think I had anything to do with that? Jesus . . ." His voice petered out in a plaintive squeak.

"I'm not sure. Did you?"

"*No!*" Leon said. "I swear! I'm telling you the truth. How can y-y-y-you th-th-th . . ." In his frustration, he hammered on the table with his fist. This was no simple, frightened stammer, Gideon saw, but a profound speech impediment, surfacing under pressure.

"All right, Leon, all right, but there's a connection; I'm sure of that. Whether you know what it is I don't know."

"I *don't.* You've got to buh-buh-believe me!"

"Okay, calm down. That's up to the inspector to look into, anyway."

"You have to tell him about it?"

"You better believe it."

Leon twisted restlessly in his chair, then jumped up and walked to the other end of the table, picking up a couple of as-yet-unglued pottery shards and aimlessly pressing them together while he stared out the window. Gideon could see he was trying to pull himself together as well, and he let him take his time. Leon's surprising collapse into stuttering panic had unnerved Gideon, had made him feel unaccustomedly mean.

After a long time Leon spoke in a subdued, calm voice. "I'd like to be the one Nate hears it from."

Gideon hesitated, but the idea appealed to his sense of justice, or possibly of poetic justice. "All right. But I want to be there."

"Can I do it tomorrow morning?"

"No, I think it had better be today. This evening," he amended. That would give Nate a chance to sober up. "And the others are going to have to be told too. We'll call a meeting after dinner, say seven o'clock, and get Nate there. You can tell everyone at once."

With his back still to Gideon, he nodded stiffly. "God!" he said with muffled fervor.

"I'll tell them if you don't want to," Gideon said.

Leon shook his head. "No, let me, please. Really, it isn't the way you think it is—not exactly. You'll see."

"All right. But I still have a few more questions—"

"One more favor?" Leon interrupted. "Can I answer them tonight? I promise I'll be there, and I promise to answer everything. I give you my word. I just . . . I need to psych myself up. But right now, I . . . I mean I can hardly stand to hear myself talk."

Gideon felt much the same. "Okay, Leon," he said after a moment's hesitation. "Tonight."

"Thank you. You won't regret it. Would I be pushing my luck if I asked you not to tell anyone about it before then?"

"Why not?"

Leon shrugged, turning the brown ceramic fragments over and over. "I don't know. It just feels right for me to . . . to 'fess up on my own." He smiled weakly. "And right after the meeting I'll go to the police station with you. Or tomorrow morning if they're not open. Please."

For the third time Gideon hesitated, and for the third time he acquiesced, this time against what he knew to be his better judgment. He knew why he was doing it too. At the back of his mind was an image of Randy asking for his help on the misty hillside and Gideon stiffly putting him off—and a second image of Randy the next time he saw him, on the mortuary table. Irrational as it might be, Gideon found it hard to be adamant with Leon.

"All right," he said. "I'll keep it between us. But only until seven P.M. If you're not there right on the button, then I tell them.'"

"Fair enough. But I'll be there. And thanks."

At the door, Gideon stopped Leon by placing a hand on his sleeve. "Leon, there's something I don't understand."

Leon turned mutely toward him.

"Why, a Polos wrapper, of all things? Didn't it occur to you someone might connect it with you?"

Leon's smile, if it could be called that, reminded Gideon of the stiffened rictus sometimes encountered on a corpse. "I never meant him to find the damn thing. It was an accident, can you believe it?"

"I still don't understand."

Leon sighed. "Look, Randy and I spent a whole night up there, getting the skull in the ground just right, you know? Then the next afternoon we were going to check it out again just to make sure it looked all right—no footprints or trowel marks, that kind of thing. And *then* we were going to leave some junk around to catch Nate's eye—an old pop bottle, a milk carton—"

"So why the Polos?"

Leon made an impatient little clicking noise with his teeth. "I told you—it was just an accident. I must have dropped the thing there while I was working on the skull. I would have found it the next day when I checked things over, but Nate found it first—absolutely by accident."

He laughed wonderingly. "Still, it added up to the same thing, didn't it? Nate found the skull and went off the deep end. Everything went just the way it was supposed to, until . . ." His eyes, which had been fixed on the floor, rose to meet Gideon's. "Ah," he said softly, "what the hell. I guess I've got it coming." His eyes remained locked on Gideon's. "But I *didn't* kill anyone."

As soon as he walked with Leon back out to the dig and then took Abe aside, Gideon regretted his promise.

"You want to have an all-hands meeting at seven o'clock, but the reason is a secret?" There was real surprise in the old man's voice. "From me, it's a secret?"

"Well, it's just . . ."

Gideon glanced down in the pit at Leon, who, with a rake in his hands, was watching him anxiously, his face still pale.

"It's just that I made a promise."

"To who did you make a promise?" Up went a peremptory hand. "Hup! Never mind. Excuse me I should ask. A secret is a secret."

"Come on, Abe," Gideon said miserably, "it's a promise. Give me a break."

Both of Abe's hands went up now, palms toward Gideon, and the frail shoulders shrugged. "Not another word. Why should your old teacher—who taught you everything, and who helps you on your cases all the time, and who's supposed to be running this dig—know what's going on?"

"Good," Gideon said more firmly. "I'm glad you feel that way. We're liable to have a problem with Nate, by the way. He ought to be there, and he was pretty well soused when I left him an hour ago."

"*Nate?*"

"Yes, indeed. He's sleeping it off, I think."

Abe made a decisive little nod. "When we're finished here, I'll go down and fix him up. I'll make him take a guggle-muggle."

"Come again?"

"An old remedy. You mix whiskey, hot tea, molasses, and raw eggs, and swallow it in one gulp."

Gideon made a face. "It sounds terrible."

"That's why you got to drink it in one gulp. You call it a guggle-muggle because that's what it sounds like when it goes down: Guggle, muggle. Believe me, by seven o'clock he'll be fine."

He walked a few steps to the pit and called for attention, his voice thin in the crisp air.

"Hold it a minute, please! We need to have a meeting tonight at seven o'clock. I hope it doesn't interfere with anybody's plans."

Only Sandra appeared annoyed. "How long will it be?"

Abe looked at Gideon, who said, "An hour; maybe more."

"No problems?" Abe asked the group, and waited. Sandra sighed gustily. The others were quiet. "Let's meet at the Queen's Armes, in that room next to the lounge, with all the sofas."

"The sitting room," Gideon said.

"Right, the sitting room. I'll see there's something to nosh on; a little coffee and some Danish."

Gideon started for the shed to do some pottery sorting but had gone only a few steps when he remembered his promise to Julie. He turned around.

"I just remembered. I can't make it at seven. How about eight?"

No one objected. Leon gave him a small, pallid nod. Only Abe spoke. "And why not at seven?"

"Because . . . well, it's just hard for me."

"A secret?" Abe asked drily.

"No, not a secret," Gideon growled. "I just promised my wife I'd walk out with her to Dyne Meadow and, uh, watch the moon come up. At seven-oh-four."

Everyone seemed to look at him for a long time before Abe clapped his hands together. "Okay, folks," he said, "let's get the backfilling all finished up. Leon, you look a little green around the gills. You're all right?"

"I . . . I'm not sure."

Abe nodded knowingly. "The fish paste. You want to lie down? Maybe you should go home early?"

"No—yes, I think maybe that'd be a good idea."

"Go ahead; get some rest. You'll be at the meeting tonight?"

"Definitely." Leon's grayish lips stretched in a sickly smile. "I wouldn't miss it."

By four o'clock the rest of the crew had also left, and Abe and Gideon locked up the gate and walked down the hill together. "Abe," Gideon said as they approached the bottom, "I've been thinking about that femur."

"I've been thinking too."

"In spite of everything else, Nate seems to have run a pretty professional dig. That means that what*ever* it was Leon found, it would have been photographed right away. There must be photographs of it. I think we ought to look through the whole photographic file—"

"This I already did," Abe said. "Nothing."

"Huh," Gideon said.

They walked across the wooden footbridge over the Char, their feet making homely, muffled thumping sounds. Abe stopped suddenly.

"Wait a minute. Tell me something. The boy that got killed—Randy—he was the technician, right? He took the photographs?"

"Right."

"So, tell me, Mr. Skeleton Detective: If the police were investigating his murder, wouldn't they develop any film he had in his camera? In case it should give them a clue?"

"I don't know."

"Of course they would. I read it all the time in detective books. Randy got killed when?"

"November thirteenth, probably."

"And Leon's card got filled out November first. So the pictures were maybe still in the camera. I think you should give Inspector Bagshawe a telephone call."

"I think you're right," Gideon said after a moment.

He called from a red telephone booth on Lower Sea Lane

and got Sergeant Fryer. Abe had been correct. They had
indeed found that Randy's camera contained film, and had
developed it. To their disappointment, the pictures had all
been of rocks, potsherds, and other such useless things. If
Gideon wanted them, he could have them. Inspector Bagshawe
had to pass through Charmouth on his way from work and
would no doubt be glad to drop them off at the Queen's
Armes. Would eight o'clock or thereabouts be convenient?
Eight o'clock, Gideon said, would be perfect.

Abe nodded with satisfaction when Gideon hung up and
told him. "Good," he said, stopping under a sedate sign
that read *Dampiers of Charmouth. Licensed Grocers. Provi-
sion Merchants*. "Maybe we'll find out something. Now I
got to buy what goes into the guggle-muggle, and then
maybe I can get Nate to have a bite before the meeting."

Ten minutes later Gideon was hammering on the door of
the Queen's Armes, hoping that Julie was inside and could
hear him. Andy and his wife, he'd remembered too late, had
gone off shopping again, and Gideon had neglected to take
his key with him. Abe, who probably had one, was of
course at the Cormorant, pouring his horrific concoction
into poor Nate. Whether it sobered him up or not, Gideon
thought, it would surely cure him of any incipient tendency
toward alcoholism.

As far as he knew, there were no other guests at the hotel
to come to his rescue, and the George, which looked so
inviting across the street, would not be open until five,
thereby ruling out the expedient of a cozy pint before the
fire. Gideon was just beginning to feel sorry for himself
when the heavy door swung inward. Paul Arbuckle stood
there, looking, as usual, surprised and gently perturbed.

"Well, hi, Gideon."

"Paul—I thought you weren't due back until tomorrow."

"No, getting back from Dijon is complicated. I had to
leave there today." His eyes brightened. "Boy, Gideon, we
came up with *another* Acheulian scraper, and some worked
Dama clactonia bones. It's fantastic! You ought to come and
see it!"

Gideon, envying him, smiled. "How about letting me in? It's a little chilly out here."

"Sorry." Arbuckle laughed and stood aside.

They walked down the long entry corridor, lined with dark wooden walls, still redolent of cedar after five hundred years. Gideon stopped opposite the Tudor Room.

"Listen, Paul, have you taken any official action on this mess yet?"

"No, not till tomorrow."

"Good. Are you free at seven o'clock tonight?—eight o'clock, rather?"

"Yes, why?"

"There's going to be a meeting of the whole crew here in the sitting room. Something's come up that you're going to want to hear about."

"What?"

"Well, I made a promise that I'd keep the thing under wraps until then," Gideon said, feeling silly, "but you're going to want to rethink the action against Nate when you hear about it."

"And it's a secret?" Arbuckle looked doubtfully at Gideon, then broken into his doughy smile. "All right, I guess I can wait till eight. But don't get your hopes up too high. Nate really has behaved like a fool. Robyn believes he should be drummed out of the corps entirely, and . . . well, to be perfectly frank, I think the poor dumb bastard has it coming." He colored slightly at this excess. "I don't know what your surprise is, but I hope it's a good one."

"It's a good one," Gideon said. Nate might be a poor dumb bastard, but at least he wasn't a dishonest, fraudulent dumb bastard, and that ought to count for something.

"No," Julie called from the bathroom, "I never heard you knocking. I was washing my hair." She came out, with a towel wrapped turban-style around her head, her pretty face freshly scrubbed. She was one of those people who look clean when they're dirty, and when she was newly washed she positively glowed. "What are you looking for?"

Gideon was on his knees and elbows, poking about unde the bed. "My tennis shoes," he said. He got up, went t the bureau in the corner, and looked through the drawers fe a second time. "I thought I'd wear them on our wal tonight in case it's still muddy; they'll be easy to wash." H stood looking around the room, hands on his hips. "Nov where the heck are they? Or did I bring them with me a all?"

Standing before the mirror, Julie tucked her blouse neatl into her gray slacks. "Yes, Gideon," she said patientl "you were wearing them this morning. When you couldn find your slippers."

"Well, I found my slippers. They were under the bec But my tennis shoes are gone. Don't bother looking in th closet," he said as she went to it, "I've already looked i there."

"But you don't always see things when you look."

"I'm telling you they're not there," Gideon grumblec "I may be a little absentminded when I'm thinking abou something important, but—"

With her head still in the closet, Julie stuck out an arr and waggled a large, white, blue-trimmed tennis shoe.

"Sonofagun, that wasn't there two minutes ago," Gideo said.

Julie laughed. "All I can see is this one. We'll find th other one after dinner. You know, you're sure lucky yo have me too take care of you. What did you do before yo found me?"

He came up behind her and wrapped her in his arm: "God only knows," he said.

□ 18 □

Since Abe was ministering to Nate and Arbuckle was having dinner in a Lyme Regis restaurant, they had the cozy dining room to themselves. Gideon was able to put Stonebarrow Fell out of his mind, and they enjoyed a relaxed, dreamy meal.

Then, after another unsuccessful search for the missing sneaker, they walked out to Dyne Meadow. At the end of Barr's Lane, they turned off the flashlight that Hinshore had lent them, and tried to edge gingerly past Bowser's pen, but of course the thing came bounding out, throwing himself hysterically against the chain-link fence.

Once past the formidable hindrance, however, they walked to the meadow and found the big log they had sat on before, damp now in the evening dew. All that was left of the day was a thin, ruddy streak in the west, against which a rolling shoulder of hillside and the ravage silhouette of an ancient stone barn stood out as crisply as an artificial horizon in a planetarium. The rest of the sky was black and as yet moonless, with only a few dim stars, so that they could see little of the meadow around them. A knee-high fog hung over the ground, wispy and vaporous, like mist onstage in a play. The only sounds were the thin plashing of an unseen stream and the soughing of breeze-stirred branches.

In a few minutes the northern sky grew lighter, and then

the top of a stupendous orange moon rose behind distant
trees and swam up with marvelous speed. At the first sight
of it, Julie gasped and reached for Gideon's hand. He put
his other arm around her and pulled her closer, and she
leaned her head on his shoulder. He could smell the clean
fragrance of her hair and, more faintly, that sweet, damp,
grassy bouquet of rural England. How adolescent this was,
he thought, and how heart-wrenching perfect. He sat as still
as he could, wanting nothing to change, and watched the
moon, as three-dimensional as an enormous golf ball, float
upward, paling to a cool alabaster and shrinking as it rose.

When he first heard the sound, he hardly noticed it—a
distant, deep tolling like the pealing of a great, faraway bell.
And then, when it finally did register, it was not in the
neatly organized, orderly convolutions of the cortex, but
somewhere deep in the dark and brutish brain stem that he
perceived it. Before he even knew what it was he heard, the
skin on the back of his neck raised itself, in obedience to
primeval laws, and sent a long shiver crawling down his
spine. He leaped to his feet, turning in the direction of the
sound.

Julie jumped up too. "What *is* it?" she said, her voice
hollow. "Oh, my God—the *dog?*"

For it was unquestionably the dog, and he was unquestionably loose and closing on them, his frenzied baying
nearer now. Speechless, they stared toward the tortured
echoing howl. The moon was behind them, throwing some
light; they could see before them about a hundred feet of
misty meadow, and beyond that the edge of a beech spinney
through which the path from Barr's Lane came.

Paralyzed, his blood like cold sludge in his veins, Gideon
stood stupefied, mindlessly waiting. Now, in addition to the
wild, swelling howl, there was a rapid, rustling patter, and
with the new sound Gideon suddenly found he could move
again. He bent, looking desperately for anything that would
serve as a weapon, and picked up the weathered stub of a
thick branch, as big around as a loaf of bread. Gripping the
damp, heavy wood, he turned toward the awful sounds and
moved in front of Julie, who stood as if petrified.

Julie moved closer to Gideon and put her hand on his arm. She was still wan and tousled, and her black eyes were very bright. "You're really all right?"

"Sure, honestly. *You* are, aren't you?"

"Uh-huh." She smiled tentatively. "You were . . . magnificent."

He laughed. "Told you I had him in the palm of my hand." But he had to close his eyes to fight down a wave of giddiness.

Conley returned and put two objects on the table. "That," he said, "is the chain that holds the back gate shut. It's been cut through, as you can see. And that," he said, indicating the second object, "is a canvas shoe—yours, I should guess."

Gideon picked it up. "Where did you find it?"

"It was in the bushes, not far from the stile. I was lucky to see it. Obviously, someone used it to set the Beast on your scent."

"Is that possible? Can you just walk up to a dog and let it sniff someone's shoes—and then it goes tearing off after him?"

"A hound like Bowser? Most certainly. And with the ground as damp as it is, the dog wouldn't have a problem in the world. They do better in moist weather, you know."

"Someone *wanted* Bowser to kill you?" Julie asked incredulously. "But who? Why would anyone want you dead?"

The answers couldn't have been more obvious. Gideon stood up—a little too suddenly; his vision blurred and a hundred places in his body twinged and burned, as if he'd been rubbed all over with heavy-grade sandpaper. But he was anxious to get going. There were still plenty of things he didn't understand, but now he had a personal score to settle and he wanted to get on with it.

"Let's go," he said to Julie. "It's after eight."

Conley looked startled. "But . . . you can't simply go like that. . . . You must let me—here, let me write down my name and address." He pulled over a notepad that had been near the telephone and began scribbling. "I absolutely insist that all bills be sent to me. And—here—I'll write a little statement that wholly accepts responsibility: "I, Grahame Baldwin Conley. . . ."

Gideon stood there, swaying slightly, his mind still hazy. "No, that isn't necessary. . . ." Standing up so suddenly had been a mistake. He was dizzy as well as muddled. He steadied himself with both hands on the table and made himself focus on the crisp, white pad of paper against the purple check of the plastic tablecloth. Conley's square hand moved purposefully over it.

"You write like a left-hander," Gideon murmured.

"What?" Conley looked up. "I *am* left-handed. Look here, are you sure you're all right? Would you like to stay the night? I can have a bed made up in no time."

Gideon shook his head, smiling. The motion actually seemed to clear his thoughts. "No, thanks." He gestured at Conley's writing hand. "I just seem to have a one-track mind."

"Oh, I see," the colonel said, clearly failing to see.

"And, please, don't worry about any bills. It wasn't your fault."

"I'm afraid I must insist. And shouldn't we call the police?"

"I'll take care of it. Thanks for getting there when you did. You saved our lives."

"Well, of course, old fellow. I'm awfully sorry about all this. I hope you're not too terribly angry."

"Not at you, Colonel." And then, as a rumbling woof from in back shook the house, "And not at Bowser, either."

Not really.

He strode so quickly down Barr's Lane that Julie had to trot to keep up.

"Who wanted to kill you?" she demanded.

"Leon Hillyer. That bastard."

It had to be. And how unbelievably stupid he, Gideon, had been. He'd trustingly promised to tell no one about the skull before eight o'clock—giving Leon a full five hours to figure out a way of getting rid of him. Then, to make it easier, he'd announced in front of all of them that he would be in the dark and deserted Dyne Meadow at precisely 7:04 P.M. And now, with 8:00 come and gone, Leon was no doubt sitting in the Tudor Room, munching Danish pastries, wondering with the rest of them where in the world Gideon Oliver was, and looking as befuddled as anyone else about the reason for the meeting.

Julie jumped in front of him and placed her palms against his chest.

"Whoa."

Impatiently, he stopped.

"Just take it easy," she said. "I've never seen you like this. You're really mad, aren't you?"

"Goddam right I am!"

Goddam right he was. That vicious, fast-talking kid had not only tried to kill *him;* he'd coolly decided to sacrifice Julie, too, no doubt on the off-chance that Gideon had told her about his tawdry little fraud. And, my God, how close it had been!

"Wait a minute," Julie said, "I'm not sure you're thinking clearly. I want to ask you some questions."

"Later. Come on, Julie, get out of my way."

She paid no attention. "First of all, are you saying that Leon not only tried to kill you but murdered Randy, too?"

"Probably. I don't know. I don't have it all figured out yet."

"Then what was that bit about Colonel Conley being left-handed? I thought you suspected him."

"Conley?" Gideon said, surprised. "*Conley?* Not at all. My mind was wandering, that's all. I've got left-handers on the brain. Today I looked in a mirror and accused Leon of being left-handed. I was wrong about that, but I was sure right about—"

And all at once, everything fitted; everything clicked sharply into place, was with the final twist of a Rubik's Cube.

"He *is* left-handed," Gideon said, bedazzled, not sure if he was marveling at his own brilliance or at his own obtuseness.

"Leon? But you told me he was right-handed."

"He *is* right-handed."

Julie peered worriedly up into his face, trying to see his eyes in the dark. "Gideon, darling, don't get angry, but I think you're still a little—"

"I'm not a little anything. What I'm trying to say is that Leon *used* to be left-handed, probably as a kid, but was made to switch over. Parents do that, you know. Only it wasn't complete—it hardly ever is. And so of course he might have swung a mallet with his left hand, particularly if he was excited."

"But how could you possibly know that?"

They began to walk again, more slowly. "Look," Gideon said, "you know the way a left-hander typically holds his hand when he writes?"

"Sort of scrunched over, you mean?"

"Right, with the hand curled around like a hook; inverted writing posture, it's called. It's the way Conley was writing."

"Yes, I know," Julie said with transparent confusion. "But not all left-handers write that way. My sister Karen doesn't."

"That's true, but most of them do, possibly because of the way they're taught to slant their paper in school. But almost no right-hander does."

"I believe you, but I think something is escaping me."

Gideon stopped as they came from the mud and gravel of Barr's Lane to the concrete sidewalk of The Street, Charmouth's concisely named main thoroughfare.

"Julie," he said, "when I looked at Leon in the mirror today and thought he was writing left-handed, it wasn't the mirror-image that made me think so; it was the *way* he was writing—hook-handed. But with his right hand."

"So . . ." Julie frowned, seeing what he was driving at. "You think he learned to write that way as a child—a left-handed child—and then just kept the same position when he was made to change, because that was what he was used to?"

"That's exactly what I think."

"That makes sense, but isn't it kind of . . . well, tenuous?"

"But there's more. There are some problem characteristics that follow when left-handed kids are forced to change hands, at least some of the time, according to a lot of psychologists. And Leon Hillyer's got 'em." Purposefully, he started across the quiet street toward the Queen's Armes.

"Well, what are they?"

"He stutters when he's nervous, and he has a tendency to transpose numbers. He'd written a 'twenty-one' on that find card I told you about, then had to cross it out and put in a 'twelve.' He laughed it off and told me he does it all the time. Damn! And I never figured it out!"

In the dark doorway of the Queen's Armes, she stopped him again, standing in his way. "Gideon, you never stop astonishing me. How do you know such things? Transposed numbers, inverted writing posture—after all, you're an anthropologist, not a—"

"Julie, do you think I don't know what you're doing?"

Even in the darkness he saw her widen her eyes innocently. "Doing?"

"You're temporizing. You're trying to keep me out of there because you think I'm mad enough to do something dumb."

"Well, aren't you? Gideon, if you really think he's a murderer, what you ought to do is tell the police about it."

"I'll tell the police later. First, *I* want to talk to him. Now, are you going to get out of my way?"

It seemed to Gideon that he said it with convincing menace, but she didn't move, except to fold her arms. "Will you stop being so ridiculously macho?" she said. "What are you going to do, for God's sake, beat him up or something?"

"No, I'm not going to beat him up," he said angrily, but Julie's arms-crossed, feet-planted, no-nonsense barring of the door made him laugh and then relax. "I don't know what I'm going to do," he said sheepishly. "I guess I haven't thought it out."

He laughed again and put his arms around her. "Hey, you were pretty magnificent yourself out there in the meadow."

Headlights suddenly loomed, flooding the entryway with

light, and they jumped apart like a couple of kids caught necking. A dark car pulled up to the curb, the light blinked out, and a bulky form slowly emerged.

"Well now," Inspector Bagshawe boomed softly, "no need to look so guilty. I don't suppose that's the first time this old doorway's seen a bit of slap-and-tickle. Mrs. Oliver, I presume? No offense, ma'am."

"Yes, this is my wife," Gideon said, "happily for us all. Julie, this is Inspector Bagshawe."

Bagshawe murmured something and lifted his hat, the first time in a long while that Gideon had seen a man do that. In his other hand he had a large manila envelope. This he handed to Gideon.

"I've brought you your photographs. Twenty-four in all; the undeveloped film in Randy Alexander's camera. Much good may they do you."

"Inspector," Julie said, "there's something we need to tell you." She glanced nervously at Gideon, who didn't object; of course she was right.

"It's Leon, Inspector," Gideon said.

There was a fractional pause. "Is it, now?"

"I'm sure of it. He killed Randy, all right." He smiled. "And he's left-handed, by the way—sometimes, anyway."

"Well now. And am I to be told how you came to these conclusions?"

"You sure are, but later. Right now, why don't we go in and talk to him?"

"You mean he's in there? All wrapped up for me, so to speak? By all means, let's go in then. Wouldn't want him scarpering at this point."

As Gideon opened the door, the light from the entrance hall fell on him. Bagshawe's mildly chaffing manner vanished. "Good Lord!" he exclaimed. "What's happened to you? You look like bloody hell!"

But Gideon was staring at the reception desk at the far end of the ancient corridor. There, Andy Hinshore stood, livid and popeyed, dialing the desk telephone and shaking so hard the two parts of the instrument rattled against each other in his hands. He stared at Bagshawe, somehow recognizing him for a policeman.

"Police?" he said. He stared stupidly at the telephone. "But how . . . I was just calling. . . . Someone's been—there's been a killing!" He blinked twice, and his Adam's apple went ratcheting up and down his throat.

Trembling, his hand rose to point to the age-blackened door of the Tudor Room. "In there."

They flung the door open and burst into the room only to stop short on the threshold, stumbling over each other in a Three-Stooges-like scramble that would in other circumstances have been comical.

Behind them, in an awed voice, Hinshore said unnecessarily: "By the fireplace."

The room, lit only by the dying fire, wavered between darkness and fluttering, warm orange. Objects on the walls—plates, pictures, old copper utensils—danced in and out of focus. Only the hearth itself was clearly lit, and there, on the stone flooring before which people had sat these five hundred years in comradeship and warmth, a man's body lay sprawled, his chin tilted rigidly upward, the golden beard glinting like copper wire in the firelight.

"Leon Hillyer," Bagshawe said with interest, and turned on the light.

□ 20 □

"Now, you just calm yourself, Professor Frawley, and drink some tea," Bagshawe said supportively.

Frawley nodded, brought the steaming cup to his mouth cradled in both hands, and bent his head over it, as a man who had been lost in the snow for two days might lift a mug of brandy.

As soon as Bagshawe had had a quick look at the body, he had called police headquarters, having pretty much to wrest the telephone from the benumbed Hinshore. Sergeant Fryer, lean and dour, quickly arrived with a uniformed constable, and soon after that Dr. Merrill had come. Merrill and the sergeant had at once busied themselves in the Tudor Room with Leon's body, while the constable stood just outside the open door to the sitting room, keeping watch on the dwindling personnel of Stonebarrow Fell.

Bagshawe had taken over the dining room. First he had conferred hurriedly with Gideon, who brought him as up-to-date as he could in ten minutes. Then he called in Jack Frawley. The pot of tea had been politely requested by the inspector—partly, Gideon thought, to calm Frawley, who looked hideous, and partly to give the agitated Hinshore something to do.

Frawley finally put down his cup. "Thank you. I think I'm all right now," he said without conviction.

"Fine, fine," Bagshawe said. "Now, if you'd just go over it again...?" A small pad was before him on the table, and the tip of his tongue emerged to lick the point of a stubby pencil. He was all friendly patience.

"I came in early," Frawley said dully. "Nobody was in the sitting room yet except Nate and Dr. Goldstein, and Nate was... well, not entirely sober, to be perfectly candid. It was a little uncomfortable, so I went into the Tudor Room—just seeing the place, you know." He was speaking in a very low voice, breathing in and out between the sentences. Now he closed his eyes for a moment. "Leon was lying there all... well, you saw him. I think I just stood there, sort of in a trance. Then I heard the front door open and some people come in. I guess I shouted and everybody came running in. That's all."

"And who," Bagshawe said pleasantly, "is everybody?"

"Everybody: Dr. Goldstein, Dr. Arbuckle, Sandra... Barry, I think."

"You think?"

"Well, I wasn't really... I was pretty upset. I think Barry was there. The man who owns the place too. They all came."

"Professor Marcus?"

"No, not Nate. He's really not in very good shape." Neither was Frawley, from the look of him. His face was the color of parboiled chicken.

"And then?" Bagshawe asked. "Did you touch anything?"

"Me, you mean? Oh, no. I could see he was dead; there wasn't anything to do." He turned moist and pleading eyes on Bagshawe. "Inspector, I don't feel very well. If I could lie down..."

"Just a few moments more, sir, if you please. What happened next?"

"I really don't remember too well. Dr. Arbuckle ran in and felt his heart. Then he gave him CPR—" A violent shudder jerked Frawley's shoulders.

Gideon understood his reaction. Leon had been an awful sight. A torn, bloody dent had grooved his forehead and crushed the bridge of his nose, and the very shape of his head was awry. Blood was in abundance, and the poker that had only too clearly done it all lay a few feet away. Julie had fled from the room at once and Gideon had very nearly followed her, but he had made himself remain with the pacific, unperturbed Bagshawe, using his old device of looking without quite looking.

". . . and then," Frawley was saying, "Mr. Hinshore said nobody better touch anything, and he was going to call the police. We all went into the sitting room, and then you came."

"I see," Bagshawe said. "I'll just get that down, if you please."

While he did so, Frawley said, "If I could go now—"

"Very shortly, sir. I believe Professor Oliver has something to ask you, about the Poundbury skull."

"The Poundbury skull?" Frawley repeated dimly, as if he'd never heard of it.

"And your conversation with Randy," Gideon said.

Frawley had the teacup near his face. He clapped it shakily down. "Inspector," he said in a feeble show of spirit, "I really think we could go into this another time."

"No, sir, I think now would be the right time. We could do it at headquarters if you prefer."

"No," Frawley said hurriedly, "we can do it here." He looked mournfully at Gideon. *Et tu, Brute?* said the look in his expressive eyes.

The best approach seemed to be to wade in, and Gideon did. "Jack, this morning you said Randy told you that Nate was behind the fraud."

"That's right, he did. I already told you—"

"Today Leon told me that *he'd* pulled off the Poundbury hoax—with Randy's help. If that's true, why would Randy tell you that Nate did it?"

"How would I know? Who knows what he was thinking? I told you what he said, and that's the truth."

"You've told two different stories," Bagshawe put in. "First you told me that the young man hadn't talked to you at all. And then you said—as Professor Oliver here has pointed out—that he'd accused Professor Marcus—"

"I believe I already explained that. I, ah, may have been in error in withholding information at first, but I meant no harm. I stand firmly on what I said."

"Which time, Jack?" Gideon asked.

"Inspector, do I have to stand for that? I'll swear to what I've said, if necessary."

Bagshawe looked searchingly at him. "Professor Frawley," he said slowly, "I think I must tell you that anything you say may be used—"

Frawley's complexion went from blue-white to dull red. "Is that what's called the usual warning?"

"The Usual Caution, yes, sir."

"All right, then," Frawley said with sulky aggressiveness, "at least I know where I stand."

"I'm not sure you do, Jack," Gideon said. "The Usual Caution is about the same thing as telling you you're about to be arrested for murder."

On that rather large liberty, he looked surreptitiously at Bagshawe and saw the massive eyebrows lift, but the policeman said nothing. Gideon went ahead: "You're in a lot of trouble, Jack, believe me. If you haven't told the truth, you'd better do it now."

Frawley inclined his head. Gideon looked down on bent shoulders and a crown of thinning hair. "Come on, Jack," he said more gently.

Frawley sat up with his eyes still closed. He spoke in a monotone. "When Randy talked to me that morning, he told me . . . what you said."

"That he and Leon had stolen Pummy and put it there for Nate to find?"

Frawley nodded, his eyes still closed. "I guess he had a change of heart, and he wanted me to intercede for him with Nate. I refused; I told him he'd made his own bed and he had to tell Nate himself."

"But he didn't?"

"I guess not."

"And you didn't feel you should tell Nate?"

"No." His eyes popped open and Gideon saw a sullen glimmer in them. "Why should I? Nate made it clear to me enough times my advice wasn't needed. And if he was so obsessed with his theories that he couldn't see through a sophomoric trick like that, he deserved to take the consequences."

His speech had brought color to his cheeks, and he looked belligerently about him. "I don't see that I've done anything so terrible."

"That remains to be seen," Bagshawe said sharply. "Did it never occur to you, while you so judiciously withheld your information, that Mr. Alexander's murder and his part in the hoax might be related?"

"No! I didn't even know there'd *been* a murder until you told us a couple of days ago. I just thought he'd gotten cold feet and run out." He shrugged. "It didn't surprise me."

"And *since* you've learned there's been a murder?"

"I . . . how could I come forward? After not saying anything before? How would I look?"

Bagshawe's beefy but expressive face told him. "And so you were content to leave us with a fabricated and misleading story that cast suspicion on Professor Marcus. I take an *extremely* dim view of this, sir."

In response, Frawley pouted and muttered under his breath like a chastened child who has capitulated—but not quite. Gideon heard, ". . . don't think . . . done anything so wrong . . ."

"Be that as it may," Bagshawe said, and consulted his notes. "This meeting, I understand, was to be in the sitting room. What were you doing in the Tudor Room?"

"I already told you. I was just seeing what the place looked like."

"And you just happened to wander into the Tudor Room and just happened to find Leon Hillyer's body."

"Yes!"

"I think we've finished here, Professor Frawley."

"You mean I can go back to my place now?"

"I'd rather you stay here in the Queen's Armes. If you still need to lie down, tell P. C. Piggott. I'm sure a bed can be found."

* * *

"I don't know about you," Gideon said when Frawley had left, "but I'm a lot more confused than I was an hour ago. I would have bet anything on Leon's being the murderer."

"And so may he be," Bagshawe replied. "Getting killed oneself is hardly proof of innocence, now is it? No, I rather like your little theory of an hour ago, left-handed mallet wielder and all."

"But then who killed Leon?"

"Tea?" Bagshawe asked. He leaned comfortably forward, lifted the cozy from the pot, and poured two cups. "Who killed Leon," he mused. "That's the question, all right. Well, it might have been the gentleman who just left, mightn't it? He didn't know, after all, that Leon had already spilled the beans to you, and he might have killed him to keep him from doing so. Do you remember what he said?" He flipped a page to look at his notes. " 'How could I come forward after not saying anything before? How would I look?' He could have killed Leon to protect his reputation, such as it is." Bagshawe sucked some tea from his cup and rolled it around his mouth.

Gideon was doubtful. "Maybe. I don't doubt Frawley's base motives, you understand, but I have a hard time visualizing him strangling someone or crushing a head with a poker. Now, poison would be something else."

As the inspector grimly smiled his agreement, Constable Piggott ambled by the dining-room entrance. Bagshawe called to him. "Would you give my compliments to Dr. Arbuckle and ask him if he'd be kind enough to step in for a few moments?"

"Sir!" said P. C. Piggott, and in a few seconds Arbuckle came hesitantly in, looking shaken. In him this showed itself as a constrained stiffness of manner, a quiet stolidity slightly more pronounced than usual.

"Now, Dr. Arbuckle," Bagshawe said, after he had ceremoniously poured the tea and Arbuckle had taken an apathetic sip, "if you would tell us what you saw, I'd be obliged."

"I was in my room upstairs," Arbuckle said, looking at the table, "and I heard somebody shout; Dr. Frawley, I

think. It took me a few moment to—to collect my wits, and
then I ran downstairs to the Tudor Room. Everyone was
standing in a huddle near the door, not moving.'' He groped
for his cup and drank some more. ''In a state of shock, I
suppose. It was horrible. He was lying there, all . . . all . . .''

''Yes, of course. By 'everyone' you refer to . . . ?''

''All of them. Everybody that's in the sitting room now.
Well, except Dr. Marcus, of course.'' There was a prim
little twitch of his lips, and he pushed his glasses up on his
nose. ''He wasn't in any condition to come.''

''I see,'' Bagshawe said, writing. ''And what happened
when you got there?''

''I thought maybe I could do something for the boy. I
went to him—I'm afraid I had to push some people out of
the way—and did my best. I tried to start his heart, tried
mouth-to-mouth resuscitation, but . . . I don't think there was
anything anybody could do.''

''Very commendable, sir,'' Bagshawe said. ''It must have
been extremely unpleasant.''

''I just felt I had to do it.'' Arbuckle said simply.

''Considering the state of the body,'' Bagshawe said,
''your clothing is remarkably clean.''

''It is now, yes. I ran up to my room to wash and change.
I got blood all over my shirt, my hands, my . . . mouth. And
it wasn't only blood. . . . You know, I've never seen a violent
death before. . . .'' For the first time his rigid posture crumbled slightly. He lifted his eyes from the table, and in his
darting glance around the room there was horror.

''And the clothes you were wearing at the time?'' Bagshawe
asked. ''Where are they now? I don't mean to press you.''

''It's all right,'' Arbuckle said, regaining his tenuous
self-control. ''I just threw them on the floor, I think.''

''I see. It might be necessary for us to take those away.
Would you have any objection?''

Arbuckle seemed surprised. ''No, but why?''

''Well, it's always possible that in brushing against the
body something important might have adhered to your
clothing. One never knows.''

"You're welcome to them." Arbuckle shivered. "God knows I'm never going to wear them again."

There was a light tap at the door and Dr. Merrill looked in, his florid, friendly face arranged into an unnaturally serious mien to fit the occasion.

"Terribly sorry to interrupt, Inspector, but would you have any objection to my sending Miss Mazur along home? She's on the near edge of hysteria. I'd like to give her a sedative and see that she's put to bed."

"Damn," Bagshawe said, "I want to talk to them all. You haven't given her anything yet?"

"No."

"Is she capable of answering a few questions, then?"

"Oh, yes. It's just that she's working herself up into a bit of a state. It appears that she and the young man were—"

"Yes, I know. Damn. Well, let me talk to her for five minutes, and then you can have her, all right?"

"Yes, I think so. Only I wouldn't put too much pressure on her right now."

Merrill left and Bagshawe said, "Dr. Arbuckle, would you mind if we continued this later?"

"Again, you mean? Yes, sure." Arbuckle said unenthusiastically. "Certainly."

Gideon was not long in following Arbuckle from the room. He had already noticed on his own that Sandra was uncomfortably close to some sort of emotional histrionics—all bony, exaggerated motions, stiff-fingered smoking, and quavery grimaces—and he had no wish to sit in on her interview. Anyway, he doubted if he'd be much help; he certainly hadn't contributed to Arbuckle's interrogation, and had, in fact, felt both extraneous and intrusive. No, he'd be happy to leave the murder investigation to Bagshawe at this point. Besides, he wanted to have a look at the photographs from Randy's camera and see if that human femur, left, partial was to be found.

Bagshawe accepted his withdrawal with his usual equanimity, and Gideon went into the sitting room with the manila envelope of photographs. This rectangular room had been tacked onto the original structure a few centuries earlier, first to serve as a Methodist school, then as an antique shop, and finally as a second lounge for hotel guests. It was a pleasant, intimate place, much like the living room of a private home, with couches and armchairs, a television set, and cases of books.

The atmosphere was anything but intimate when he entered. Frawley was sitting in one of the armchairs, chewing his lip and looking wretched. Barry sat in the chair next to him, with an open magazine on his lap, staring nervously into space, no doubt anticipating his turn in the dining room. Arbuckle was in a third chair, near the silent television set, occasionally and inattentively turning a page of a large picture book in his lap: *A History of Dorset*. Near him Nate sprawled, propped upright against the back of a couch like a board, his skinny legs out straight before him and his hands thrust into his pockets. He looked less intoxicated but more ill than when Gideon had seen him last, and Gideon suspected he'd been happier before the administration of the guggle-muggle.

On the other couch, Abe and Julie sat together, talking quietly. On the fringes of the room, Andy Hinshore was bustling nervously about, straightening things, brushing off spotless tabletops, and generally fussing. A tray of tea things and several bottles of beer were on one of the tables, untouched. Gideon pulled a chair up to Julie and Abe, sat down, and opened the manila envelope.

"These are Randy's photographs," he explained.

They both looked uncomprehendingly at him.

"It was your idea, Abe. The photographs that were in Randy's camera—we wanted to see if that femur turned up in them."

"Oh," Abe said, and Julie smiled blankly, just with her lips. Gideon couldn't blame them for their scant interest. An inconsistency on a find cared didn't seem terribly important at the moment.

They were large black-and-white photographs, about eight inches by twelve, and Gideon began to go slowly through them. It took him a little while to figure out what he was looking at, because the backgrounds seemed unfamiliar. But he soon realized that they were pictures not of the wedge-shaped trenches, but of the square test pit that had been dug near the shed and then abandoned. If he remembered correctly, it had been sunk near the beginning of the month, so at least the timing was right; Leon's find card had been dated November 1.

In the twelfth photograph he found what he was looking for. The four pictures that followed showed different perspectives of the same object, but there was no mistaking what it was: the head, neck, and a little of the greater trochanter of a human left femur, lying *in situ* in the pit.

He handed it to Abe.

"What do you know?" Abe's interest perked up at once. "So it's real. And a steatite carving it's definitely not, which means Leon was lying about it."

"It looks like it." Gideon turned in his chair. "Paul," he called, "didn't you say you visited the site around the beginning of the month?"

"What?" Arbuckle surfaced vaguely from his book. "Yes, that's right; on an audit."

"Do you remember anyone turning up a human femur?" He waved the photographs at him.

Arbuckle shook his head. "I was only there a couple of hours."

Gideon returned to the photographs. Something about the look of that bone was vaguely bothersome, but what? It was human, all right, and yet . . . what was wrong with it? It was a little too heavy, a little too—

The thought shook him like a jolt of electricity. This was from the test pit—*the test pit!* Not the Bronze Abe barrow but the test pit, with its Riss glacial sixteen inches below the surface! This bone had been found at twenty-five inches, so it was at least two hundred thousand years old; from the very dawn of Homo sapiens, the obscure, Middle Pleistocene dawn over which anthropologists still quarreled—and from which nothing but some artifacts and a few scattered, fragmentary cranial remains had ever been recovered; never—until now—a leg bone.

"Good God!" he exclaimed without meaning to.

"What is it?" Julie said, her hand at her throat. "What's the matter?"

"It's nothing," Gideon said quickly. "That is, nothing about the murders. But this bone—it's fantastic! It's a Second Interglacial leg bone!"

"Is that important?"

"Important?" Gideon couldn't keep from laughing. "We hardly know anything about those people—we don't even know if they were people, properly speaking, or the last of Homo erectus. We don't know . . ."

He turned again to Arbuckle. "Paul! Did you hear what I've been saying? We've got a Mindel-Riss femur at Stonebarrow—a new Middle Pleistocene site!"

"That's great, Gideon," Arbuckle said, and bent dully to his *History of Dorset*. He was in a very deep funk indeed, if news like this couldn't bring him out of it.

Hinshore had glided noiselessly up behind Gideon to look over his shoulder at what was causing all the excitement. "Oh," he said, "A fossil, eh? Yes, I've seen that one before."

Gideon sat perfectly still, replaying the words. Then he looked up at Hinshore. "You've seen this before?"

"Why, of course. I recognize the little thingummy on the side." He indicated the bulge of the greater trochanter. Gideon stared at him, and Hinshore smiled broadly back.

"Where did you see this?" Abe asked.

"Well, I'm not sure. In the newspapers, I suppose, or on the telly."

"Andy, you never saw this on television," Gideon said.

"I didn't?" He studied the photographs some more, but warily, evidently made uneasy by Gideon's persistence. "Well, I guess I made a mistake then." He shrugged and moved off, but before he'd gone three steps, he snapped his fingers loudly and turned around. "*I* remember!" He looked at Arbuckle. "Why, that's the fossil you had on the table, isn't it?"

Arbuckle appeared to have drifted away from the conversation. "I beg your pardon?"

"Don't you remember? You were studying it, all absorbed, in the Tudor Room—" He faltered under Arbuckle's vacant, ill-focused stare, then appealed to Gideon. "I was telling you about it, don't you remember? You and Mr. Robyn. About how I'd almost put a mug down on it and Professor Arbuckle here nearly skinned me alive."

"I'm sorry, Andy," Arbuckle said mildly. "I didn't know what you were referring to then, and I don't know now."

" 'Course you do," Hinshore said exasperatedly. "It was the second night you were here—on your first trip, I mean. November 1, it would have been. I remember because the month started on a Thursday, and the missus . . ."

November 1, For the second time in two hours everything fell sharply into place, but it was a different fit. Gideon took a long, hard look at Arbuckle, his heart thumping.

"You killed him, didn't you?" he said, forcing the words from a suddenly constricted throat.

For several long seconds Arbuckle stared at him. "Randy? What are you talking about?" He laughed, then frowned abruptly. "Gideon why are you saying this?"

"No, not Randy." Gideon said. "Leon."

"*Leon?*" He glanced hurriedly around the room for support. "What are you talking about? What are you trying to do?" The room was as still and silent as a painting. Arbuckle laughed again. "Oh no, you can't—I see what you're doing. . . . I want to talk to Inspector Bagshawe!" he shouted, presumably for the ears of the constable in the hallway. His forehead was suddenly oily with sweat. "Why would I give him CPR if I was trying to kill him? Tell me that." The question was thrown to the room at large.

"I think I know the answer to that, Paul." The sitting room was, if anything, more hushed than before, and Gideon's heart beat louder than ever in his ears. At the edge of his vision he saw Inspector Bagshawe heave noiselessly into the doorway and remain there, with the constable just behind him.

"I think," Gideon said, "that you gave him CPR because when you'd killed him a few minutes before, you'd gotten blood on your clothes, or your hands, or maybe you'd left your fingerprints on him. By leaning all over him again after he was dead, you had a credible explanation for any of that.''

"But—that's patently ridiculous." Arbuckle's round glasses fogged as suddenly as if they been sprayed, and he took them off to wipe them with a handkerchief. Without spectacles his blue eyes were washed-out and expressionless, the disturbing, ineffectual eyes of a scholar, a recluse. "I tried to save his life, and you're making it sound as if—"

"Come on, Paul. The bridge of his nose was rammed two inches into his cranium—it didn't take a physical anthropologists to know he was dead. There was no possible chance he was alive, and you knew it."

Nate had not yet moved or even opened his eyes. Now, without doing either, he spoke, seemingly to himself, in very much his normal voice. "I don't believe it. *Arbuckle?* Jesus H. Christ."

Arbuckle, stolidly ignoring this, put the wire-rimmed glasses back on his face, meticulously adjusting each earpiece, then wiped his forehead with his crumpled handkerchief. He closed his eyes briefly, and when he opened them, he stared stiffly at Gideon for a few more seconds. Then he sagged against the chair, seeming to grow smaller, to deflate. *A History of Dorset* slid from his lap and slapped against the floor.

"I never, never meant it to happen," he said. "All I was trying to do was to get that"—he turned toward the sprawling Nate Marcus, and his timid, viscous voice quivered—"that coarse, mindless *idiot* off the dig!" He glared at Nate, who remained relaxed and unresponsive in his chair; then he continued more quietly: "I arranged the Poundbury thing, I admit that, but . . . the deaths . . . my God, I never meant . . . it never occurred to me—"

"And the dog?" Gideon said.

"Dog?"

"In the meadow."

Arbuckle squirmed, looked more embarrassed than guilty. "Well, yes, the dog. But really, that was Leon's idea, believe me.... I just happened to know a little about hunting dogs...."

At his point Bagshawe stepped pachydermously into the room. "Dr. Arbuckle, would you mind stepping outside with me, please, sir?"

"Oh," Arbuckle said. "Of course."

In the total silence he rose on rickety legs, his pudgy features somehow smudged and out-of-focus, like a photograph taken at too slow a speed. Gideon dropped his eyes, unable to look at him. Bagshawe stood aside to let the archaeologist out the door, then followed him.

From the hallway the rumbling chant could be heard clearly.

"Paul Arbuckle, I arrest you for the murder of Leon Hillyer. You will be taken to the police station in Bridport and so charged. Anything you say now or then will be taken down and may be used in evidence..."

□ 21 □

ABE PUT DOWN his cheese-and-pickle sandwich and leaned back in the chair. "Let me get this straight. It was Leon who killed Randy and Paul who killed Leon?" He lifted his eyes to the ceiling. "*Oy*, I can't believe I'm saying such things. And it was really Paul Arbuckle behind the hoax with Pummy?"

"That's right," Gideon said.

"That much I can follow," Julie said, working on a ham-and-cheese sandwich. "Where I get lost is *why*."

Gideon had been having a little trouble with that part too, but he had just concluded a mutually informative telephone conversation with Bagshawe, who had called at 11:30 P.M. after witnessing a confession from Arbuckle, which had been made over the objections of a solicitor obtained in his behalf. While Gideon had been downstairs talking at the desk telephone, Hinshore had delivered a midnight meal of sandwiches and beer to Abe's room, and they had fallen on it hungrily.

"I guess it would help if I started at the beginning," Gideon said.

"I guess it would," said Julie.

Gideon, who was ravenous, washed down the last of a roast-beef sandwich with a swig of lager from the bottle, and picked up a sandwich of sliced cucumber and butter. "Okay, the beginning was November first. Leon was working alone in the test pit and he turned up that femur."

"And wrote up a find card," Abe said, "like he was supposed to."

"Right. And Randy photographed it, not having any idea of what it was. But Arbuckle, who was wandering around on his audit, saw the thing and realized exactly what it was—not Bronze Age but Middle Pleistocene. He got Leon to give him the bone—I'm not sure whether he paid him, or just talked him into it, or what—and he took it away with him, back to the hotel. That's when Andy saw him gloating over it."

"I see," Abe said, putting down his own bottle of beer. "The find card just got left quietly and forgotten. Frawley never saw it, and the bone neither, so it never got put in the field catalog. About that at least he was telling the truth."

"Well, *I* don't see," Julie said. "What could he do with the bone anyway, no matter how important it is? And what does it have to do with the killings? And the hoax? And—"

"Let's start with Pummy," Gideon said. "First of all, you have to remember that Paul is fanatically interested in Middle Pleistocene Man—it's his whole life. Well, here he is, marking time, moping around this Bronze Age site—"

"Boringly recent by his standards."

"And he can hardly wait to get back to his own Middle Pleistocene dig in Dijon. Then, out of the blue comes a two-hundred-thousand-year-old bone not even two feet below the surface—and he and Leon are the only people in the world who know they might be standing on the most important early-man site ever found. So—"

"Let me guess," Abe said. "Paul found out that Leon had it in for Nathan because of his dissertation problems, and he convinced him that it would be very nice if it should come to pass that Nathan gets fired—in a hurry." With a finger, he pushed the final corner of his sandwich into his mouth. "So they stole Pummy from the museum, and Leon buried it and fooled Nathan—not the smartest man in the

world, I'm starting to think—into proclaiming his wonderful
discovery, and so on and so forth.''

"That's it. Paul wanted the dig terminated as quickly as
possible, before someone stumbled on another early-man
bone or artifact. Then, in a year or two, when it had blown
over, he was going to reopen the site under his own
direction, and step right into the very first rank of Middle
Pleistocene archaeologists.''

"So my idea about Nate being set up was right?" Julie
asked.

"Oh? Was that your idea?" said Gideon. "Really?"

"You're darn tootin'. I believe you thought it was unnecessarily rococo.''

"A simple question," Abe said. "What's all this got to
do with Randy getting murdered?''

"Well, it was Randy who actually stole the skull from
Dorchester. Leon was smart enough to keep his hands clean
of that. He talked Randy into it for a lark, and then, later
on, when Randy had second thoughts, they argued about it
up on the fell. Randy told him he was going to tell me about
it that night, and I guess they got into scuffling. The mallet
was right there, and Leon broke his arm with it—accidentally,
maybe; who knows? Then, in a panic, he grabbed him by
the throat to keep him from screaming and wound up
strangling him. After that he rolled him over the cliff. In the
fog, nobody saw a thing." Gideon shrugged. "The whole
thing's guesswork, you realize, since the two of them are
dead, but it sounds like the truth to me.''

Julie shuddered. "So Paul had nothing to do with
that?''

"Not in a direct way, no. He claims he was horrified.''

"But horrified as he was," Abe put in, "it sure didn't
keep him from killing Leon.''

"It sure didn't. That part's still a little confused, but from
what Bagshawe could make out, Leon started to get panicky
tonight—again. This was after they thought the dog had
taken me out of the picture, you understand''—a sudden
contraction around his heart made him reach out to squeeze
Julie's hand—"and you, too. They argued in the Tudor

Room, and when Leon started going to pieces—which I can believe, because he was pretty close to it when I pinned him down this afternoon—Arbuckle panicked too and hit him with the poker.''

Abe oscillated his head grimly back and forth. ''I'm sure he was horrified all over again.''

''I think he was,'' Gideon said. Suddenly drained, he sat heavily back against his chair. Merrill had given him some codeine earlier, but his bruises had begun to ache again, and his scrapes to burn. ''Anyway, that's the whole story.''

''No, it isn't,'' Julie said. ''I still have questions. Right after that business with the dog, you were sure Leon had sicked it on us. But then, in the living room, you seemed to think it was Paul. Or did I misunderstand?''

''No, you're right. I started thinking about the timing, and it was obvious. Whoever stole that sneaker had to have done it this afternoon, because we didn't decide to go out Barr's Lane until about two. Well, the hotel was locked up all afternoon because the Hinshores were in Bridport and nobody without a key could get in. That let out Leon, but it didn't let out Paul, because he was already here.''

''But how could he get hold of your tennis shoe?'' Julie said, her brows knit. ''I was in the room all afternoon.'' She touched a finger to her lips. ''Oops. Except for twenty minutes or so, when I went across the street for some stamps. I guess that'd be long enough.''

''More than long enough, what with my key hanging on a peg in the entry. I guess Leon called Paul and told him we were going to go into the woods, and the two of them hatched the idea.'' He began to stretch, then stopped with a wince. ''Ouch. I think I'm about ready to call it a day.''

''Me, too,'' Julie said, putting down her half-finished sandwich. ''Just one more question. Was it Paul who was giving all that information to the *Times?*''

''That's right. He figured the more prepublicity it all got, the worse it would be for Nate when it blew up.''

''Yes, I can see that. But—not that it matters—how in the

world did he ever find out you were coming to Stonebarrow Fell?''

''That I still haven't figured out.''

''That's easy,'' Abe said. ''I told him.''

''*You?*'' Gideon said. ''But I asked you—''

''You asked me did I tell anybody on the dig. Paul's not on the dig; he's an administrator from Horizon. Why shouldn't I tell him?''

''For Christ's sake, Abe, maybe if you'd told me that, we'd . . . Hell, never mind.''

''Maybe if you would have told me *why* you wanted to know,'' Abe said, made testy by Gideon's tone, ''I could have told you.''

It was rare for them to snap at each other, and Gideon was immediately contrite. ''I'm sorry, Abe. I'm obviously not at my best. There was no way for you to know it was important. I didn't know, myself.''

''That's all right,'' Abe, too, hurried to patch up the small rift. ''It's my fault. I just forgot.''

''No, my fault,'' Gideon said. ''Boy, am I ready for bed.'' So ready that he couldn't quite find the energy to gather himself up and go.

''Oh yeah,'' Abe said, ''something else I forgot. From back home.''

A certain familiar lilt made Gideon look up, to find Abe grinning widely, at Julie as much as at him.

''I was talking to Michaelis at the university,'' he went on, ''and he was telling me they're thinking of starting a graduate anthropology department at the Port Angeles campus next year. So he says to me, do I know a good physical anthropologist who'd be interested in teaching up there, maybe with a full professorship if he's got the right experience.''

''I appreciate it,'' Gideon said tersely, ''but I don't want any strings pulled for me. I can find my own jobs.''

''Strings?'' Abe repeated, appealing to Julie. ''Who's pulling strings? Boy, this guy has a temper!'' He leaned agilely forward with more vigor than Gideon had at the moment, and clapped him gently on the knee. ''What kind of strings? You're not a good physical anthropologist? You wouldn't be interested in teaching on the Olympic Peninsula? Is it my fault he's interested in you? Why wouldn't he be interested?''

Julie leaned over and put her hand on his other knee. ''Gideon, it would solve all our problems. I could work at the Park Service in Port Angeles.'' She sounded breathless and softly excited. ''There was a house I saw for sale, with a view of Hurricane Ridge on one side and Ediz Hook on the other. . . .''

''And also,'' Abe said, ''Port Angeles isn't so far from Sequim. To me it doesn't matter so much, but I know Bertha would like to see you sometimes. . . .''

Gideon nodded. It must have been the grueling and extraordinary day that made him not quite trust himself to speak.

''You'll fly up and talk to him?'' Abe said.

Gideon nodded again. ''I sure will.'' He rubbed his hand over his forehead and finally forced himself to stand, a surprisingly drawn-out process. ''And, Abe, thank you.''

''Perfectly all right.'' Abe was beaming. ''My pleasure.''

''And what will happen to Nate?'' Julie asked Abe. ''Will Horizon reinstate him?''

''Oh, I think so, at least if I have anything to say about it. To finish up the Bronze Age excavations anyway. Nathan's a good boy at heart, and I think he learned a good lesson here. As for Frawley, the *shtunk,* we'll let Nathan figure out what he wants to do about him.''

With Julie, Gideon had made his painful way to the door before he turned around. ''And the Second Interglacial strata, what about them? There could be a hell of a Middle Pleistocene site here, Abe, and it ought to be dug too.''

''Absolutely. I was thinking of organizing an exploratory dig for the foundation next summer—for a couple months, maybe—and bringing in some first-rate prehistoric archaeologists: Hernandez, Passarelli, Ingraham. . . . And of course I might lend a hand myself. It would be a nice place to spend the summer.''

It certainly would, Gideon thought with ungrudging envy.

"That's great, Abe; you'll be right back in the thick of things."

"I certainly will. The only thing I'm missing is a grade-A physical anthropologist." He reached for a pickle slice on his plate and popped it into his mouth.

"Listen, Gideon, I was thinking . . ."

MORE MYSTERIOUS PLEASURES

HAROLD ADAMS
The Carl Wilcox mystery series

MURDER	#501	$3.95
PAINT THE TOWN RED	#601	$3.95
THE MISSING MOON	#602	$3.95
THE NAKED LIAR	#420	$3.95
THE FOURTH WIDOW	#502	$3.50
THE BARBED WIRE NOOSE	#603	$3.95
THE MAN WHO MET THE TRAIN	#801	$3.95

TED ALLBEURY

THE SEEDS OF TREASON	#604	$3.95
THE JUDAS FACTOR	#802	$4.50
THE STALKING ANGEL	#803	$3.95

ERIC AMBLER

HERE LIES: AN AUTOBIOGRAPHY	#701	$8.95

ROBERT BARNARD

A TALENT TO DECEIVE: AN APPRECIATION OF AGATHA CHRISTIE	#702	$8.95

EARL DERR BIGGERS
The Charlie Chan mystery series

THE HOUSE WITHOUT A KEY	#421	$3.95
THE CHINESE PARROT	#503	$3.95
BEHIND THAT CURTAIN	#504	$3.95
THE BLACK CAMEL	#505	$3.95
CHARLIE CHAN CARRIES ON	#506	$3.95
KEEPER OF THE KEYS	#605	$3.95

JAMES M. CAIN

THE ENCHANTED ISLE	#415	$3.95
CLOUD NINE	#507	$3.95

DAVID STOUT
CAROLINA SKELETONS #829 $4.95

REX STOUT
UNDER THE ANDES #419 $3.50

REMAR SUTTON
LONG LINES #830 $3.95

JULIAN SYMONS
CONAN DOYLE: PORTRAIT OF AN ARTIST #721 $9.95

ROSS THOMAS
CAST A YELLOW SHADOW #535 $3.95
THE SINGAPORE WINK #536 $3.95
THE FOOLS IN TOWN ARE
  ON OUR SIDE #537 $3.95
CHINAMAN'S CHANCE #638 $4.50
THE EIGHTH DWARF #639 $4.50
OUT ON THE RIM #640 $4.95

JIM THOMPSON
THE KILL-OFF #538 $3.95
THE NOTHING MAN #641 $3.95
BAD BOY #642 $3.95
ROUGHNECK #643 $3.95
THE GOLDEN GIZMO #831 $3.95
THE RIP-OFF #832 $3.95
FIREWORKS: THE LOST WRITINGS #833 $4.50

COLIN WATSON
SNOBBERY WITH VIOLENCE: CRIME
  STORIES AND THEIR AUDIENCES #722 $8.95

DONALD E. WESTLAKE
THE BUSY BODY #541 $3.95
THE SPY IN THE OINTMENT #542 $3.95
GOD SAVE THE MARK #543 $3.95
DANCING AZTECS #834 $4.95
TWO MUCH! #835 $4.95
HELP I AM BEING HELD PRISONER #836 $4.50
TRUST ME ON THIS #837 $4.50
The Dortmunder caper series
THE HOT ROCK #539 $3.95
BANK SHOT #540 $3.95
JIMMY THE KID #838 $3.95
NOBODY'S PERFECT #839 $3.95

AVAILABLE AT YOUR BOOKSTORE OR DIRECT FROM THE PUBLISHER

Mysterious Press Mail Order
129 West 56th Street
New York, NY 10019

Please send me the MYSTERIOUS PRESS titles I have circled below:

103 105 106 107 112 113 209 210 211 212 213 214 301 302
303 304 308 309 315 316 401 402 403 404 405 406 407 408
409 410 411 412 413 414 415 416 417 418 419 420 421 501
502 503 504 505 506 507 508 509 510 511 512 513 514 515
516 517 518 519 520 521 522 523 524 525 526 527 528 529
530 531 532 533 534 535 536 537 538 539 540 541 542 543
544 545 601 602 603 604 605 606 607 608 609 610 611 612
613 614 615 616 617 618 619 620 621 622 623 624 625 626
627 628 629 630 631 632 633 634 635 636 637 638 639 640
641 642 643 644 645 646 701 702 703 704 705 706 707 708
709 710 711 712 713 714 715 716 717 718 719 720 721 722
723 724 725 726 727 728 729 801 802 803 804 805 806 807
808 809 810 811 812 813 814 815 816 817 818 819 820 821
822 823 824 825 826 827 828 829 830 831 832 833 834 835
836 837 838 839 840 841 842 843

I am enclosing $_____ (please add $3.00 postage and handling for the first book, and 50¢ for each additional book). Send check or money order only—no cash or C.O.D.'s please. Allow at least 4 weeks for delivery.

NAME _____

ADDRESS _____

CITY _____ STATE _____ ZIP CODE _____
New York State residents please add appropriate sales tax.